BETRAYAL OF GENIUS

COVENTRY SAGA BOOK 3

ROBIN PATCHEN

JDO PUBLISHING

For Sharon and Terri.
There's nothing like having friends along on the journey. I'm glad
we get to travel this road together.

CHAPTER ONE

Everything was ruined.

Jacqueline Beal froze in the doorway of her lab and stared at the wreckage of her life's work.

She'd known Don was frustrated. After the funeral a month past, red-eyed with grief, veins pulsing in anger, her former partner had threatened legal action. Trouble was, he had no legal leg to stand on.

Apparently, he'd realized the same thing.

The lab they'd once shared hadn't just been searched, it had been destroyed.

Jacqui stepped deeper into the room. With her toe, she nudged aside an iPad and stepped over the remnants of its shattered screen. A monitor lay on its side, dented as if someone had taken a baseball bat to it. Microscopes, test tubes, and syringes had been tossed everywhere, some smashed to pieces, others just ruined by littered glass.

CPUs, ripped apart and gutted.

Equipment worth hundreds of thousands of dollars, wrecked.

She sucked in a breath, barely holding back the sob trying to escape, and waited for the nightmare to end. Surely this wasn't real.

Surely the man who'd been like a grandfather to her hadn't done this.

She skirted a metal worktable and bumped into the oscilloscope. Pain exploded in her shin. Ignoring it, she bent to examine the metal box with its lifeless screens. Its back was destroyed, its wires ripped out. She barely resisted an urge to kick the expensive machine and add even more damage.

Maybe all wasn't lost yet.

Careful to avoid further injury, she picked her way across the room until she reached her desk. She and Don had thought, when they first rented the space right after she'd earned her masters from MIT, that they'd eventually build offices. But they'd worked so well together, neither of them had been eager to erect walls between them. Instead, their desks were pushed together so they could see each other. How many times had he sent her an idea over email, then watched her face as she read it?

How many times had she made a suggestion and seen him process it, intelligent eyes narrowing under his salt-and-pepper hair?

How many times had they brainstormed solutions to seemingly insurmountable problems across those two desks?

They'd been a great team.

No more.

He'd taken a knife to her leather chair, and stuffing peeked out of the slashes. She tamped down a rise of fear at the violent act, kicked debris out of her path, and rolled the chair back to her desk.

How had it come to this?

Stomach roiling, hands shaking, she sat and dialed 911.

Jacqui was in the middle of explaining the carnage to the operator when the door opened, sending fresh adrenaline to her veins. But it was her assistant who stepped in, not her former partner.

Braden Reilly's jaw dropped. "Holy cow. What in the world?"

She lifted her finger to silence him and turned her focus to the phone call.

"Police are on their way," the woman said. "Are you in any immediate danger?"

"I don't..." Don was angry, furious, but he wouldn't hurt her, would he? She gazed at the destruction all around her. The man who'd done this had lost all reason. The man who'd done this—he could do anything.

No. He'd had a moment of fury, but he was still the same man who'd believed in her and encouraged her, who'd taken a chance on her when she'd graduated, giving her a job well beyond the positions being offered her.

He needed help, no question, but he was still the same man.

The operator said, "If you believe the perpetrator is there—"

"He's not here. And my assistant just arrived. I'm not alone."

Jacqui answered a few more questions before hanging up.

Braden seemed to shake off his shock and bent to pick something up off the floor.

"Don't touch anything," Jacqui said. "The police are on their way."

He crossed to the safe and crouched down to look inside. The door was open, the contents removed. "Did he get it?" Braden's South Boston accent was always more pronounced when he was upset, and it was thick right now. "Is it over?"

She was still coming to grips with what had happened. Thank God, thank *God* for the dream He'd given her. She'd woken up the morning after the funeral for Don's wife with a lingering memory of it—Don taking her device and running, always just out of reach as she tried to follow. She wouldn't have believed Don could do something like this under any circumstance. But the warning had been so strong, almost palpable. She'd come straight here, gathered the invention and the research she'd done over the course of years, and hidden them.

Her brownstone had top-notch security, and unlike the lab, Don didn't have a key. Her research should be safe there, for now.

"You're serious?" Braden straightened to face her, eyes wide. "It wasn't in there?"

"No."

"Where is it?" He shook his head. "Never mind. I don't need to know. It's yours, not his, and certainly not mine. I'm just glad it wasn't here."

"It's all of ours, and I intend to treat it that way."

"You're under no obligation—"

"A man is worthy of his wages. You've worked very hard for us, and when we sell it, you'll get a nice bonus—for your loyalty and your hard work. And Don?" She ran a hand through her hair, forgetting the ponytail until it was too late. She yanked out the hair band, gathered her long hair, and put it up again. "Don will be compensated, too, though I'll be deducting the cost of this"—she gestured at the ruins surrounding her—"from his share."

"Why would you do that? Do you have a contract?"

"When he sold me his shares, I agreed to give him half the profits from the device. It seemed like the right thing to do, since he was instrumental in its development. We didn't put it in writing. He knows he can trust me."

Braden nodded slowly at her words, processing. "Too bad you can no longer trust him."

She was glad Braden realized that. He admired Don Burgess, who'd hired him fresh out of college and mentored him until Don's wife had been diagnosed with cancer. At that point, Don had quit caring about Braden. And Jacqui, and their business.

He'd quit working. He'd quit contributing to their partnership. And then, he'd quit the partnership altogether, begging Jacqui to buy his shares and swearing he wanted nothing else to do with the company. Because of their high debt, which they'd incurred to buy the equipment that now lay scattered and ruined, she hadn't had to scrape together too much to buy him out. She'd had the money. Barely.

She'd promised the shares would be Don's when he wanted them back. And she'd promised he'd reap the financial benefit of everything they'd built together.

At the time, he'd sworn he didn't care. Now that Lola was gone, it seemed Jacqui's promises weren't enough for Don. The man she'd once looked up to seemed to have buried his reason along with his wife.

Braden leaned a hip on Jacqui's desk. "You're sure it was him?"

"Who else?" She looked at the ruined space, all the destroyed equipment. "Maybe, if anything had been stolen, I might believe it was a random burglary." But as far as she could tell, everything was there. Even the most expensive equipment hadn't been removed. Just smashed.

"He's lost in his grief," Braden said. "No matter what the doctor said, Don never believed Lola would die. He's looking for someone to blame." Braden's voice was low and tender. As young as he was, he could be very insightful. When Don had hired Braden, Jacqui had been skeptical that a twenty-two-year-old fresh out of college could do much but grunt work, but Braden had proved her wrong.

Tears pricked her eyes. For Lola. For Don and the life he'd lost.

For the mentor and friend Jacqui and Braden had lost.

She'd hoped that, after Lola's passing, Don would grieve, heal, and return to work. Obviously, that couldn't happen now.

Braden said, "Do you mind if I suggest you go easy—?"

"Easy?" She stood and gestured to the remains of Don's temper tantrum. "Look around you. This wasn't just about getting his hands on the research. He destroyed years of work. Not just mine but yours too. He destroyed hundreds of thousands of dollars' worth of equipment."

"In his anger and grief," Braden said. "But he's a mentor, a friend."

"This isn't the work of a friend."

"I realize that. I just think mercy—"

"Mercy?" Jacqui couldn't keep her voice from rising. "He doesn't deserve mercy."

Braden tilted his head to the side. "If he deserved it, it wouldn't be mercy."

She sighed, not in the mood for a theology lesson. "Mercy isn't mine to give today. All this equipment is going to need to be repaired or replaced. Our insurer sure isn't going to be merciful."

He dipped his head, offering her the point. Not that she'd won anything. There would be no winners in this situation.

The police arrived, took their statements, and snapped photos. After they left, Jacqui and Braden assessed the wreckage, making a detailed list of all that was destroyed or damaged. From high-tech equipment to old-school Bunsen burners, hardly anything had escaped Don's fury.

It was after seven by the time they were finished with the little they could do before the insurance adjuster came by the following day.

They had worked through the dinner hour, so she ordered takeout, and they ate at her desk, mostly silent. What was there to say? When she was full, she carefully wrapped the second half of her meatball sub and offered it to Braden. "Why don't you take the rest of this home?"

His eyebrows lifted. "I've never known you not to keep your own leftovers. Waste not, want not and all that."

Her lips twitched in an almost-smile, the first of the horrible day. "Seems the least I can do after all the work you've done. And considering what's going to happen next."

He took the sandwich and set it aside, his gaze never straying from hers. "What do you mean by that?"

She gestured at their ruined lab. "Obviously, we're not going to get a lot of work done around here for a while. Until we get a settlement—"

"Are you letting me go?"

"I'll keep paying you until you get another job."

"I don't want another job."

"Really?" She couldn't understand why the man wouldn't want to find a less volatile place to work. Now that they'd finished their biggest project, now that his mentor would definitely not be returning, she figured Braden would jump at the chance to leave.

He had to know she'd give him a glowing recommendation. "You don't have to stay on my account. I'll find someone else."

"I want to keep working for you. But you don't have to pay me. I have some money saved up, and I can always go back and work for my dad for a while."

She should know what his father did. Somewhere in the back of her mind, she knew Braden had once told her. She didn't want to ask.

But he'd worked with her long enough to read her expressions. "He owns an auto body shop."

"Oh, yeah. I knew that." Typical. Minute details about the inner workings of silicone chips never left her brain, but important details about the humans in her life sloughed off like dead skin cells. It wasn't that she didn't care. It just appeared that way to everyone she met. "Be honest, Braden. You're not going to hurt my feelings. Now that Don's not coming back—"

"I love working here. I thought, when Don stepped away..." He didn't finish the thought, and Jacqui wasn't surprised.

"It's fine," she said. "I know I can be a little intense."

"I've come to appreciate your style." His words sounded so sincere, she was tempted to believe them. But she knew she wasn't exactly personable.

Braden's eyes narrowed. "You are going to start up again, right?"

"Of course." She'd been born to do this. No way would she let Don Burgess or anybody else scare her off. "If you want to keep working for me, then I'm going to keep paying you. Those are my terms."

He laughed. "I don't think you understand how the negotiating process works."

She wished she could feel lighthearted enough to offer even a chuckle. "I never was very good at the business end." That had been Don's responsibility. So much of what made them successful had been Don's responsibility. She'd learned enough to keep them afloat for a while, but now she'd have to learn more. Or hire someone.

Those were problems for another day.

"Do we have a deal?" she asked.

"If you insist. I'll be on call when you need me, but I'll be back in Dorchester with my family. I think they could use an extra set of hands right now anyway."

"That'll work." Her phone rang, and she snatched it up. "Jacqui Beal."

"Detective Klein." The police detective had come by earlier that day to investigate. He was an older man with dark skin and pale blue eyes. He had a gentle manner she'd especially appreciated as she worked to process what had happened. "We wanted to let you know we questioned Don Burgess, but aside from your belief that he's the one who broke into your lab, there's no evidence—"

"It wasn't a break-in," Jacqui said. "The door and the lock weren't damaged. He's the only one besides me who has a key." She'd never even shared a key with Braden, and he'd worked there for almost two years.

"Mr. Burgess claims he lost his keys a couple of days ago. He had to contact his car manufacturer to replace the one for his car— and he has a record of having done that. Also, he has a video camera at the house that shows when he came in and left. He was home all night."

They had a video camera at the lab too. But it had been tampered with, the recordings destroyed. Even the ones stored off-site had been hacked and deleted. Only Don could have accomplished that. She'd explained as much to the detective already.

"He obviously planned the break-in and claimed his keys were lost. The man's a technical genius." Jacqui worked hard to keep her voice level. "He could easily have climbed out the window, or even tampered with the video to make it look—"

"I know your theories, Ms. Beal. I'm having someone look at

the recording to see if it's been altered. Until we get some real evidence, though, Mr. Burgess won't be arrested."

She rubbed her temples. "When do you think—?"

"We've got a backlog of cases. We're doing our best, but even if we can get enough evidence to make an arrest, it'll be weeks, maybe longer."

Why was she surprised? Sure, her business had been destroyed, but nothing had even been stolen. This was just another day at the office for Detective Klein. "Okay, then. Thank you for—"

"The thing is," Klein said, "after seeing your lab today, I recommend you take extra precautions."

"What do you mean?"

"Whoever did it, whether it was Burgess or someone else... Whoever it was, it was personal. And violent. I'm suggesting that maybe, next time, it won't be equipment he attacks."

CHAPTER TWO

T HREE MONTHS LATER

~

T HE THOUGHT of letting go made Reid Cote physically ill.

"Next!" the TSA agent called.

Ella tugged on his hand, but he didn't release her. "Daddy, it's my turn."

He wasn't a bit surprised his ex wasn't where she'd promised to be, which was why he'd gotten the pass from the ticket counter to allow him to accompany his daughter all the way to the gate. If it were up to him, he'd accompany her all the way to California.

Truth be told, if it were up to him, Ella wouldn't be going in the first place.

After one more look to the other side for Denise—where was she?—he bent to Ella's level and pointed past the security checkpoint. "Wait right there and don't move."

His six-year-old kissed his cheek. "I promise." He reluctantly let go of her hand, and she skipped into the scanner and held her hands over her head like the agent told her to. She had flown back and forth to California to visit her mother a couple of times, but this was the first time since she'd been kidnapped the previous summer. The visits had always made Reid nervous, but what he was feeling now was a new level of fear.

Ella made it to the other side and waited where he'd directed while he hurried into the machine. He had to take his eyes off her and face straight ahead for the scan to work. If he screwed up and had to do it twice, it would be that much longer before he could get to his daughter.

The chances that she would be snatched and whisked away under the noses of eight TSA agents and countless perfectly safe business travelers and families were close to nil, but his heart wasn't listening to his head.

Finally, the agent waved Reid through, and he rejoined his daughter, feeling out of breath as if he'd run a marathon.

Ella, on the other hand, seemed perfectly fine. She'd already collected her backpack from the conveyer belt. Now, she slid her hand into his, her trademark smile in place. "Mommy came, right? Isn't she supposed to meet us here?"

He forced a smile and a nod. "We'll find her."

They navigated the crowd in the terminal at the Manchester airport until they reached the right gate. Denise had flown in earlier and was standing in front of the windows. Outside, rain dripped down the glass, and Reid sent up a prayer for an uneventful flight to LA. *No turbulence, please, Father. It'll frighten my little girl.* And he wouldn't be there to comfort her.

When Denise saw Ella, she kneeled and held her arms wide, her grin—so much like Ella's—in place.

Once again, Ella tugged to get free of Reid's grip, and once again he reluctantly let her go.

His beautiful little girl ran into the arms of the woman who'd broken both of their hearts. Denise removed her oversize sunglasses but kept a big floppy hat in place as she hugged Ella as if she really loved her.

Maybe she did, in her own way. But Reid had heard once that

children spell love T-I-M-E. If that were the case, then Denise's love was a paltry offering.

Not that Reid was complaining. No chance he'd give Denise more time with his daughter. It was bad enough that this visit had been extended to a month, twice as long as their typical summer visits. Reid's attorney had advised him to allow the longer visit after reminding him that Denise could demand much more if she were so inclined. Reid had agreed, but he didn't know how he would survive an entire month away from Ella.

And how would she do away from him? Sure, right now she was enthralled with her mother and chattering like a magpie. But at night, when Ella was alone in a strange room and the nightmares came, would she call for him?

How could he comfort her from three thousand miles away?

This was a mistake. He shouldn't let her go. He couldn't.

But he had no choice.

Finally, Denise stood and faced him, sliding her sunglasses back on her face. She patted Ella's shoulder. "Tell your daddy good-bye, and then we'll go get a snack for the flight."

Reid worked very hard to keep his expression neutral. "Where were you? I told you to meet us at security."

"You're earlier than I thought you'd be."

"I texted when we were in line. She was standing there alone—"

"Daddy, your face is turning all red."

He sent his daughter a tight smile. "Sorry, sweetie." He let it go. Denise didn't understand—couldn't seem to grasp—how hard this was for him and Ella. Nothing he said would change that. "Just a few things first."

Denise seemed to be exerting as much effort as he was to maintain her polite expression. "What more could there be after the dissertation on the phone last night?"

He ignored the sarcasm. They'd been on FaceTime during their talk, and he'd seen her attention wander often, typing something into her tablet as if the latest social media post couldn't wait ten minutes. He'd go over it all again with her now. "She needs a regular sleep schedule. You don't have to stick to our schedule, but whatever you do, you need to be consistent. It's very important she gets enough rest."

Ella piped up. "Everybody stays up later in California, right, Mommy? Can we this time? Maybe all the way until nine?"

Denise slid her hand down Ella's braids. "Nine o'clock? You think you're old enough for that?"

"I'm six now. I can handle it."

Reid could already see this going off the rails. "The thing is—"

"Nine o'clock is perfect." Denise shot Reid a *don't even think about arguing* look before focusing on Ella. "That'll give us time after dinner to watch movies. I'm way behind on my animated flicks."

"It's not healthy for children to watch TV right before bed," Reid said. "Ella packed some of her favorite books."

Denise waved away the words. "Of course, we'll read before bed. Right after the movie. Right, sugar?"

Sugar. As if Denise were a Georgia peach instead of a New Hampshire country girl. But it'd been years since she'd shed her— what had she called them? Redneck roots?

Ella beamed at her mother. And who wouldn't? The woman was beautiful and rich and famous and promising the moon. Whatever Ella wanted, Denise would provide, whether it was good for her or not.

He sent up a prayer for patience and faith and continued the instructions. "You can't leave her alone, ever. For her own safety and—"

"Feeling of security." Denise's fake smile was back. "I understand the situation."

"Do you? Because you weren't around for the *situation.* Couldn't be bothered to—"

"Ella, sugar." Denise dug into her gigantic purse and pulled out a tablet. "I loaded some games on this. Why don't you sit over there and find one to play while your daddy and I talk?"

Ella looked from him to her mother and back. She gave him a *be nice* look before taking the iPad and climbing into a chair about five feet away.

Reid angled so he could keep his eye on her and lowered his voice. "Great parenting, that. Just give her a screen to stare at to get her out of the way."

Denise stepped close enough that he could smell her no doubt uber-expensive perfume. A decade ago, when Denise got this close to him, his hormones had raced and his brain function had shut down. As recently as seven years past, he'd have given everything he had and whatever he could beg, borrow, or steal to make this woman happy.

Now, he clenched his fists to keep his temper in check.

She lowered her voice. "She doesn't need a front-row seat to our arguments."

Ella looked up, and he gave her a lighthearted wink he didn't feel. She smiled, her precious dimples in place.

Meanwhile, Denise glared. "You've thrown that in my face quite enough, thank you." Her voice was both low and vehement, a whisper-shout if he'd ever heard one. "You don't understand what was—"

"God forbid a director should be inconvenienced by your daughter's kidnapping."

Denise's expression didn't change, but the color leached from her face. "You don't understand."

"Explain it to me then."

"My life is none of your business."

"My daughter is none of yours."

In the past, Denise would have backed down by now. She knew her limitations. She knew she was no good for Ella. But today, she squared her shoulders and lifted her chin. "*Our* daughter. I carried her. I gave birth to her. I nursed her."

"And then you left her and barely looked back."

She crossed her arms. "Did you have more instructions for me? Not what you told me last night. I wrote all that down."

He started to shoot back a response, then snapped his jaw closed. Written it down? When?

Denise must've seen his shock. "I was taking notes on my phone." She pulled it from a pocket, pressed a few buttons, and turned it toward him. He glanced at the bullet-pointed list.

She had been paying attention. Close attention.

But why? What was she after? Because this was not Denise's typical modus operandi.

She shoved the phone away. "If there's nothing else—"

"There's plenty *else,* but I'll go for now. I'll call every evening to talk to her. Be sure to answer."

"I don't have to do that," Denise said. "This is *my* time with her. You get her the rest—"

"You forfeited your rights a long time ago."

Denise's head dipped and lifted too slowly to be called a nod. Certainly not agreement. It was more like she was considering what he'd said, letting it settle in her mind. When she spoke again, her words were measured as if chosen carefully. "To forfeit means to give up. If a team forfeits a game, they can never go back and play it over. A forfeit is permanent, and the forfeited item or idea can never be regained."

Fear dripped over Reid as if someone had dumped a pot of sludge on his head, hot and sticky. The shallow, selfish woman who'd left him to pursue an acting career would never have used those words. That woman didn't care about her daughter or her parenting rights or anything but herself and her own ambitions.

This woman.

Something had changed.

Reid was no lawyer, but he understood Denise wasn't uttering some off-the-cuff idea. This was no whim. She was making a point, one he wouldn't be dumb enough to challenge right then.

The acid that had burned his stomach since he and Ella left the house that morning churned. Denise was up to something, and that was never good.

"I never *forfeited* my rights to my daughter. I just haven't fought for them." She leaned in, close enough that her breath brushed his ear.

He'd have stepped back, but he felt frozen, hanging on the edge, waiting for her to finish her thought.

"We're not even to halftime yet, Reid. The game's a long way from over, and I have a lot of fight in me."

CHAPTER THREE

Jacqui hefted a huge container of ice cream from the walk-in freezer and carried it into the shop, where she guided it into position in the glass-fronted case. So many unique combinations, but most people chose the simple ones—chocolate, vanilla, cookie dough. She'd sampled every flavor in the store—all thirty-five, though they only ever offered twenty-four at a time—and she still hadn't decided on her favorite. Why get vanilla when you could choose butter pecan? Why settle for chocolate when rocky road was a choice?

Oh, she understood some people preferred simple and old fashioned. But she was a fan of the new and fresh.

This hiatus from her normal life, though she wouldn't have chosen it, had been a blessing. She hadn't realized until her lab was destroyed how much time she'd spent there. Or, if not there, hunched over her laptop in her brownstone. She'd converted the basement—designed as the servants' kitchen and quarters back in the late nineteenth century—into a home workspace. With only the high, squat window that gave a view of people's feet as they walked by, the flickering fluorescent lights did little to dispel the dark and dank feeling of the space.

It had been years since Jacqui had spent any real time out-of-doors, and her seven-minute walks to and from work barely counted. Most of that time, her brain had been focused on the latest challenge, and she'd hardly noticed the weather, the unique city around her, or the people walking by.

Not that today was ideal to spend outside. The rain was steady, and the shop was empty. A little drizzle didn't stop the tourists, but not even the most rugged among them wanted to get drenched in a cold summer rain for a scoop of ice cream. She imagined people holed up in their cabins and their B&Bs, snuggled under blankets and enjoying card games.

Though it seemed so many people these days spent more time looking at screens than they did at each other. That was one of her many observations since she'd awakened from her work-induced stupor. Maybe she wasn't that different from the general public after all.

Jacqui took out a sample cup. What would chocolate banana taste like paired with cherry bomb?

She got a bit of each on her spoon and tasted it. She wanted new and better. She wanted to innovate.

She let the flavors meld in her mouth.

Huh. She'd discovered one more flavor combination that didn't work.

Chuckling at her own foolishness, she tossed the remains into the trash and gazed around at the tidy shop, looking for something to do. She was being paid to be here. She should be working.

She thought of the laptop back at her cottage, the sketches she'd been noodling with the last few weeks. The first month after she'd abandoned her wrecked lab and fled to the White Mountains of New Hampshire, Jacqui hadn't been able to work at all. Knowing that the most troublesome problems were often solved by her subconscious mind, she'd put her problems on the back burner and poured herself into learning the duties at this shop, ensuring she could manage the place so the owner—a friend of her parents— could spend some time with his grandkids in Texas. Truth was, the store's assistant manager could handle it just fine, better than

Jacqui. But the owner hadn't wanted to leave his life's work in the hands of a high school kid.

It had been months, though. Jacqui needed to act, to *do* something. She'd been stunned by Don's betrayal, but she had to quit waiting for the next step to present itself. She uttered a prayer for direction—one she'd repeated many times.

She was the innovator. Don was the businessman. Sure, he understood the technology and the science, but not like she did. He'd brainstormed with her, given her ideas, and helped her hone her own. But when it came down to turning those ideas into reality, she'd taken the lead, directing Braden and the techs every step of the way.

This past winter, she'd perfected an invention she'd been working on for years, one that could change thousands—potentially hundreds of thousands—of lives, but she didn't know what to do with it.

She did know that Don's plan was wrong, no matter how much money it might bring in. This couldn't only be about money. Until she figured out the next step with her artificial neuron, she would run this shop to the best of her ability.

Which was harder than it looked. At first, she'd rolled her eyes at her father's suggestion that she come up here. She hated to admit this and wouldn't confess it to anybody, but it had seemed beneath her. She was an inventor. She had a graduate degree from MIT, for heaven's sake. And now she was going to schlep ice cream?

But running this shop had been harder than she'd anticipated. It was business, and business wasn't her forte. Give her complex math equations, no problem. But simple balance sheets—when they didn't balance—made her crazy. And then there were the people. She had to manage the employees, all high school students, and deal with the customers. The assistant manager, Bree, had just turned eighteen and was about to enter twelfth grade. She'd worked there a couple of years. Not only did she know the business better than Jacqui—embarrassing as that was to admit—she was great with the customers. She remembered people's names and what kind of ice cream they liked. She interacted with the kids, who thought she, with her blue hair and nose ring, was *totally awesome*.

In her whole life, nobody had ever considered Jacqui totally awesome. Certainly not children. As an only child, she'd always felt more comfortable in the company of adults and never had much use for the other kids in school. In fact, the only kid she'd ever felt any kinship with was the daughter of one of the customers at the ice cream shop.

Ella always made her smile, and for some reason Jacqui couldn't comprehend, the girl seemed to like her. Ella was an anomaly, though.

Jacqui was learning that there were different kinds of intelligences. She was smart. According to a test she'd taken in eighth grade, a genius.

But she could hardly remember anybody's name, and their favorite ice cream flavor? Not a chance.

Bree, though? That barely eighteen-year-old girl was a genius in her own way. A genius at interacting with people in a way Jacqui never could.

She spotted a tiny cobweb high in the corner near the front windows. It wasn't a challenge, and it wouldn't take any innovation, but it was something to do.

Her cell phone rang. After she glanced at the Caller ID, she slid one ear pod in her ear and answered. "Hi, Mom."

"How's it going up in the wilds of New Hampshire?"

"It's not the old west," Jacqui said.

"Are you keeping warm?"

She laughed. "It's June." Though, to be fair, the temperature that day, with the pouring rain, hovered in the sixties. It hadn't been raining when Jacqui walked to work that morning. She'd regret that decision when she had to walk home.

While Mom updated her on the goings-on at the country club in Hilton Head, Jacqui hauled the ladder from the storage room, set it up beneath the cobweb, and climbed, feather-duster in hand.

After checking to be sure the eight-legged weaver wasn't waiting to pounce, she swiped the duster over the area.

At a break in the conversation, Jacqui asked, "How's Dad doing?"

"Oh, you know your father. He spends more time consulting on cases than ever."

She missed her parents so much. Her mother's easy smiles, and the way she doted on her, always made Jacqui feel cherished. Dad was more like Jacqui, reserved and quiet, always churning some idea. "I thought when you two decided to stay in South Carolina indefinitely, maybe Dad was slowing down."

Mom chuckled. "Your father doesn't know the meaning of the phrase."

"I'm sorry. That must be frustrating for you."

But Mom sounded at peace. "Your father is who he is. I wish he didn't feel compelled to work so many hours, but he loves it. And I have friends down here. I stay busy."

Jacqui wished Dad would be more attentive to Mom, but she'd always identified more with her brilliant workaholic father than with her gentle, tenderhearted mother.

"I wouldn't have minded having you come stay with us," Mom said. "I hate that you're stuck up in New Hampshire alone."

Still on the ladder, Jacqui dusted the framed artwork—close-ups of kids enjoying frozen treats. The owner had told her the photos had been taken right across the street. Normally, she loved staring out the wide windows at the beauty—the grassy park, the brightly colored playground equipment, and the clear blue waters of Lake Ayasha. Under today's thick clouds, every-thing was gray.

"I've made a couple of friends here. And I needed to stay within driving distance of the lab. This was really the perfect solu-tion." What she hadn't told her mother was that she hadn't wanted to be anywhere Don could find her, and her parents' house would be the first place he'd look.

Mom sighed. "I know. I do miss you, though. Your father does too. The authorities still haven't figured out who broke into your lab?"

Don had been friends with Jacqui's parents since before Jacqui was born. She hadn't had the heart to tell them that she was convinced he'd been behind the destruction of her lab. She'd only told them that her whereabouts were a secret and asked them not to tell anybody. She could trust her parents to respect her request, even if they didn't understand it.

"Not yet. Which is just as well. I've agreed to stay here until mid-August." Jacqui spotted another cobweb against the ceiling and reached for it.

The bell over the door jingled, surprising her. Her jolt caused her to lean a little too far, and the ladder started to tip.

"Whoa, there." A deep voice came with strong hands that settled the ladder back in place. "You all right?"

Through the phone, Mom said, "Sweetie, what happened? Are you hurt?"

Her heart pounded. She gripped the cold metal ladder and breathed deeply. That would have done some damage.

"You need help down?" The man was still behind her, his voice familiar. Was it really him?

She hadn't expected to see Reid again for a month. His daughter was out of town, wasn't she? Why would he come for ice cream on a cold and rainy day, and without Ella in tow?

Even as her mind voiced the question, her heart gave her a very hopeful answer.

"Jacqui?" he said.

"Sweetie?" Mom said.

She touched the ear pod to indicate to Reid that she was on the phone. "I have to go, Mom. I have a customer."

"Are you okay?"

"I'm fine. I'll call you tomorrow." She ended the call, pulled the ear pod from her ear, and shoved it into her pocket. Once she was back on solid ground, she turned to him. "You startled me."

"Sorry about that."

"Not your fault. I'm the one who was too lazy to move the ladder."

Reid smiled, his straight white teeth bright against his tanned skin. Most New Englanders didn't have a tan yet in mid-June, but with as much time as Reid and Ella spent outside, his made sense. His dark brown hair was cut short, showing off his strong jaw and those pretty hazel eyes. She hardly ever noticed people's eye color, but his were so unusual—sometimes more brownish, sometimes more greenish, and always with that hint of gold. Right now, his brows lifted over them.

She was staring. A stupid grin crossed her face, but she couldn't stop it. "What are you doing out on a day like this?"

"Wasn't ready to go home to an empty house just yet."

In the three months she'd been in Coventry, she'd met a few people. James Sullivan owned The Patriot, a restaurant down the street, and a company that offered backpacking tours to tourists. He'd introduced himself to her shortly after she'd started and offered his assistance if she ever needed anything. His wife, Cassidy, worked at the youth center just a few blocks away and came in often, usually with one of the girls she mentored. Chelsea, who owned HCI, the clothing manufacturer that employed half the town, had come by a few times with her husband, Dylan. He seemed intent on making sure his wife took a break from work every now and then. All these locals and more had made Jacqui feel welcome here.

She liked them, but the visitors she most looked forward to were this man and his little girl.

Reid shrugged out of his raincoat and draped it over a chair, glancing at the empty space. "Big crowd today."

"You're my first customer."

"Bored much?"

"It's torture. How'd it go this morning?"

He slumped into a chair. "Not great."

"Was Ella nervous or—?"

"She was thrilled." Reid looked anything but.

Jacqui sat across from him. "That's good, right? As long as she has to go, she might as well enjoy it." Surely he wouldn't be glad if his daughter were miserable.

"Yeah, of course. I want her to be happy. I want her to enjoy her mother."

"Just not too much," Jacqui guessed.

His lips quirked at one corner. "You know me so well."

She didn't, not really, but she'd like to. After folding the ladder, she headed behind the counter and returned the ladder to the storage room. When she was back in the store, she stood behind the glass case. "I know exactly what you need."

"Not one of your *innovations*." He slapped his hand over his stomach. "I don't think I can take any more disappointment today."

She let her jaw drop. "I'm offended! You should have tried chocolate banana and cherry bomb."

"I'm begging you."

She chuckled. "Your loss, then. What'll it be?"

"I'd say surprise me, but I've made that mistake before. How about mint chocolate chip?"

She feigned a giant yawn. "Coming right up."

He sidled into one of the four soda-fountain barstools at the far end of the counter and watched as she mounded two scoops into a waffle cone, then headed for the toppings. "Jimmies?"

"Let's not meddle with perfection."

She rolled her eyes and handed over his cone. "No charge." She wouldn't charge him, but she'd pay for it herself. It wouldn't be right to give away someone else's product, and Jacqui always tried to do the right thing.

He licked the treat. "You're not joining me?"

"If I eat any more ice cream, I won't fit into my jeans."

He studied her, tilting his head a bit. "You do look good in them." His eyes widened the slightest bit as if surprised he'd said it.

Was he flirting with her? She'd never been great at picking up on things like that, but she was fairly certain.

On the other hand, he seemed sorry he'd said it.

How was she supposed to respond? Should she be offended? Some of her friends from school would've been, but the man had complimented her, hadn't he?

And she liked Reid. He was handsome and kind, and there was something heartwarming and attractive about a man who doted on his child the way he did. Who knew good fathers could be so... sexy?

When was the last time she'd thought the word sexy? Had she ever?

She had no idea what she was doing. She needed to get back to her lab, where it was safe. Yet, even as she considered, she knew that, at this moment, there was no place she'd rather be.

Reid's playful look faded. "I'm sorry. I'm not very good at this."

"This?" Oh, why had she asked? What was wrong with her?

He shrugged and licked his treat.

She needed to say something to move them past the awkwardness. "Shouldn't you be working?"

"Tactical error on my part." He seemed to have forgotten about the ice cream until it dripped down his fingers. She snatched a napkin and handed it to him. "Thanks. Maybe a cup?"

She handed him one of those and a spoon, and he set the cone inside and wiped his fingers.

"Tactical error?" she prompted.

"I should have found a job that kept me busier in the summer. Ella usually only goes for two weeks. I figured I could help James with his backpacking tours to kill the time. But a month?" He shook his head. "I have no idea what to do with myself."

"Hmm. I need someone to work the counter in the evenings."

"I'm not *that* desperate. Not yet, anyway."

"Don't blame you. Besides, I interviewed a sixteen-year-old yesterday. Kid's cute and has experience. Not sure you could beat him out for the job."

"I always wondered what it would feel like to hit rock bottom."

She chuckled. "Seriously, are you going to be okay? I can only imagine how hard this is for you."

Reid hadn't said much about what had happened with Ella the previous summer, but other locals had filled her in on the child's kidnapping and rescue.

It explained why Reid seemed intent to never let Ella out of his sight. Sending her to California with her mother must be torture.

"I just have to keep busy." He looked outside at the rain. "Unfortunately, James's backpackers cancelled, which leaves me with way too much time on my hands."

"My situation is nothing like yours, but I understand how it feels not to have anything meaningful to do. It's been hard since I left—"

The bell over the door tinkled, and two women walked in. Beyond the glass, a coach bus idled at the curb, gray exhaust pumping into the chilly moist air.

One of the women looked around, turned to the other, and said, "Perfect. Bring 'em in."

Reid muttered, "You did want to be busy."

The other woman marched back outside and stepped into the bus. A moment later, people streamed out and walked inside. They were older, some gray-haired, some using canes, many grumbling, a few smiling, and all heading her way.

Reid asked, "You need my help?"

He almost sounded hopeful, but she wasn't supposed to let anybody behind the counter who didn't work there, and Jacqui had to follow the rules if she expected others to do the same. She hated to see him go, but by the looks of things, she was about to get very busy. "I can handle it. Maybe I'll see you later?"

"What time do you get off?"

"Bree's coming in at four."

"Dinner?"

Dinner? With him. Like a date?

The thought sent both anxiety and anticipation to her heart. She ignored the first and smiled. "I'd love to."

CHAPTER FOUR

Reid wasn't ready to face an empty house. After he left Jacqui, he went to The Patriot and set up his laptop at the lunch counter to work, chatting with James whenever the man had a free moment. Reid's oldest friend had been spending more time at the restaurant he'd inherited after his father's death than he had in years. When the previous manager retired, rather than hiring a new one, James had taken over. Now that he was married, now that the mystery of his sister's death had been solved, he was healing, no longer trying to avoid human contact at all costs. The fact that his new wife, Cassidy, worked just a few blocks away was incentive for him to stay close to home these days, which was why he'd been eager for Reid to handle a couple of the backpacking tours. The two were practically inseparable.

Reid was answering customer emails when a shadow crossed his workspace. He caught a glimpse of a towel seconds before it hit him in the head.

He rubbed the spot, not that it'd hurt. "Real mature, man."

James's grin had returned shortly after Cassidy agreed to marry him, and he showed it off now. Reid was happy for his friend, only sorry when he had to witness the two lovebirds all snuggled up and in love.

"You looked like you needed a distraction," James said.

"Just work. You know." His new online clothing retailer wasn't setting any sales records, but he could pay his bills. And when he couldn't, he had savings. They were making it. Not that he'd ever be able to compete with his ex.

But why would he care about that? He was the better parent in every way that mattered. So what if Denise was worth millions?

"How'd it go this morning?"

Reid snapped his laptop closed. "Denise is up to something."

James's amusement faded. "What do you mean?"

"You know how she is, flighty and flaky and utterly self-absorbed."

James tipped his head from side to side. "She had some good qualities, too, you know. You loved her. Surely you can remember a few of them."

If he tried really hard, he might be able to come up with one or two. She was beautiful. She was fun. She was also irresponsible and childish and... He blew out a breath. "Not anymore."

Someone must've been leaving because James lifted his hand and called, "Thanks for coming."

"Great food," a woman said. "We'll be back."

Reid turned in time to see the little family of five scoot out the door and onto the covered sidewalk. The rain had picked up since Reid had been inside. Had Jacqui walked to work that morning? She'd told Ella that she usually did, but the rain had only been a drizzle that morning. Now, it was a downpour.

"Nothing, huh?" James asked.

Reid shook thoughts of Jacqui from his mind and tried to remember what they'd been talking about.

"Not saying I want you to fall for her again," James continued, "but it probably wouldn't hurt Ella if you didn't loathe her mom."

Denise. Right. Reid had spent way too much time thinking about his ex over the years. "She wasn't here, James. Her daughter was kidnapped, and she didn't even come home." Their daughter had been in the hands of a monster, and Denise couldn't be bothered to take a few days off work to fly in.

James held Reid's gaze. "It's possible there's more to her story than you know."

"What does that mean?"

James regarded him a long moment, eyes narrowed. Finally, he said, "She reached out to Cassy. Cassy hasn't told me anything, just that there's more to Denise's story than any of us understand."

Reid's blood boiled. "Your wife is friends with—"

"Calm down, man. They're not friends. She reached out after Ella's rescue. That's it. They text every so often. I'm not even sure Cassy understands what was going on with Denise at that point, but—"

"Nothing, absolutely nothing Denise was going through was more important than finding our daughter."

James lifted his hands in surrender. "I'm not disagreeing. I'm just saying." He dropped his hands to the bar. "Why do you think she's up to something?"

Reid explained about the detailed notes Denise had taken, but James only smirked. "All these years, you've been frustrated that she didn't take parenting seriously. Now she is, and it bothers you?"

"If it were only that, but she implied that she might try to fight for better visitation rights or maybe..." He couldn't even say what he was thinking.

She wouldn't dare try to get custody, would she?

James started to respond, but, despite the mid-afternoon hour, people were coming in. James had extended the restaurant's hours through dinner for the summer, just to see how it worked. It was normally a breakfast and lunch place, but he was testing to see how they'd do in the evenings. If a crowd at two in the afternoon on a rainy day was any indication, they'd do just fine.

Now that Reid had put into words—or at least into thoughts—

his fears about Denise, he couldn't focus on work. He sipped his soda and waited until James returned.

When he did, he asked, "Can she do that? I thought you two had a pretty solid agreement."

"Even if we did, she could challenge it. But we don't. She left and filed for divorce and never pressed for any of her rights regarding Ella. I have full custody and always have. I've sent Ella to her every year for a couple of weeks because I never wanted Denise to take the issue to court. But, as she reminded me today, she has rights too." He pressed his fingers into his too-short hair. One of these days, he was going to get a real haircut by a real barber, not settle for what he could manage with his electric razor. But haircuts took time, which was usually in short supply.

For the next month, he'd have plenty of that, at least.

"Seems to me," James said, "what happened last summer, and Denise's absence, works in your favor."

"Yeah. Maybe."

"Do you have a lawyer who can advise you?"

"Yeah. He's the one who talked me into letting Ella go for a month. Thought it would be better to placate Denise than fight her. If I fight her, I risk losing."

"No way, man. You've been with Ella all this time. You've taken care of her. This is her home."

"You're not seeing this the way a judge will," Reid said. "Denise is Ella's mother. She's rich, she's famous, she's probably got a team of lawyers at her disposal. She can offer Ella so much more than I can."

"Money isn't everything. Money matters very little when it comes to raising a kid. What matters is that Ella is safe and secure."

"From a judge's standpoint, Ella can be safe and secure in California as easily as she can in New Hampshire." Reid swallowed the anxiety rising in his throat. "Pray Denise changes her mind about this. Because if it comes down to court, I think I'll lose. And so will Ella."

~

REID WASN'T A STALKER. He was just bored. And lonely.

Ella had been gone—he glanced at his watch—approximately six hours, and already he had no idea what to do with himself.

Maybe showing up at the ice cream shop earlier—in a rainstorm and without his daughter in tow—had been odd.

But sitting out here now, waiting for Jacqui to get out of work? That was downright stalkerish.

Was that even a word?

But if Jacqui had walked to work in a drizzle this morning, she'd have to walk home in a downpour. No raincoat or umbrella would be enough to protect her in this weather. And anyway, he didn't know where she lived or what her phone number was, and how could he take her to dinner if he couldn't reach her?

The little voice in his head told him he could easily have called the shop, but he was here now. If she thought he was too forward? Well, that would end this, whatever *this* was.

Was it really so awful to offer a woman a ride home in the rain?

He didn't know. He hadn't dated anyone since Denise, and he'd been in high school when they started seeing each other. The rules had changed in the years since then, but nobody had given him a playbook.

That he was even considering dating now said a lot about how alone he felt. He had to find a way to fill the long hours until his daughter returned home. Previous summers, he'd worked full-time, but going back to work after the kidnapping had been torture. Ella had needed him. He'd continued on at HCI for months, but that spring, as the end of the school term neared, he'd resigned from his job and started an internet clothing retail business.

A thriving business, except in summer when many of his customers were on vacation.

Thanks to the heavy cloud cover and the bright white interior of the ice cream shop, he could see Jacqui chatting with Bree. She disappeared into the back, reappeared wearing a raincoat, and headed for the door.

When she stepped onto the sidewalk, Reid opened his car door and climbed out. "Can I give you a lift?"

She must not have heard him over the pouring rain. Hood up, head down, she turned and walked away.

He shouted, "Hey, Jacqui!"

She paused and glanced his way but didn't seem to recognize him. He glimpsed a flash of fear in her eyes an instant before she picked up speed, practically running the other direction.

What in the world?

Should he follow or let her go?

Before he could talk himself out of it, he climbed back in his car, turned it around, and followed. He leveled with where she'd slowed back to a walk on the sidewalk, lowered his window, and tried again. "It's Reid. You want a ride?"

This time, she took a longer look, then hurried to the passenger door and climbed inside. After the door slammed, she said, "I don't even think ducks like this weather." She turned to face him, tight smile in place. "Sorry about that." She motioned to the dampness on his armrest. Her face was pale, and the shadow of fear remained.

"It'll dry." He waited until she'd settled and put on her seatbelt. "What was that about?"

"What do you mean?"

"You heard me. When I called before, you ran."

"I didn't realize it was you."

He opened his mouth, then snapped it shut. That was only half an answer. It didn't explain her fear.

"Did you just happen to be driving by?" she asked.

That would explain away the stalker behavior, but he didn't want to lie. "I was working at The Patriot. I mean, not working there, but on my business, with my laptop. Anyway, I remembered you once said you always walked to work, and I thought you might want a ride home. Plus, I never got your number, and we'd talked about dinner, and..." Now he was babbling.

But her smile turned genuine. This woman, with her dark red hair and light brown eyes, with those high cheekbones and full lips. He'd thought her beautiful the first moment he'd met her. That she was kind to his daughter hadn't hurt.

The way she was smiling at him now, she was stunning.

"That was very thoughtful," she said. "Thank you."

He forced himself to stop staring. "Where to?"

She directed him to a house on the lake about a mile from the shop. He pulled into the driveway and parked as close as he could to the walkway. "Nice place."

"It is, isn't it?" She gazed at the cottage. "I rented it sight unseen and was very pleased when I moved in."

"Can I pick you up about six?"

"That'll work." She undid her seatbelt and turned to him with another one of those heart-stopping smiles. "Thanks again."

Reid watched until she was safely inside, already counting the minutes until dinner. Jacqui would be the perfect diversion while Ella was out of town. He just needed to make sure they kept this casual because, once Ella was home, he'd have no time for a relationship, no matter how enchanting Jacqui might be.

CHAPTER FIVE

Jacqui studied the menu at the Italian restaurant Reid had chosen. It had a casual atmosphere—wood tables and chairs, walls painted light blue, exposed beams overhead. Her favorite feature was the stone fireplace in the center and the flames crackling within.

She'd had a salad delivered for lunch, but hours had passed since then. The scents of tomatoes and garlic and onions hanging in the air made her stomach rumble. "What do you recommend?"

"Everything," he said. "I usually order the spaghetti, but I've never had a bad meal here."

"Why am I not surprised." She tapped the unique combinations on the menu. "All these yummy possibilities, and you go for the mint-chocolate-chip of Italian food."

He chuckled. "What can I say? I'm a simple guy."

She wasn't sure about that. He'd changed into a pale green button-down shirt that brought out the gold in his eyes. He'd shaved since she'd seen him that afternoon, but most of the time, he had scruffy whiskers as if he couldn't be bothered. Or perhaps he didn't have time. Being a single father couldn't be easy, and as much time as he spent with his daughter—Jacqui saw them a couple of times a week in the ice cream shop or in the park across the street—he probably didn't have a lot of spare moments. He was incredibly handsome, more so because he clearly didn't try very hard.

They chatted about the food until they got their drinks and placed their orders.

She sipped her water and set it down. "Have you heard from Ella?"

Reid's easy smile faded. "Not a word." He checked his watch. "It's only three thirty there, though. I'll call when it's closer to bedtime."

"And her mother lives in California, did you say?"

He nodded once, then added, "Beverly Hills."

"Posh."

Reid shrugged, then blew out a breath. "I probably never told you this."

He seemed less than eager to tell her now, whatever it was.

"Her mother is Denise Masterson, but the world knows her as Denise Masters."

Was Jacqui supposed to recognize that name?

His eyebrow quirked. "You don't know who that is?"

"Should I?"

He laughed, a genuine, joy-filled laugh. "Nope. Not at all. In fact, I think that's my favorite thing about you so far."

"You have a list?"

"I definitely have a list." His eyes twinkled. "Maybe I'll share it on our second date."

"There's incentive."

They gazed at each other over the table, Jacqui mesmerized by those gold flecks in his irises, until Reid cleared his throat and broke eye contact. "Anyway, she's an actor, my ex. She's in those superhero movies. Maybe you've seen them?"

"I haven't seen a movie since..." Jacqui thought back. After a moment, she admitted defeat. "I don't even remember the last movie I saw. Probably in college."

"That long?"

"I'm not *that* old."

"Oh." He laughed. "That's not what I meant. What do you do for entertainment?"

She shrugged. "Read, sometimes."

"What do you like to read?"

"This and that." She thought about the medical and tech journals stacked on her nightstand at home. She wasn't ready to reveal how much of a nerd she was. "How did you meet Denise?"

His smile dimmed a little. "We were high school sweethearts. After graduation, we went to Plymouth State, right down the road. She got pregnant our senior year. I'd figured we'd marry anyway, so I proposed, and we eloped."

"Romantic."

The way his lips slipped into a smirk, she didn't think he agreed. "That fall, Ella was born, and we bought a little house in town. I went to work for HCI, and she stayed home with the baby. I thought she was happy. Or at least, not miserable. She had some postpartum depression, but everybody said it would go away. Eventually."

"I hear it generally does." Jacqui had done some research on depression for an idea that hadn't panned out. So many of them didn't.

"I'd always known Denise wanted to be an actor but, once Ella came along... I fell instantly in love with our daughter. Denise?" His Adam's apple bobbed. "She didn't seem to feel the same way. She lamented her lost acting career. She blamed me and Ella and God, I think."

"That must've been hard. Newly married, young, and with an infant."

"I tried to encourage her. She could've found acting gigs nearby. There are theaters around, or she could've done some local ads, that kind of thing. I never understood. All those years we were together, and I guess I never really knew her."

"Whatever happened, I'm sure it wasn't your fault."

"I won't take all the blame, but I probably didn't try hard

enough to understand. I was young and stupid and, frankly, annoyed at her attitude. Here we'd been given this precious child, and Denise could barely tolerate her. Or me." He tapped the side of his water glass. She kept silent, figuring he was gathering words to continue. "Ella was four months old. I came home from work to find Denise had packed her belongings. Her parents were there, trying to talk her out of it. But she was determined. She left for California that night. We all thought she'd crash and burn and be back within a year. Instead, she got a small part on a TV series. And then another. And then the movies and now—"

"She's Denise Masters, apparently famous."

He grinned. "Apparently not *that* famous."

"You know I'll be looking her up tonight."

"Just don't be fooled by the airbrushed photos. She was always pretty, but not like they make her look."

"Must be hard on Ella, being so far from her."

"They barely know each other. Ella's gone out there to visit a couple of times. Last year, after Ella was kidnapped, I refused to let her out of my sight. Denise came here and stayed a few days, apparently all she could fit in with her tight schedule. One visit a year does not a relationship make."

"This time, it's a month, right?"

"Is it wrong that I'm hoping Denise has a terrible time? That she realizes how hard motherhood is and decides she doesn't want to be bothered with it?"

Reid seemed to be half-joking, but the other half? Jacqui wasn't sure how to answer him. She could make him feel better, or she could tell the truth. She shrugged and pulled one of the rolls from the basket in the center of the table.

"I take it that's a yes," he guessed. "I am a terrible, terrible person."

"You're a really engaged father who wants his daughter home."

"And safe," he added. "I don't trust Denise to protect her."

"That doesn't make you a bad person. But..." At Reid's raised eyebrow—just the one, an unspoken invitation to continue her sentence. She broke a bite off her roll, buttered it, and popped it in her mouth.

Reid didn't say a word, just kept staring at her with that eyebrow quirked like a question mark.

"Girls need their mothers," Jacqui finally said. "Even a less than ideal mother is better than no mother at all. Ella needs to have somebody to talk to about girl things. At six, she can tell you anything, but when she gets older, she's going to need a woman in her life, somebody to confide in and ask questions of. There are some things dads simply can't help with."

That eyebrow lowered. "She has two grandmothers who dote on her. Cassidy's become like an aunt to her. She doesn't need Denise."

Jacqui wasn't sure that was true, but she said, "Okay," and hoped the subject would drop.

Because she didn't want to say what she was thinking, that girls did need their mothers. She couldn't imagine life without her own mom. Dad had been so busy, pioneering medical procedures and then teaching those procedures around the globe. Mom had been enough, though. She'd stayed home with Jacqui, cared for her, protected her. Jacqui'd never had a lot of girlfriends, but Mom had always been her confidant. While she and her father could talk about medical advancements for hours, when she had questions about life or people or relationships or anything else, she called Mom.

Even without her mother as a big part of her life, Ella was fortunate that she'd never have to wonder about her father's devotion. There was no question Reid adored his little girl and would do anything for her. That was true of Jacqui's own father, even if he'd never been very good at showing it.

A group came in the doorway, bringing a cold breeze with them. Jacqui shivered and aimed her chilled hands at the cozy fireplace not six feet away.

"Are you cold? You want me to get your jacket?" He'd hung it by the door when they came in and started to stand to retrieve it.

"I'm fine," she said. "I love a wood fire."

His eyes narrowed the slightest bit. "Wood as opposed to…?"

"My place in the city is old, and the fireplaces all need work. I had the one in the living room converted to gas, but flipping a switch isn't exactly the same as that." She nodded to the crackling logs. "I keep thinking I'll get them repaired, but…" Her explanation didn't seem to satisfy Reid. His mouth opened, then snapped shut. "What?"

"Fireplaces?" Emphasis on the plural. "How many do you have?"

Oh. She'd said too much. "A few. You know how those old places are. It was built before central heat."

"So this ice cream gig in Coventry is only temporary?"

Right. They hadn't talked about that. They'd spent a little time together, but Ella had always been at the center of those conversations. Just the two of them—it was different.

Not awkward or uncomfortable. Just different.

"I own a business in Boston. We had a bit of a mishap. Rather than hang around and wait for the insurance money to come in, I thought I'd get out of the city for a little while."

"What kind of mishap?"

She didn't want to share the details about her business or her former partner. She was trying to keep a low profile, rarely even sharing her last name and always being careful not to be photographed. She didn't know Reid well enough to tell him the whole truth about why she was there. "Let's not talk about that tonight. Tell me about what you do."

He launched into an explanation about the business he'd started. She'd successfully diverted him this time, but eventually she was going to have to decide if this handsome stranger was worthy of her trust.

~

By the time the tiramisu they'd shared was no more than crumbs on the plate, Jacqui felt a little smitten with her dinner companion. Ridiculous, considering she barely knew the man. But, after he'd told her a little about his business, which was already successful even though he'd only been at it a couple of months, he'd launched into stories about Ella that had her laughing out loud.

The man was smart and industrious and, most importantly, head-over-heels for his little girl.

There was something incredibly attractive about that.

They were just climbing into his car when her phone rang.

She reached in her purse and glanced at the screen. Braden? What could he need at this time of night?

She rejected the call. She'd reach out when she got back to the cottage, which would be too soon for her taste. Though she and Reid had lingered over dessert, she wasn't ready to go home.

Maybe it would be more honest to admit she wasn't ready to leave Reid's company.

Reid stopped at a light. She glanced his way and caught him looking and only barely suppressed her smile.

He snapped his attention back to the road. "Everything okay?"

"I'll call him back later."

Reid nodded. "Him?"

"My assistant. I have no idea—"

Her phone rang again. Again, she pulled it from her purse. Again, she saw Braden's name.

"Go ahead," Reid said. "I'll try not to eavesdrop." That last part was delivered with a smile.

Reluctantly, she swiped to answer. "Is this an emergency?"

There was a pause, then, "Not exactly."

"Because I'm—" On a date? No, that was none of Braden's business. "Out with a friend. I'll call you tomorrow."

"Don came by the shop today."

The very mention of her former partner's name sent acid to her too full stomach. "What did he want?"

"He told me about the deal he put together for our neuron. He said you rejected it. It sounded like a good deal."

Now it was *our* neuron. Never mind that Jacqui had invented it. And Jacqui owned the majority share in the business that'd paid for its development. Never mind that Braden had exactly zero right to question her about this.

But Don could be persuasive, and Braden was young and inexperienced, and he'd practically worshipped the man. She sent up a quick prayer for patience and said, "And?"

"What Don did to the lab was awful, and I'm not saying you should forgive him. But he put together a good contract. I don't understand why you're not agreeing to it."

"Did Don tell you the name of the company that wants to buy it?"

"No." His voice lost a bit of its confidence. "Does it matter?"

"Have you heard of Tarim Biomedical?"

"No, but—"

"The company matters, Braden. Look, I get that we're a for-profit enterprise, but I'm in this to change lives."

"According to Don, it's one of the biggest pharmaceutical companies in the world. They have the resources to develop—"

"Slow down and think about what you just said. Tarim is a *pharmaceutical* company, not a medical device developer."

"Don says they're planning to put together an entire team just to develop technology for the artificial neuron. You've said yourself you're not good at the business end of this. He is. I don't understand why you're rejecting his plan out of hand."

A car cut them off, and Reid hit the brakes, jolting Jacqui out of the conversation and back to the present—and the present company.

Reid didn't need to hear this.

"Look," she said, "I'm happy to discuss this with you, but I'm busy right now. I'll call you tomorrow."

"What about the conference? Are we still going to be there?"

She'd completely forgotten about the research-and-development conference later that month. That was another part of the business Don had always managed. "We don't have a booth, right?"

"Not this year, but Don thinks we should attend. I can go, if you want me to. I mean, I think you should be there. You can do a lot more good than I can. I just wasn't sure. I think he expected you and him to go together, at least before Lola died."

"What would...?" She felt like an idiot for saying it, but, "What would be the point? I mean, what exactly would we do?"

"Meet people, tell them about what BNB has been up to, tell them about the neuron and generate buzz. Basic networking."

Networking. Her nemesis. "Okay, yeah. Plan to go."

"You'll be there, too, right?"

"Yes, I suppose. Will you get the details and send them to me? Figure out exactly what's expected and how we're supposed to dress and what we should bring and all that?"

"You've been to these things before, haven't you?"

"I've always just shown up with Don. He does all the work, and I stand there until somebody asks me a question. It really isn't my thing."

"Yeah. I'll do what I can. It's not my place to ask, but where are you? I haven't seen you in months. I went to your place today, and a stranger answered the door."

Annie, her house sitter, a woman she'd hired on the recommendation of a friend.

"I told you I didn't want to get another job," Braden continued, "but you haven't even started rebuilding, and if you're not planning on coming back—"

"I am coming back. I'm on hold until I get the insurance money, and I'm taking a sabbatical, that's all. If you don't want to wait any longer, I understand. Start sending out resumes, and I'll write you a glowing recommendation."

There was a pause before Braden blew out a long breath. "I'm sorry. I don't want to get another job. I shouldn't have questioned—"

"I understand. I'll call you tomorrow." She swiped to disconnect and tossed the phone in her purse, wishing she could toss all the problems Braden had brought up. But avoiding them wasn't helping. "Sorry about that."

Reid cast her a quick glance. "You want to talk about it?"

She was surprised to find she did, but they were nearing the edge of Coventry. They'd be at her cottage in ten minutes. "It's late. Maybe another time."

"It's eight thirty. We're not exactly burning the midnight oil."

That was true. What was he suggesting, though?

He glanced her way. "Never mind. You're probably ready to get home."

"What are the options?"

"Hmm. It's a little wet for a walk. I'm not much of a drinker."

She was glad to hear that. "Me, either."

"Coffee?"

"Is there any place open?"

He smiled and took the next turn. Three minutes later, they were parked in front of a little house that had to have been standing for a hundred years. Only the swinging sign sporting a black-and-white image of a steaming mug told her it was a business and not a home.

"Cuppa Josie's. Best-kept secret in town." Reid parked on the street in front of the old place and turned to face Jacqui, a serious look on his face. "I'll take you here as long as you promise not to tell anybody about it. The tourists haven't discovered it yet."

"I didn't know the locals were so against outsiders."

"Not outsiders, just tourists. People who stay more than"—he paused to think—"three months no longer fit the category."

"Phew. I barely made it."

He grinned and opened his car door.

Jacqui reached for her handle, then stopped as Reid rushed around the front. A moment later, he pulled her door open.

Her father still opened her mother's car door and helped her from the car. Jacqui loved that about them. Her parents were so different from one another, but they adored each other.

Rarely had Jacqui met a man with manners as good as her father's. Reid had impressed her in that area as he had in so many others that evening.

She took his hand and let him help her from the car. His grip was somehow both firm and gentle, his skin warm despite the cool evening. She expected him to release her as soon as she was safely out of the car, but he held on as they climbed the front steps. Only after he'd opened the door for her did he let go.

How long had it been since a man had held her hand?

Probably as long as it'd been since she'd seen a movie, if not longer.

The aroma of coffee hit her the moment she stepped inside. She wasn't sure what she'd expected, but not this. Worn couches and comfy chairs filled the small room in front of her. A door to her right opened to another room, this one with a few café tables. Patrons sat in various places, sipping drinks, some staring at laptops, others chatting with companions. It didn't feel like a coffee shop as much as an inviting home that happened to sell coffee.

She wasn't sure where they were going to sit. There didn't seem to be any open spots.

Reid settled his hand on the small of her back and guided her across the hardwood—it had to be original—to the glass case ahead, which held a small selection of cupcakes, though it had plenty of room for more.

"You hungry?" Reid asked from behind her.

After the meal she'd just eaten? "You're kidding, right?"

He chuckled, the sound deep and rumbly, which caused her heart to do a girlish little flip. "Just as well. Looks like they're nearly cleaned out."

A slender woman stood on the far side of the counter. "What can I get you?"

"Do you have decaf tea?" Jacqui asked.

"Earl Gray okay?"

"Perfect."

The woman looked past her. "Your usual?"

"Just decaf tonight."

When their drinks were ready, Reid led Jacqui through a door to her right into a smaller room she hadn't noticed. Like the others, this one was filled with a mishmash of furniture. Unlike the others, there were no patrons in here.

"Where do you want to sit?" Reid asked.

She chose a smallish armchair in front of the cold fireplace, and he settled in the one across from her. "This place is charming."

"Ella loves the cupcakes."

"I wish I were hungry."

"We'll come back, then." He looked around, then met her eyes with an amused grin. "This is a good place for me to share that list of things I like about you. But not tonight—that's definitely a second-date conversation."

She couldn't help but return his smile. "Let's see how this one plays out first."

He lifted his coffee in a sort of salute. "I'll be on my best behavior."

Her tea was already strong and a little too hot to enjoy, so she set the teabag on the saucer with the cup and put them both on the small table between her and Reid. Though it looked as if it could be an antique, its top was stained with drink rings, which didn't detract from its beauty but somehow added to it.

"So, you were going to tell me about that phone call?" Reid prompted.

The evening was far too pleasant for such an unpleasant conversation. On the other hand, tucked in this cozy shop in this faraway town across from this man, she felt safe, truly safe, for the first time since she'd stepped into her wrecked lab three months earlier.

She felt like she could breathe.

"My business develops products for use in medical devices."

"Okay." His head tilted to the side. "But not the devices themselves?"

"My research is smaller than that, more like microchips."

"Like Intel? Isn't that what they make?"

"My focus is on the medical field. We developed an artificial neuron."

His eyebrows rose. "I should've paid more attention in biology. A neuron—that's a type of cell, right?"

"A nerve cell." She wasn't great at explaining things in layman's terms, but she'd give it a shot. "It's the cell that transmits and receives nervous impulses."

Reid was nodding slowly. "And you made an artificial one? What will you do with it?"

"There are so many possibilities. Think of it for paraplegics who can't move their legs, not because their bodies aren't capable but because the nerves are damaged. This is just one step, but it could lead to a cure."

"Wow."

She launched into an explanation of the different uses for her invention—everything from heart failure to autism to Alzheimer's. She hadn't spoken about it—had hardly let herself think about it— for months, and once she got going, she found it difficult to slow the flow of words.

Reid was nodding along, asking questions and generally encouraging her to talk. Which she did, more than she had in far too long.

When he set down his empty cup, she realized she'd forgotten about layman's terms, forgotten to read her audience. "I'm sorry. I went on a tangent there."

"It's fascinating." He seemed like he meant it, but Jacqui could tell by the look on his face that she'd lost him.

And here she'd determined not to let on what a nerd she was until at least the second date.

CHAPTER SIX

Reid had no idea what Jacqui was talking about.

He'd followed at first—an artificial neuron that could work with existing neurons to get them to function properly. But then she'd started using vocabulary he hadn't heard since chemistry class.

Some of her words, he'd never heard at all.

Jacqui was obviously brilliant. It was only a matter of time before she figured out what a dolt he was. And anyway, confused as he was, he thoroughly enjoyed watching her.

Her eyes sparkled with passion. Her hands joined her words in what he assumed would have been a perfectly intelligent explanation to somebody who'd done more in high school biology than play finger-football with James and stare at Denise across the room.

Reid must've done something to let on that she'd lost him because the sparkle in those bright eyes dimmed. "Anyway, it could be groundbreaking."

"Sounds amazing."

She shrugged and sipped her tea, her gaze slipping to the cold fireplace.

"I'm guessing based on the phone call earlier that all is not well."

"Right. Sorry. I got off topic."

Reid leaned forward, forearms resting on his legs. "Even though I didn't understand half of what you just said, I love your passion. I love your desire to serve people, to heal people. It's beautiful."

"Oh." Her pale skin turned pink. "Thank you."

Her passion was beautiful. She was beautiful. What this gorgeous, genius creature was doing with him, he had no idea.

He sat back, trying to figure out how to get her to keep talking, but Josie stepped into the room, focus on Jacqui. "Did you not like it? I'll be happy to get you something else."

She'd hardly touched her tea. She took a second sip. "It's very good, thank you."

Josie turned to him. "Refill?"

He lifted his cup, and she poured the steaming brew into it. He was in no hurry to end this evening.

After she stepped away, Reid nodded to Jacqui. "Are you planning to develop any of the products you just talked about?"

"That's outside my area of expertise. There are much better people for that job."

"So, what happens next?"

"That's the million-dollar question. My assistant was calling to tell me that my partner—former partner—went to see him today and told him about an offer we received, an offer I refused. Braden wanted to know why."

Her words raised more questions than they answered. He figured he'd start with the most obvious. "Former partner?"

She sighed. "Long story."

He lifted his full cup of coffee. "I've got nowhere to be." And, based on the wealth of information she'd just given him and the worry on her face right now, Jacqui needed to talk.

"Don was one of my father's mentors. Apparently, Dad had been bragging about me. You know, like fathers do." Her eyebrows lifted, and he chuckled.

"I have been known to brag a time or two."

"How could you not? Your daughter's amazing."

Reid was learning that Jacqui's father's daughter was pretty amazing herself.

"Anyway, Don wanted to start a small research lab and recruited me right out of college. Though he understands the science and can help with the big picture, he's not great at the details, the nitty-gritty work."

"The actual inventing part of invention," Reid guessed.

She lifted one shoulder and dropped it. "But he gets things I don't, like the sales side of it. He can reduce the most complex things to terms anybody can understand. Not only that, but Don's really good at spotting young talent and helping people achieve their potential. I could never have built our company alone."

"Sounds like he could never have built it without you."

Her head dipped slowly, an acknowledgement. "He was like a grandfather to me. I trusted him completely."

Reid didn't miss the switch into past tense. He said nothing, just waited for her to continue. After another sip of her tea, she did.

"Two years ago, his wife was diagnosed with cancer. Don was certain she'd recover, despite what the doctors were saying. I've never been vocal about my faith. I know I should be. I know the Great Commission is called that for a reason. But Boston's not exactly the spiritual hub of the universe, and in my profession..."

Reid had seen Jacqui at church nearly every Sunday since she'd moved to town. It was good to hear that it wasn't just a Sunday morning activity for her but a response to true faith.

Being surrounded by atheists and agnostics every single day couldn't be easy. Reid had dealt with that in college, and he'd lost his faith for a little while, overly impressed with the intellectual arguments against God he heard so often. And then Ella was born. One look at her perfect face and Reid knew that there was a God, and He was good.

Between Boston's academia and its science community, Jacqui must be bombarded by false beliefs every day. He was impressed she'd held onto her faith. So many would've given it up.

"When things started to look bleak for Lola," she said, "I visited her and told her about the Lord. I'd tried to talk to her and Don about it a little before, and they'd always brushed me off. This time, though, she listened. We prayed together." Tears filled Jacqui's eyes. She shook her head slightly as if to rid it of dark thoughts before she continued.

"My folks spend most of their time in Hilton Head. Don and Lola became my family in the city. They have kids, but they're not close. Both of them have kind of gone off the rails, I guess. His son spent some time in prison. His daughter narrowly escaped it. Anyway, Don and Lola sort of made me like an adopted grand-daughter. I spent most of my holidays with them. We celebrated birthdays together. But as Lola got sicker, Don got... I don't know how to explain it. Darker, I guess. He was desperate to save her life and insisted she get into this drug trial. It was very expensive, and she wasn't the perfect candidate. But he had a friend who pulled some strings. It did nothing but make her feel sicker than she would have otherwise. She died in February."

"I'm sorry. It must have been hard for Don, that balance between doing everything you can without sacrificing the person you're trying to save."

"Exactly." She dabbed at her eyes. "Lola agreed to the trial for Don's sake. The problem was, they didn't have the money for it. I was against it from the start. Lola's body wasn't going to recover at that point. But it was important to Don, so I offered to loan him the money he needed."

Medical trials were expensive. Where would Jacqui have gotten the funds?

He wasn't going to ask, but Jacqui must've seen something in his expression, because she said, "I don't have a lot of expenses. Most of what we'd made in the business, I'd put away. And I had some family money. It wasn't that much."

He doubted that but nodded for her to continue.

"Anyway, Don was angry at me. He was furious that I'd told Lola about Jesus and furious that she'd 'found religion.'" Jacqui made air quotes around those words.

"You're kidding. Why?"

"Because God gave her peace. She agreed to the trial to placate him, but she was no longer afraid of death. She got to the point where she welcomed it. She was ready to meet her Savior. Don believes she died because she gave up fighting, and he blames me for that."

"That's"—Reid groped for a good word and landed on —"insane."

"I'm afraid that's exactly what it was. He wasn't in his right mind. The more she deteriorated, the more bizarre his behavior became. He wouldn't accept a loan. He swore he was done with the business and done with me. So I bought him out, all but ten percent, which I absolutely refused to buy. I wanted him to know he'd always have a place with BNB, whenever he was ready to return. We had the company restructured, making me the managing partner and him a silent partner. All the while, I'd planned to let him buy back those shares whenever he was ready."

"That was generous of you, all things considered."

"I wouldn't be where I am without Don. Without him, I'd be working for someone else's company, following their vision instead of my own. I owe so much to him. And Lola."

"I can see that. But it seems to me like he owes you too. Am I overstating things if I say that, without you, he'd never have invented your artificial neuron?"

She shrugged but said nothing.

"There are a lot of great business people in the world." Reid had discovered he was one of them. He'd learned a lot working for HCI. Since he'd struck out on his own, he'd learned a lot more. One of the things he'd learned was that he had a knack for it. But then, so did millions of other people. "The ability to spot talent—

that's less common but not exactly rare. But I bet there aren't a hundred people on the planet who can invent an artificial neuron."

Her lip quirked up at the corner. "More than that."

"A hundred and ten, then. The point is, he couldn't have built it without you. He seems more... I don't mean to sound callous here, but he seems more replaceable than you are in your company."

"I didn't want to replace him." Jacqui sighed. "I was sure that, once he processed his grief, he'd want to come back, get things back to normal."

"I'm guessing that's not what happened."

She gazed past Reid, and he waited, wondering what was going on behind those beautiful eyes.

Finally, she said, "All that time, even though he swore he wanted nothing to do with BNB, he was putting this deal together. Per our verbal agreement, Don gets half of the profit from the neuron."

Reid sat up straighter. "Half? He only owns ten percent."

"When it was being developed, he owned half. Maybe I was too generous. I was sure he'd come back. I wanted him to come back." She pushed her hair away from her face, then dug in her pocket. "Sorry. It's driving me nuts." She pulled it into a ponytail and secured it with a holder. "I can't stand it down for very long. I should probably cut it."

She definitely should *not* cut that gorgeous hair. But he didn't say so.

"Anyway, Don has a vested interest. He found a buyer, a buyer willing to pay far more than it's worth." By the tightness in the corners of Jacqui's mouth, that was not good news.

Reid set his coffee down and leaned forward. "I take it there's something wrong with the buyer."

"Tarim Pharmaceutical. It's a foreign company. Don't get me wrong—there are good foreign pharmaceutical companies. That's not the problem. But other nations don't have the same regulations as we do here. Now, I'm not a huge fan of regulations, and I think some of the regs in the U.S. are too strict, but they're in place to protect the public. This company is known for pushing the limits even by their country's standards. They perform drug trials among the poorest populations on the planet. They've done some in their own country, but often they'll find some remote village, hang around long enough to test their drugs, and then leave. Even if the drugs are successful, patients need follow-up care. You can't just start somebody on a life-saving drug, give them hope, and then abandon them to die. In one case, the drug ended up killing twenty percent of the test subjects. Did Tarim care?"

Reid started to respond, but Jacqui continued.

"Usually the patients—victims might be a better word—are poor and uneducated. They don't know what they're getting them-selves into. They see a bunch of men in suits with *doctor* in front of their names, and they trust them. They sign away their rights so that, even if they had the financial resources to sue, they have no legal recourse. Tarim's CEO gave an interview on the subject and chalked up the bodies they leave in their wake to *progress*. He pointed to the life-saving drugs they've developed. And they have developed those drugs, but their practices are unethical and, in some cases, inhumane. And unnecessary. There are safe ways to do drug trials, safe and ethical ways. They're just costlier."

"I can see—"

"But that's not the worst of it." Jacqui leaned forward as if to press her point. "It's a *pharmaceutical* company. Remember all those uses for our artificial neuron that I mentioned?"

"Sure. Paralysis, heart conditions, autism—"

"Alzheimer's," she added. "Tarim is a leading manufacturer of a drug widely prescribed for Alzheimer's patients. It's their bread-and-butter drug."

Reid was starting to get it. "You're saying they have a vested interest in seeing that your neuron isn't developed."

She flipped her hand toward him as if he'd made her point.

"Exactly." She sat back and blew out a long breath. "You get it. You're the first person who gets it without me spelling it out."

"Even if their intentions were honorable—"

"There's nothing honorable about the people who run that company."

"I'm just saying," Reid said, "that even if there were, BNB belongs to you, right? You get to decide where to sell your invention."

She sipped her tea. It had to be cold by now, but she didn't seem to mind. "Don wants to sell the patent license to the highest bidder and get our paycheck up front. I've always trusted his judgment on these things, but he's not thinking straight. I understand where he's coming from. He has all those medical bills and—"

"Wait. Your buying him out didn't cover those? Not that I have any idea what your company is worth, but I would have guessed..." He let his words trail when she shook her head.

"The trial was expensive. All of Lola's care was expensive. And his kids are always coming with their hands out, needing money. I have no idea what he did with the money."

"But you think it's gone."

"His behavior is desperate. I wish I understood what was going on. Maybe then I could help him."

"Desperate how?"

"Oh. I guess I haven't..." Looking beyond Reid, she lifted her hand and called, "Can you warm up my tea?"

A moment later, Josie arrived with a steaming carafe. "Anything else?"

"No, thank you." Jacqui dipped the teabag she'd set aside into the steaming liquid and sipped. "That's better." After Josie walked away, Jacqui said, "I went to see Lola a few days before her death. When I was leaving, Don told me about the deal he'd put together. It sounded too good to be true, and when I learned the name of the company that made the offer, I realized it was. I rejected it. We argued."

Reid's stomach twisted. "Did he hurt you, or—?"

"No, nothing like that." She took a deep breath. "At his house after the funeral, I tried to offer my condolences. He pulled me into his office and threatened to sue me. I was heartbroken, but I wasn't worried. He had no legal leg to stand on. I guess he figured that out because a week later, he... went to the lab."

By the way her voice hitched, by the way she'd tripped over the words, Reid knew there was more to that story.

After setting the teacup on the table, she pulled out her phone, pressed the screen, then handed it to him.

Reid stared at the photo.

Smashed computers, broken glass, papers strewn everywhere. Somebody had destroyed it.

"You can flip through the next few."

He did, seeing machinery on the floor, monitor screens cracked. Drawers taken out and dumped, their contents scattered. A white leather chair had been slashed with a knife, its stuffing poking out the holes.

A rush of adrenaline had his blood pumping as he handed her the phone back. "You're sure it was him?"

"Positive, though the police can't prove it."

"Was he looking for your invention?"

"I think so. I'd always stored it and all our research in the safe. But after the funeral, I moved it all to my house. My guess is that he went to the lab to steal them and, when he discovered they weren't there, he lost his temper."

Reid pointed to the phone still in her hand. "That's more than a lost temper, Jacqui. Anger passes. That took time. Maybe the first thing he threw on the floor, maybe that was rage. Maybe even the second. But after that? He was trying to destroy everything. He was trying to destroy..." He swallowed past the rise of protectiveness, of sheer worry for this woman. "Jacqui, the man who did that is not stable or safe or—"

"The detective said the same thing. Even though he's not convinced it was Don, he told me that whoever'd done it was dangerous. That's why I'm here. I mean, the lab was destroyed, so I can't work. My insurance company hasn't settled my claim."

"What? Why?"

"They're waiting until the police finish their investigation. The detective sent the video camera recording to some lab to see if it had been tampered with. Obviously, it has because it didn't record anybody there at the time of the vandalism."

That word didn't begin to cover what Reid had just seen.

"The lab didn't do that to itself," Jacqui added.

"So what's the holdup?"

She made more air quotes. "'These things take time, ma'am. You're not our only case.' My attorney assures me there's nothing to worry about, that as soon as the police finish the investigation, my insurer will pay. We just have to be patient."

"Meanwhile, you can't work."

She smiled for the first time in an hour. "Maybe it doesn't seem like it to you, but running an ice cream shop is no picnic."

He chuckled. "I suppose, but it's not exactly the same."

Her expression shifted back to somber. "No, it's not. And without Don, to be honest, I'm floundering. He took care of the business end of things. Usually, when I have a problem, I let it simmer on the back burner, if you will, while I do something else, and the solution presents itself. Well, this problem's been simmering for three months, and I still don't know what to do. Don's the businessman, not me. I know exactly zero about that end of things. I need to quit doing nothing, though. I need to..." Her words trailed, and she sipped her tea.

"What do you need to do?"

"That's just it. I'm not sure. I guess I need to find companies to pitch the neuron to. But I don't want just any company. It's got to be one that has the people and the resources to develop great products. They have to be people with the vision to make it happen."

For the first time since they'd started this conversation, Reid felt he had something to offer besides words of encouragement. "I could help. I'm good at research, and I get the business aspect. I don't understand your neuron, but I understand profit and loss, risk and reward." And it would give him something to do besides skulk around the ice cream shop and wait for his daughter to call.

Jacqui studied him through narrowed eyes. "Do you have time for that?"

"I've got nothing but time."

CHAPTER SEVEN

Jacqui was in the middle of catching the assistant manager up on the day when a familiar gray sedan parked at the curb outside the ice cream shop.

"You were saying about the delivery?" Bree prompted, penciled eyebrows rising over too-thick mascara. The girl always wore a full face of makeup to go with her perfectly curled blue hair.

"Driver called," Jacqui said. "They're running late but should be here by five. Do you need me to stay, or—?"

"I've been here for deliveries before. No problem. Anything else?"

"Nope. It's been steady so far."

Bree tied on her apron. "Okay then. See you tomorrow."

"Call if you—"

"Need anything." The girl winked. "I know the drill."

Jacqui stowed her apron, grabbed her purse, and hurried out into the muggy, overcast day. By the time she reached Reid's car, he'd come around and opened the door. "Your chariot, milady."

She stifled a giggle, settling onto the leather seat. "Thank you, kind sir."

He closed her door, rounded the car, and sat beside her. "How was the ice cream today?"

"Cold. How was the"—she searched for a word and landed on —"website?"

He laughed. "Quiet." He hit the turn signal and angled into the busy traffic.

"Did you talk to Ella last night?"

"She finally called at eleven."

"Is she having fun?"

His lip quirked at the corner. "Yes, but she misses me 'lots and lots.'"

"Which makes you happy."

He quit trying to hide the smile. "We've already established that I'm a terrible, terrible person."

The sound that came out of her mouth was closer to a giggle than a laugh. "You're a sweet daddy who wants his little girl home."

He glanced her way. "Her being gone hasn't been *all* bad."

Heat filled her cheeks. She didn't know what to say, so she said nothing.

Reid parked in her driveway, and she led the way into her cottage, where she hung her bag on the hook by the door before continuing through the great room to the kitchen. She turned to direct him to the table, but he hadn't moved past the entry.

"It's bigger than it looks."

He took in the floor-to-ceiling stone fireplace, the remodeled kitchen, and the modern-farmhouse furnishing. "Impressive."

If he found this two-bedroom impressive, she wondered what he'd think of her place in Boston. "Just a rental. I got a good price because I rented it long-term back in March." She indicated the kitchen table. "I thought we'd set up here."

As he settled in a chair, she asked, "Anything to drink?"

"Scotch and water."

Her shock must've shown on her face, because he laughed and said, "Hold the scotch."

She fixed two glasses of ice water and set them on the table. "Be right back."

She hurried up the stairs and grabbed her MacBook from the desk in the second bedroom, which she used as an office. By the time she returned, Reid had his computer plugged in and open. "Wifi password?"

She found the little book that had come with the rental, opened to the right page, and rattled it off. Within minutes, they were both settled, fingers on keyboards, and ready.

He seemed to be waiting for her to take the lead. She was embarrassed to admit the truth. "I don't know where to start."

"I think we're getting ahead of ourselves." He pushed his computer away and pulled a notebook and pen from his bag. "Why don't you give me a list of the companies you're considering."

She rattled off the few that came to mind, and he wrote them down. "There are so many more, but those are the ones in Boston. I know people at those places."

"They all have good reputations?"

"Excellent."

He tapped the paper with his pen a few moments. She was about to suggest they split the list and start researching when he set his pen down and met her eyes. "I don't understand something. I'm sure it makes sense, but do you think a single company will be able to come up with devices for all those things you mentioned last night? I mean, is one company going to develop a device for a paraplegic and a device for Alzheimer's and—?"

"Insightful question." She pushed her laptop aside. "Ideally, rather than sell the rights to the artificial neuron to a single device developer, we'd offer a limited patent license to any company who wanted to buy it. That way, multiple companies could invent devices for multiple things, and we'd make a portion of the profit from all those inventions."

Reid was nodding slowly. "That makes sense. But that's not your plan because...?"

When she thought about the answer, she hated to admit it. "That's not what Don wanted to do."

Reid's only reaction was a slight narrowing of his eyes. "Why?"

"He had all sorts of reasons, but honestly, I think he needs to get the money up front. If we grant patent licenses, we'll make a little on the front end, but in the long run, our income is dependent on what other companies do with it. If they end up not developing anything, we get nothing."

"But the upside potential—"

"Is enormous, of course. But so is the downside. Right now, we only know that the artificial neuron works in the laboratory in very specific conditions. We can't guarantee that it'll work in any device. Don's idea was to license exclusive rights to the patent for ten years, and then offer the patent licenses to other companies after that."

"Get a payday up front and a payday down the road." Reid made a note on his yellow pad. "Smart business. So even if you were to sell to that company Don chose, you'd be able to sell the patent rights again in a decade, right? So it seems—"

"But that's ten lost years, Reid. Ten years. Do you know how many people will die of Alzheimer's in the next ten years?"

"I under—"

"Not to mention heart failure. Do you know how many suffer with autism, with paraplegia?"

He lifted his hands as if surrendering. "I'm not arguing. I have a friend whose brother is a paraplegic. The ability to move his legs would change his life. I'm just trying to understand."

Her pulse was pounding as if she were in a fight. "You're right. I'm sorry. The last time I had this argument, it was with Don. I guess..."

He gave her a gentle smile.

Oh, that smile.

It knocked down all her defenses.

"So, let me just understand what you're saying here." Reid

skimmed his notes, his pen tapping a rhythm on the paper. "You aren't opposed to finding a single company to sell the neuron to—"

"Not the neuron, the rights to use it, and only for a limited time."

"The rights, which you would eventually get back."

"Not necessarily get back. They just wouldn't be exclusive after that set time."

"Okay. I see. You want to license exclusive rights to the neuron for a set timeframe in order to give the buyer a competitive edge to develop products. The buyer pays up front for that edge. After that set time, you'll license those rights to companies that want to buy them."

She processed the question, then nodded. "Yes. That's right." Except... "The truth is, I never bothered with any of this stuff. I'm telling you what I remember from the single class I took on this in college and the things Don has told me. To be honest, I was only ever partially paying attention to him when he explained those things. That's not my raison d'être."

"Should we seek out somebody who has experience with this?"

"My attorneys will be able to help us with the legal ins and outs when the time comes. Right now, I feel like we need to find out if anybody's interested in buying what we're selling."

He made a note on his pad. "Okay. We'll put a pin in that. Our first step is to find someone to license the exclusive rights to because you need to be paid for your work. Like any business, you have overhead and employees. You need to keep the lights on."

"Yes. We've licensed a couple of patents in the last few years, but we've poured all the profit, every bit of capital we have, into developing the artificial neuron. Obviously, we've taken salaries, but modest ones."

Not that Jacqui couldn't keep the lights on and the business going all by herself. But she hadn't touched her trust fund, and she didn't want to now. It was bad enough she lived in a home her parents provided. She refused to be one of those trust-fund kids who couldn't make her own way in the world.

Her father had taken what his parents gave him and turned it into a successful business. He worked hard and built something that mattered, and he managed to do it without touching his trust fund. He'd taught her to do the same. She wouldn't let him down.

Reid made another note. "The business is located where?"

"Boston, near the hospitals."

"Expensive real estate. So, like any business, you need to make money. You need to be paid back what you've invested."

"But I'm in this to save lives first. My assistant, our other techs —we're all in this to save lives. Even Don was mostly in this to save lives. But he needs the money, and now that we've been offered so much?" She blew out a long breath. "I need to find a company I can count on to do the right thing *and* pay us what the exclusive rights will be worth."

"Best guess, are companies going to be clamoring for this?"

She shrugged. "The way Don talked, yes. But then, Don could sell it to them. Don could explain it in ways anyone could understand. He has a gift—one I don't possess."

He shot her that smile again. "I think I can help you with that too. Once we find a couple of target companies, we'll come up with a sales pitch."

"You make it sound so easy."

He shrugged. "Not easy, but doable. I probably won't be anywhere as good as Don, but together, you and I can figure this out."

CHAPTER EIGHT

R eid tipped back in the kitchen chair and yawned, surprised by a wave of exhaustion. Who knew research could be such hard work? It probably wouldn't have been so difficult if he'd understood half of what he was reading. He spent much of his time trying to translate the science and medical-speak on the companies' websites.

Jacqui stood, grabbing the pizza box. She was halfway to the kitchen when she froze. "Oh, my word. It's after eleven."

Reid had lost track of time. He'd lost track of everything while sitting beside her all those hours. Her hair had gone from flowing down her back to a ponytail and then to a messy bun on top of her head. At some point, she'd traded her jeans for yoga pants and slipped on a sweatshirt. Most of the night, she'd sat cross-legged, her feet tucked beneath her. Casual as could be, Jacqui was as beautiful as ever. Even now, as she broke down the cardboard box, she was enchanting.

"It's not that late." Not that he wasn't usually in bed by ten. He always tried to wake up before Ella in the mornings to get in a workout and spend time in the Word and prayer. Even though his alarm usually sounded at five, many were the days Ella stumbled sleepily into the living room and curled up on the couch beside him while he finished his devotion time.

But Ella wasn't home. Reid could sleep all the way to seven if he wanted to. He probably wouldn't, but he could.

Jacqui shoved the folded box into the trash. "I can't believe I kept you so late. I'm sorry."

He settled the legs of the chair back on the floor and gathered their cups and a couple of empty sparkling water cans. Though he'd been with her more than four hours, he hadn't gotten enough. "Don't worry about me. I'm self-employed, and business is slow." He carried the trash to the kitchen.

"Still."

"We got a lot accomplished tonight." He set the glasses in the sink and rinsed the cans. "I think we've got a good plan." He turned, and Jacqui was right behind him, so close he could see the flecks of gold in her dark red hair. Her arms were reaching out toward him.

He lost his train of thought.

She smiled and wiggled her hands. "I'll take those." She looked at the cans, then back at him.

"Oh, right." He handed them over, and she tossed them in the recycle bin before leaning against the counter and crossing her arms. "I couldn't have done this without your help."

"My pleasure. Do you want me to call on these businesses for you, see if I can find the right contact people?"

"I'll do it. I know people at most of them who'll direct me."

"We still need to come up with your pitch."

At the mention of it, her hopeful expression faltered. "I have my share of talents, but that's not one of them."

"Lucky for you, it is one of mine."

"You're not tired of helping me yet?"

She had to be kidding. Not that the research had been fun, certainly not great second-date material, but he'd spent the time next to her. Sure, they'd worked, but they'd also shared pizza and laughs and smiles. Her smiles alone were worth the effort. Rather than admit all that and scare her away, he just said, "Not yet. I'll let you know."

She blinked, seeming shy all of a sudden, which made her all the more endearing.

Everything in him wanted to step forward and take her in his arms.

But a little voice in the back of his mind reminded him he was keeping this casual. A friendship, a couple of dates, nothing else.

Kissing felt beyond casual. Much as he longed to do it, he knew better. He didn't need to leave any broken hearts in his wake, including his own.

He guessed that too much of what he was feeling showed on his face by the way she broke eye contact and turned away.

He gathered his laptop and shoved it into his bag. "So tomorrow?"

"If you're sure you want to help."

He faced her, laptop bag in hand. "It's supposed to be beautiful out. Maybe we could go to the park and find a picnic table."

"I'd like that."

At the door, rather than linger and have to battle his impulse to kiss her, he walked out and down the front porch steps, not turning until a good six feet separated them. "Should I meet you at the shop?"

"Sure, at four. And thanks again."

He practically jogged to his car, lecturing himself all the while. *Kissing her would only confuse things. You wanted casual, not serious. It would be wrong to lead her on.*

Kissing her would be stupid.

But Reid thought maybe the voice in his head was an idiot.

Kissing Jacqui would be a lot of things, but he was pretty sure stupid wasn't one of them.

~

By the time Reid left to meet Jacqui the next afternoon, he'd put together a rough pitch for her. He'd need her to fill in the scientific and medical terms, but it was a place to start.

He parked in the lot by the lake and walked to the ice cream shop, arriving just as Jacqui pushed out the door. She saw him, and a grin lit up her features. "When I didn't see your car, I thought maybe you'd changed your mind."

"I needed to find a parking space." He held out his hand, and she slid hers into it.

Holding hands wasn't kissing. Holding hands was fine. And anyway, when he'd prayed about Jacqui that morning, he'd felt no check in his spirit.

He felt lighter for a brief moment, and then remembered that Jacqui lived in Boston. Boston was more than two hours away, and though Reid could live anywhere, Ella felt safe in Coventry. After she'd been kidnapped the previous summer, Ella's safety—and her feeling of security—were more important than anything.

Check in his spirit or no, Reid couldn't get involved with Jacqui beyond what this was—a friendship, a casual relationship, and nothing else.

The heavy traffic was always present on sunny summer days. It stopped at the crosswalk, and he and Jacqui made it to the other side of the street and walked down the sidewalk toward the gate that opened to the grassy area bordering the lake. They neared a food truck and the line of tourists waiting for snacks. "You need anything?"

"Not right now."

Dodging kids and parents, frisbees and dogs, they made their way across the tree-covered grass to an empty wooden picnic table. Reid had done this enough with Ella to be prepared. He pulled a package of bleach wipes from his bag and wiped it down, scrubbing at a stubborn spot of something he preferred not to name. When the table and benches were clean, he gestured for Jacqui to sit.

She lifted her eyebrows, clearly finding his actions amusing.

"Germs." He shrugged. "You know."

Settling on a bench, she let out a little laugh. "I wouldn't have thought of that until I got here. Of course, I rarely leave my lab."

"Whereas I spend copious amounts of time outside. If Ella doesn't run around every day, she becomes the whirling dervish of six-year-olds. It's essential that she burn her energy outside where the damage can be mitigated."

Jacqui shook her head as if he were joking. She'd clearly not spent a lot of time around kids.

He pulled a stapled packet of papers from his laptop bag and handed them to her. "Have a look."

She read, flipping from one to the next without a word, while he set up his laptop. The longer she studied what he'd done that day, the more nervous he got.

Maybe he'd overstepped. But she'd said she didn't know how to start the process. "It's probably not—"

"Shh." She lifted her finger in the universal sign for *zip it*. So he did, pulling out his phone and opening a hotspot.

She set the papers down, dug through her bag, and came out with a pen. She started making notes on the pages as fast as her fingers could move.

Okay, then.

Reid opened the document she was currently marking up with red, then navigated to his emails to see if anything interesting had come in since he'd left home.

He'd deleted a handful and was responding to a customer's question when he heard the pen hit the table. He lowered the laptop screen to find her looking at him, slight smile in place.

"This is amazing. I can't believe you did this."

"It wasn't really—"

"This would have taken me a month to write. And even then, it wouldn't have been this good."

The way she was looking at him, as if he'd pulled off some feat of enormous proportions, had heat climbing up his neck. "It's just a sales pitch. It's not that big a deal. It's not rocket science or an artificial neuron."

"Ha. Rocket science I could do. This"—she tapped the pages in front of him—"never in a million years."

"We all have our talents, I guess."

"You definitely have yours. And I appreciate that you used them on my behalf." She turned the pages to face him. "I made some notes to fill in the blanks you left. I think if we make these changes…"

Reid navigated back to the document and typed while Jacqui talked, trying to translate her technical words into plainer terms. Together, they tailored multiple scripts to work for different companies with different medical focuses and different folks within those companies—more technical jargon for the tech folks and simpler jargon for management. When she thought she was happy with them, he emailed the documents to her to look over.

Hours had passed, and the scent of grilling burgers wafted his way. Reid looked up, almost surprised to find himself at the park. He'd been so focused on the work and the woman in front of him, he'd lost himself in it.

A family had set up at the picnic table closest to theirs. A dad, a mom, and four kids. The mother was pulling food from a giant bag while hollering at the kids to behave themselves. The dad was flipping burgers on the grill and placating his wife. "Let 'em have their fun." Meanwhile, the children were engaged in a game of chase, the littlest one—no older than three—toddling after her older brothers and touching anybody within reach, yelling, "Tag!" every time.

That was what Reid wanted.

He'd been yearning for exactly what he saw in front of him when he proposed to Denise. Not an ideal family. A real family. Two people who did things together and enjoyed each other. Kids who played and laughed and chased.

When Denise left, he'd been crushed, but after a time, he'd

realized it wasn't so much Denise he'd wanted but a family like the one he'd grown up in.

Denise had shrunk from the idea as if it were a contagious disease.

Reid glanced at Jacqui and found that she'd become distracted by the family as well. She had an expression of wonder on her face. This woman who could invent a life-altering device was impressed by a man who could write sales copy. And she seemed amazed by the normal family drama playing out right next to them.

Aside from Ella, Jacqui might be the most beautiful sight he'd ever seen.

Casual, he reminded himself.

Jacqui turned his way, and he cleared his throat. "Their dinner smells good. Are you hungry?"

"I could eat."

He started to close his laptop but paused. "Are you happy with what we came up with?"

The radiant smile he might never get used to lit up her expression. "I think it's perfect, but we won't know for sure until we try it. I'll set up some appointments in the city and find out."

After what happened at Jacqui's lab, the thought of sending her to Boston to pitch her invention had his heart thumping. Would she be safe there by herself?

He wasn't ready to find out. "Why don't I come with you? That way, I can get a feel for what's missing from the pitch." And keep her safe from her former partner.

CHAPTER NINE

Monday morning, Jacqui rang the doorbell at the small split-level house just a few blocks from downtown Coventry.

The door swung open, and Reid stepped back to let her in. "I'm just about ready."

"I'm early." The stop at Cuppa Josie's hadn't taken as long as she thought it would. In the city, the line would have been out the door, but this was a vacation community. Most of the town seemed to still be sleeping.

Reid gestured up the half flight of stairs. "You can wait up here, if you like."

She climbed to the main floor. She'd had a friend in school with a split-level, and this was designed the same way. Living room on the left, eat-in kitchen straight ahead. She guessed there would be three bedrooms and a bath down the hallway to her right. Downstairs, the garage on one side, a playroom—or family room or even another bedroom—on the other.

She settled on a comfortable, oversize sofa in the living area.

"You need anything?" Reid asked. "Coffee, bottle of water?"

"I have coffee in the car. Brought you one too."

"Great, thanks." He hurried down the hallway, calling over his shoulder, "Just give me a couple of minutes."

While Reid was gone, Jacqui studied the space. He'd told her that he and Denise had bought this house right after Ella was born, and he'd never seen any point in moving. It was close to Ella's grandparents' houses, his former job at HCI, and Ella's school. The house was probably forty years old or more, but it was clean and tidy. A reasonably sized TV on a stand faced the sofa and a well-worn recliner. The coffee table held books with fairies and horses on the covers. The end table sported three framed photographs, all of Ella alone or Ella and older folks. Must have been her grandparents.

More pictures had been hung around the entertainment center, all showing Ella at different ages.

A pretty landscape painting hung on the far wall over a narrow sofa table. Had Reid decorated the place, or had someone helped him?

Denise? Another woman?

She laughed at her speculations. How ridiculous to assume a man couldn't hang a picture.

One corner of the living room was filled with toys. There was an easel complete with watercolors on its tray and a case of crayons on the floor nearby. She spotted a knotted ball of yarn and one of those things kids use to weave potholders. There were little colorful ponies and dolls and doll furniture. Jacqui stood to retrieve a Barbie Jeep and was placing the Barbie inside it when she heard a throat clearing.

Reid was watching her, amused expression in place. "Big fan, are you?"

She returned her attention to the toys. "I never had any dolls. My father didn't want me to waste my time with such frivolities."

"You're kidding."

She shrugged. "Dad and I spent a lot of time in the woods studying nature, or in his lab. I had a lot of books and microscopes and journals to record my findings."

"Sounds like great fun." Reid's tone told her he thought it sounded like anything but.

"I was up for anything Daddy wanted to do with me." She rolled the Jeep back and forth. Though she'd begged her parents to buy her Barbies because her friends had them, she'd never loved them like the other girls did. Her friends had used words like *pretend* and *make-believe*. She'd never understood the point.

She abandoned the Jeep and doll and stood.

Reid was near the stairs, duffel in hand. "Shall we?"

JACQUI HAD INSISTED ON DRIVING. Boston was her home, after all, and not the easiest place to navigate for someone unaccustomed to the roads and aggressive drivers. Though they'd gotten an early start, hitting I-93 before seven, by the time they neared the city two hours later, the cars bunched together and inched forward like miles-long caterpillars—and not much faster. But she barely noticed as she and Reid talked about everything from her childhood to Ella to both of their college experiences.

Thanks to an accident just after the I-95 exchange, they were cutting it close to make their first appointment. As they approached Boston, her anxiety kicked into gear. A call from Braden, which came in just as she exited the interstate, didn't help.

She answered through her Bluetooth. "What's up?"

"Just wondering if there's anything new on the lab or the neuron." Her assistant sounded genuinely curious. She heard nothing in his voice that gave her pause, but a glance at Reid showed his concern.

"We're visiting a couple of companies today," she said.

A pause was followed by, "Who is *we*? Surely not Don, not after—"

"I enlisted the help of a friend," she said.

"Oh. Any companies I know?"

She rattled off the first couple, but Reid's touch to her hand on the steering wheel had her glancing his way. He shook his head, serious expression in place.

"And a few others," she finished.

"Sounds like a good place to start," Braden said. "Anything I can help with?"

Again, Reid shook his head.

Why, though? Did Reid suspect Braden of something? He wouldn't if he knew the man. Braden was as trustworthy as anybody she'd ever known.

Of course, she'd thought Don was trustworthy too.

"I can't think of anything right now," she said, "but I'll let you know."

By the time she hung up, she was turning into a parking garage near their first appointment.

"Are you sure he's on your side?" Reid asked.

"Why wouldn't he be?"

Reid shrugged. "There's a lot of money at stake. I just think you need to be cautious, not tell people what you're up to in advance."

She started to argue, but Reid had a point. Braden was friends with Don, and Don could have made him all sorts of promises in exchange for information. "I'll be more careful next time."

She found a spot and had barely shifted into park when Reid pulled something from the laptop case at his feet. "I hope you don't mind. I took the liberty of..." He handed her a packet.

She flipped through it, amazed to see designs she'd sent to him, along with terminology she'd explained, laid out on colorful, glossy pages. "You made this?"

"A friend did it for me. It always helps to give prospective customers something to look at. That way, they won't be focused only on you as you talk, and later when they're thinking about it, they'll have the information at their fingertips."

She turned to another page, marveling at the simple but comprehensive design.

"Obviously, it doesn't replace the follow-up information you'll send them. Research numbers, that sort of thing. But it makes you look professional. Not that they wouldn't know that already."

Gratitude prickled her eyes. Such a silly thing to cry about. But to have somebody come alongside her, help her with this task? She didn't know how to express her thanks. She waited until the threat of tears passed but worried her red eyes would give her away when she looked up to face him. "This is amazing. I couldn't have done this without you."

He either didn't hear or ignored the emotion in her voice. "We haven't done anything yet." He opened his door and rounded the hood, pulling hers open as she gathered her things. The warm, humid air told her it was going to be a scorcher.

After he helped her out, he took her free hand. "Father, we commit this time to You. Accomplish Your will and guide us as we go. In Your name we pray, amen." He met her eyes and smiled.

"Thank you. I'm so distracted by the details, I didn't even think to pray."

He shrugged. "A habit I got into a long time ago. I don't want anything for myself that He doesn't want for me." He gestured toward the staircase at the corner of the parking garage. "After you."

They made it inside the lobby of Boylston Tech with three minutes to spare. She could hear her father's voice in her head—*If you're not five minutes early, you're ten minutes late.*

She'd already blown that one.

But she'd met the fifty-something CEO on a couple of occasions and was encouraged when the woman came to the lobby at news of their arrival, eager smile on her face. "Ms. Beal. What a pleasure to see you again."

She shook her outstretched hand. "Jacqui, please. And this is my business consultant, Reid Cote."

She greeted Reid. "Doreen Nadler. Great to meet you." She turned her attention back to Jacqui. "I can't wait to hear about this invention of yours. If it's half as good as the rumors say, it might just change the world."

"Well, I'm not sure—"

"It'll change the world for a lot of people," Reid said. "And that's the best kind of world change, isn't it? One soul at a time."

Doreen gave Reid a crisp nod. "Well said. Follow me."

Jacqui fumbled and babbled throughout her time with Doreen and the management team of the up-and-coming device manufacturer, but Doreen asked intelligent questions, and Jacqui was able to answer them somewhat coherently. When she got too technical, Reid chuckled and tried to translate for her. Not that he did a great job, but his attempts clued her in that she was speaking over her listeners' heads. How he read people's faces, she had no idea, but it seemed to be one of his many gifts.

Reid's input was invaluable in that meeting, and in the ones that followed.

Four meetings with four CEOs and then with technical teams at four different companies. They were all interested.

But were any of them good enough to trust with her invention?

It was nearly six p.m. when they settled in a booth at Jacqui's favorite restaurant. She didn't know about Reid, but she was famished and exhausted.

Across from her, Reid studied the menu. "What's good?"

"The fish and chips are fantastic. Greasy, but worth it."

"Sold." He set the menu down. "So, what did you think?"

They'd run from one appointment to the next all day, barely making enough time to grab a snack and a drink at lunchtime.

She went to a mental list she'd been compiling all day. "I think it's a good start."

"You'd accept bids from all of them?"

"I don't know. I'm not sure Boylston has the capital."

"If they don't, I doubt they'll bid."

He was probably right, but she couldn't be sure, and she didn't want her artificial neuron to go to a company without the resources to develop it into useful products. "The second company—I'd met the VP of development before at a conference. I wasn't impressed then, and I'm less so today."

Reid pulled out a notebook he'd been taking notes in. "Smithers?" He squinted at the page. "I can't read my writing. Smuthers?"

"Smuthers. Arrogant know-it-all."

"Sure, but if arrogance is a problem, we're going to be in trouble."

"Maybe. And the last company—did you see the photos in the corridor?"

His eyes narrowed. "What about them?"

"They depicted developing countries, right?"

"The plaque beside one explained how the company had brought clean water along with life-saving medical devices to that village."

"But were they testing there? I need to find out." Her stomach growled. She was so hungry, she couldn't think. And the noise level of the restaurant wasn't helping. The after-work crowd, with their laptop cases and business suits and craft beers, were getting loud as they watched a Red Sox game playing on the TVs all around.

"Would that be a deal-breaker?" Reid asked.

"Maybe. I don't know. I need to find a company I can trust with the neuron, not one that's going to hurt people. Not one that's using unethical practices. Why test devices in developing nations unless you're trying to avoid American laws?"

He seemed ready to answer, but the server delivered waters and took their orders. They both gave theirs, and when he was gone, Reid leaned forward. "You're not going to find the perfect company, Jacqui. There's no such thing because companies are made up of human beings, and every single one of those is flawed. I know you want to find the best company, but at the end of the day, this is business. American companies have to follow American laws, and didn't you tell me a couple of days ago that the US has enough regs—maybe too many—regarding these things?"

"But laws can be broken or skirted. I can't send my invention to a company that isn't going to do right by it. The neuron could save lives, but only if the people with access to it behave properly. If they don't, my invention could not only *not* work to save people, but it could hurt people. I'm responsible for ensuring that doesn't happen."

Reid picked at a piece of bread from the basket between them. "I see what you're saying. But, don't you need to have a level of faith here? I mean, the Lord gave you the talent to create this thing, and He enabled you to do it. We asked for His guidance today. Don't you think He has a plan?"

"Of course."

"So maybe it's not your job to try to figure this all out by yourself. Maybe He'll direct you when you ask Him."

"Obviously. But I have to do my part, and that means learning as much as I can about each company, eliminating the ones that aren't up to snuff."

"Based on what?"

"On..." She floundered, a flash of anger blurring her thought process. "On what I can learn."

He nodded slowly.

"What?"

He shrugged, seemed to be searching for words. "If you try hard enough, you'll find something not to like about every company, every CEO or VP or whatever. But God can use flawed people, and He can use flawed companies. I'm just saying, maybe you should rely less on your own understanding and trust Him more."

"You're saying doing my due diligence isn't trusting God?" She heard the nearly shrill tone of her voice only when it was too late.

His hands went up, the universal sign of surrender. "I have no dog in this fight, Jacqui. I'm just suggesting perhaps more prayer and less analyzing." He lifted the basket of bread and held it toward her. "And maybe a little food wouldn't hurt."

This man didn't understand at all. And if he thought hunger was driving her thought processes, he had another think coming.

To prove him wrong, she snatched a roll, glaring at him as she did so.

He only smiled as he set the basket down.

Three bites in, her anger drained.

Darn it, she hated when she was wrong.

Reid was kind enough not to say anything as he took another roll.

They avoided the subject of the neuron for the remainder of their dinner, chatting instead about Boston and her favorite places and things to do. He didn't know the city very well and seemed fascinated by what she had to say.

By the time she'd paid the check—despite his objections, and they had been myriad—they were back to their normal, easy friendship.

The sun had fallen behind the buildings, and the evening had cooled into the seventies. He took her hand as they walked back to the parking garage where they'd left the car that morning.

"I'm not accustomed to letting my dates pay for my meals," he said.

"Dates? You have a lot of those, do you?" She peered up at him beside her, and he chuckled.

"Sure. There was Denise. She and I did a lot of dating. And, uh, Ella. She never offers to pay. A lot like her mother in that respect, come to think of it."

"Those first-graders can be real mooches."

He grinned. "I had a date the other night. Italian food and then coffee. Oh, wait." He winked at her. "I guess you knew about that one."

"They don't call you Casanova for nothing."

"Oh, yeah. The ladies fall all over themselves to get close to me. Of course, the ladies are mostly about six years old and only like me because I make the bestest hot dogs in the whole wide world."

"A record holder. These hot dogs, I have to try."

"I serve them with a side of Lay's potato chips. I'm a real gourmet."

Though the food didn't appeal to her, the cook certainly did. "If this had been a date, I'd have let you pay. But it was a business meal."

His amusement faded. "I can pay for my own dinner—and my own hotel room, for that matter."

She brushed off his words. She didn't doubt Reid had the income to afford this impromptu trip to Boston, but she wasn't going to let him spend it helping her, not when she had more than she needed. "You're here consulting on my business. You won't let me pay you. The very least you can do is let me cover your expenses."

He shrugged. "It's not necessary."

"Noted."

"And ignored."

"Indeed." She tried not to laugh but failed.

After they climbed into her sedan, she opened her map app. "I know where the hotel is, but I'm not exactly sure how to get there from here."

"Just drive back to your place. I'll get a Lyft once you're safe at home."

She found the hotel and retrieved directions. "That's silly. I'll just drop you off."

He shifted in his seat to face her and took her free hand in both of his, enveloping it. "Jacqui, I love that you're not afraid. Your fearlessness is admirable."

She had a feeling that when he said *admirable*, he meant *foolish.*

"But the person who destroyed your lab, whether it was Don or someone else, is still out there, and from what I can tell, he's angry and determined. Therefore, I'd like to accompany you home and make sure you're safe, and if you want to repay me for the Lyft ride, I'll let you."

She set the phone on her lap, not sure if she should be irritated or grateful.

She felt an equal measure of both as she pulled her hand away from his. "I appreciate the offer, but—"

"I get it. You're a strong independent woman, and you don't need my help."

Exactly. But when he said it, it sounded like a rather petty argument.

His jaw worked. He started to speak, stopped, looked beyond her. Then, he leaned toward her, eyes meeting hers. "I have no doubt you don't need me at all, but I'd appreciate it if you'd indulge me. Let me make sure you're safe. I'll have a look around, ensure there's nobody waiting for you, no danger lurking in the closets. Not that you couldn't handle whatever came up, but it would make me feel better. I promise, I'll be on my best behavior."

Truth was, it never occurred to her that Reid would be anything but.

And what would it hurt to have him accompany her home and make sure her place was safe? It was a gentlemanly thing to do, and the man was the consummate gentleman.

"Oh, fine. You win."

He sat back, barely concealing a smug smile.

She couldn't help but laugh. He'd used his charms on her, and she'd fallen for it.

She wasn't complaining.

CHAPTER TEN

Would it really be so hard to be attracted to a nice, normal woman?

Approximately thirty seconds earlier, when Reid had carried Jacqui's suitcase up the steps from the sidewalk to the front door, he'd had this weird idea that, although the woman was brilliant, she was earning somewhere close to his income bracket. Her Audi was out of his price range, no doubt, but she'd explained that her grandparents had given it to her when she graduated from college. It wasn't as if she'd bought it herself.

He'd looked at the five-story brick building, just like all the rest on this street, and decided he could afford an apartment here, even afford the street parking for residents only—which must come at a premium in this postage-stamp-sized city.

He was no Cretan. His manhood wasn't threatened if a woman made more money than he did. But considering his ex-wife was a multi-millionaire, had paid off the house they'd bought together with the earnings from her first movie—a guilt move if he'd ever seen one—he felt entitled to be a little touchy.

Thirty seconds earlier, he'd been confident in his position in this... thing with Jacqui. Whatever it was.

What a difference thirty seconds could make.

He stood in the... foyer was the only appropriate word he could think of, and took in the space.

Jacqui lived in a brownstone, but it hadn't been converted into apartments.

The whole place, from what had to be original hardwood to the ornate crown molding to the winding staircase that went up, up, up, was hers.

Coventry was filled with servers and lifeguards and shipping specialists and coffee-shop proprietors who resided in modest homes and earned modest incomes and lived modest lives. But years before, Reid had gone and fallen for the only future movie star in town.

And now this.

Not that he was falling for Jacqui. And if he had been, he'd have to get over that pronto. Because, just like Denise, Jacqui wouldn't settle for an ordinary small-town guy like him.

"You can leave the suitcase there." Her heels clicked on the floor as she led the way forward. "Living room," she said, indicating the narrow front room as she passed it.

Reid settled the bag at the foot of the curving staircase and followed. A bay window filled almost the entire front of the narrow home. The wall across from him held a fireplace—this must be the one she'd converted to gas—along with shelves and a TV set. Based on the many well-worn books, Jacqui wasn't much of a TV watcher. A compact sofa was flanked by two equally small armchairs, which fit the cozy space well. At least the furniture seemed more comfortable than fancy.

Moving on, she said, "Dining room."

He continued past the antique table and chairs that looked as if they'd been there for generations.

"Kitchen's through here," she called. "You need anything?"

He followed her into a space that had probably last been remodeled a decade or so earlier. Granite countertops, travertine tile backsplash, antique brass fixtures. It wasn't brand new, but it was new enough in a house no doubt built in the nineteenth century.

Her hip was propped against the kitchen table, her arms crossed. His dismay must've shown on his face because she said, "It's not mine."

"Whose is it?"

"My parents moved in after Dad landed his first job. They decorated it. I've replaced a few things since I came, but most of the stuff is theirs."

His *first* job? "What does your father do?"

"He's a surgeon, but the place has been in our family for years. My grandparents gave it to Mom and Dad, and they've held onto it all these years because there are so few left of its kind. Most of these old brownstones have been converted into apartments, but"—she looked around the kitchen—"it's like owning a little piece of history. After they moved to Hingham, they rented it to one of his coworkers at Mass General. His family lived here for a long time. When I started at MIT, Mom and Dad let me live here."

He'd never seen anything like it, not in real life. "I'd love a tour."

Her arms fell to her sides. "That's why you're here, right? To look for the boogeyman?"

"I'm guessing there are lots of boogeyman hidey-holes in this place."

"Not really." She pulled open a door. "Pantry. Empty."

"Okay." He checked the back door and the few windows along the back wall. All locked.

After they peeked inside other doors on the first floor, he carried her suitcase to the second and stood outside her bedroom while she looked in her closet and under the four-poster bed that could have been built for the house. The space was immaculate.

"Empty and empty," she said.

He checked the office and was opening the closet door in the hallway when he said, "I feel like we should be writing down where we've searched so we don't forget."

She laughed. "It's not *that* big."

It felt that big, but he didn't say so.

It was hotter on the third floor, where they searched another bedroom, which was being used by her house sitter. Annie had gone to visit her family in Connecticut when Jacqui told her she'd be in town. Beside the guest room was a library filled, floor-to-ceiling, with books. There were even shelves built in over the door and window frames. An old Persian rug graced the floor, and comfortable chairs with a round table between them filled the center of the cozy space. He glanced at the book titles—everything from medical textbooks to encyclopedias to classic literature. From a shelf of old hardbacks, he pulled out a copy of *Bleak House* by Charles Dickens. It was a first edition, published in the mid-nineteenth century.

"My mother loves books," Jacqui said from the doorway. "Of course, Dad and I do too, but Mom's the collector."

He ran his finger across the volumes, all English and early American literature. "It's impressive."

"I don't think there are any hiding places in this room."

"Right. I'm supposed to be searching, not looking for the great American novel."

"If there is one, you'll find it in here. Help yourself if you see something you'd like to borrow."

He slid the book back into its space. "Let's keep looking." Not that he believed any intruders were in the house, but it never hurt to make sure the place was secure. Jacqui's safety was paramount, and Reid figured he couldn't be too careful.

There were two bedrooms on the fourth floor, two more on the fifth. It was clear by the stale air on the upper floors that those rooms were rarely used. Still, he and Jacqui opened every closet and looked under every bed and behind every shower curtain.

He stopped in the hallway and gazed out the window overlooking the road, which was five stories below. "Once again, I've been proved paranoid."

She indicated the staircase. "We haven't checked the lab yet. If I were an intruder looking for an invention and research, that's where I'd be."

There was a lab? How had he missed that?

He followed her down four flights, through the door beneath the stairs on the first floor, and into the basement.

He recalled the science lab at Coventry High, with its beakers and Bunsen burners. That place had nothing on this one.

Fluorescent lights overhead lit up the shiny white laminate floor, white walls, and sturdy tables supporting high-tech equipment. Test tubes and slides and microscopes, not to mention a computer with three oversize screens and other technical stuff he didn't even recognize.

"Wow."

"It's a nerd's paradise."

He faced her. "You make nerds look good."

Her smile was shy, maybe even nervous, as she watched him. "This is what I do. The only difference between me and lab rats is that I know how to work the cage's door, even if I rarely do."

This gorgeous woman in front of him, with her stunning red hair and eyes the color of milk chocolate, was about as far from a lab rat as the sun from the earth's core. Here, shy and surrounded by the things that helped her turn her genius into reality, she was just about the most beautiful creature he'd ever seen.

He held her eye contact.

She held his.

It took all his self-control not to cross the room and take her in his arms. He'd never felt so strong a desire to hold a woman close. She seemed almost embarrassed about her abilities. She needed to know she was perfect just the way she was.

But she looked away, and the spell was broken.

She crossed to a bank of cabinets and opened one. It was tall enough to hold a man, but there was nobody inside.

"Where should I look?" he asked.

She turned and pointed to a door. "Storage area. Pull the string hanging just inside the door to turn on the bulb. It's a mess, so be careful."

He followed her instructions into a room filled with dusty boxes and piles of notebooks. He flipped through one and found page after page of equations and notes and sketches.

He shouldn't be looking at her private things. He closed the cover, feeling guilty for snooping, and inched through the small, cramped space. No boogeymen hiding in the corners.

Back in the lab, Jacqui was at her computer. She turned when he stepped from the closet. "Nobody's logged in or even tried to since I left."

"Maybe your partner gave up."

She stood and turned toward the stairs. "I hope so."

"When will your house sitter be back?"

"When I told her I was coming, she decided to visit her parents for the weekend."

Reid's heart rate kicked up. "So you'll be here alone?"

She climbed toward the first floor. "I have an alarm."

Alarms could be tampered with. And how quickly would the police respond in this city? Not fast enough to protect her, if her life were in danger. "Do you own a gun?"

She glanced over her shoulder. "I've never felt the need."

Her destroyed lab should have had her feeling the need, but he didn't say so.

They made it back to the living room, where she leaned on the arm of the sofa.

He needed to order his Lyft and leave so she could get some rest. But how could he leave if she might be in danger?

"Where are you storing the artificial neuron, anyway?" he asked.

"Safe deposit box. It's protected."

But was she? "I opened one of those notebooks in your storage closet. I shouldn't have, but—"

"It's not a problem. Nothing sacred."

"Maybe, but all those notes. If Don were to come by—"

"Those old notebooks aren't important. Nobody could translate the gibberish inside but me. I converted all the legitimate research for the neuron to digital and stored it at the bank. And anyway, even if somebody got their hands on the notebooks, my company filed for a provisional patent. Nobody can steal my work."

Then why had Don broken into the lab? What was he up to, if her work couldn't be stolen? It didn't make sense.

"It's okay, Reid." Jacqui must've seen the concern on his face because her tone was placating. "This is my home. I've lived here for years. It's safe."

Places people had lived for years weren't necessarily safe. The house he'd grown up in had always been safe too, until it wasn't. Until a murderous madman had stolen Ella from the backyard when Reid's mother stepped inside to answer her phone.

There was no such thing as *safe*.

Acid filled his stomach. He tried to mask his anxiety, but the gentle look on Jacqui's face told him he failed.

"Maybe I should stay." He pointed to the sofa. "I'll sleep there. I won't bother you."

She glanced at the sofa, at the staircase, back at him. "It's not that I don't trust you, I do. Completely. But when my parents allowed me to live here, they made a few rules, rules I promised to live by."

"Lemme guess. No sleepovers."

Her lips quirked. "With boys, anyway."

"They'd prefer you in danger?"

Her smile faded. "I'm safe here, Reid. The doors on the front and the back are solid wood and have new deadbolts. The windows are wired, so if somebody breaks one, the alarm will sound and the police will come."

"If you feel so safe here, why are you staying in Coventry?"

Her eye contact slipped. She gazed around the room, not focusing on anything in particular. "I panicked after the break-in at the lab. And then I made a commitment to manage the ice cream shop. If I hadn't done that, I'd have come home already."

That would be foolish, but he didn't say so. What did he know about this former partner of hers?

Not enough. Not nearly enough.

REID WAS in the backseat of the Lyft, staring out at the jam-packed city streets and trying to trust Jacqui to God's care, when his phone rang. Denise's phone number. His first thought, that something terrible had happened to Ella, was quickly tamped down by logic and faith. Ella was fine. She probably just missed him. The thought brought a tiny bit of satisfaction as he swiped to connect.

"Hey, sweetie. How are you?"

"Not your sweetie anymore," Denise said.

This couldn't be good. "Where's Ella? What happened?"

"She's fine. I invited over some neighbor kids, and they're swimming."

"Who's watching them? She can swim, but she's young. She needs—"

"I'm watching them, Reid." Denise's voice was cold. "Not only that, but I hired a lifeguard for the afternoon."

He took a deep breath to calm his nerves. "Sorry. I'm—"

"I can take care of our daughter."

"I know." He hadn't trusted her to, but the lifeguard? That was above and beyond. "I'm sorry."

A beat passed. Denise's voice was softer when she said, "I guess you're entitled to your fear after what happened."

"Yeah." Not that Denise could possibly comprehend it.

Silence crackled between them, sparked by his unspoken accusations and her unspoken defense.

Not that she had one.

"What's up?" he finally asked.

"I'm not happy with our current situation."

He didn't want to think about what she might mean. He'd talked to his attorney, and the man had said there was little they could do until Denise made a demand.

He feared the demand was coming but pretended he had no idea what she was talking about. "I gave you a month. That's twice as long as usual. We have plans for the summer, so we won't be able to extend—"

"I don't want to extend this visit. I mean, I do, but I understand you're expecting her home." She sounded so reasonable. So unlike the Denise he knew. "It's not that. I want more time with her."

Adrenaline filled his veins, and he clenched his fists in an attempt to circumvent the anger that wanted to color his response. "What exactly are you asking for?"

"She's my daughter too."

He swallowed hard. "I understand that." *Lord, a little help?* He was tempted to throw Denise's sins in her face. She'd abandoned Ella. She'd not bothered to come home when Ella'd been kidnapped. Reminding her of those past mistakes had kept Denise in her place for a long time, but he could feel in the strength and certainty in his ex's voice that she wouldn't be...

Bullied.

He would never admit aloud the word that came to mind. He wasn't a bully, though. Just a protective father.

Nevertheless, he didn't think Denise would be altered from this course by unkind words and insensitive reminders of what they both knew. The woman who'd decided to become a movie star and then given up everything to make it happen was determined. He understood his ex's determination better than most.

The last thing he wanted was to get into a legal battle with her. If nothing else, she could outspend him on lawyers. Yes, he was the better parent. But she was the rich and famous parent.

"I'm glad you're having fun with Ella," he finally said.

"It's not about *fun,* Reid. She's my daughter. She needs me in her life."

The very last thing his down-to-earth daughter needed was a woman who put on costumes and played pretend for a living. The last thing Ella needed was to be surrounded by Hollywood wannabes and Denise Masters sycophants. Again, he tamped down the words he wanted to say. "You may be right." His response somehow sounded like capitulation and condescension, all wrapped up in one.

"I would like to handle this civilly," she said. "Rather than duke it out in front of a judge, let's come up with a solution ourselves."

"Okay." Seemed wiser to agree than to argue. "What are you thinking?"

"Since she goes to school in Coventry, you get to have her when school is in session," Denise said.

He guessed where this was going and forced his lips to stay closed.

"And I'll take her in the summers and on her vacations."

"Absolutely not." It was worse than he'd guessed. He couldn't believe Denise would even make such an outlandish suggestion. "Not a chance."

She waited a long moment before she responded. "What do you suggest, then?"

Despite his racing heart, he sent up another quick prayer. What he wanted to say was, *You're lucky I let you have any time with her at all.* He wanted to remind her that she wasn't just a bad mother, she was anything *but* a mother, that she'd written off their daughter years before and had zero right to ask for anything.

It must've been God who stayed his tongue because none of that came out of his mouth. He took a deep breath and pushed it out. He needed to talk to his attorney. He needed to spend time with God, hear His voice on this matter. Maybe he and Denise could come up with a solution they could both live with. He hated to give an inch, but if an inch would save a mile... "She could fly out to see you during spring break."

Denise, usually quick with retorts, said nothing right away. When she did speak, it was, "That's it? Spring break?"

"Spring break, and we trade off holidays. One of us gets her Thanksgiving, the other one Christmas, and we swap every year." Though the thought of not seeing his little girl at Christmas filled him with dread, if this would keep them out of court...

Another long silence answered that.

Then, Ella's sweet voice sounded in the background. "Can we have some juice boxes?"

"Sure, sugar," Denise said.

He heard some rattling on the other end, then Ella said, "And some snacks too?"

Reid swallowed a rise of nausea. His daughter sounded so happy, so carefree. She sounded just like she sounded at home.

She loved it there, and what was not to love? Denise lived in a mansion and had a pool and hired lifeguards for playdates. She didn't have to enforce rules or make Ella do her homework or chores. Denise had housekeepers for chores and cooks for mealtime. Mommy's house was always a vacation.

But Reid was Ella's father. Reid was the one who'd kept his daughter safe and protected.

The memory of her kidnapping slowed the tide of his thoughts. He hadn't always kept her safe. He'd failed, monumentally.

It didn't matter that she'd been kidnapped when he was at work. He had one job—to protect Ella—and he'd blown it.

Not that Denise would have done better. He was the custodial parent and the available parent. And the better parent in every way.

Ella's voice pulled him from his thoughts. "Thanks, Mommy! You're the best."

After the sound of a slamming door, Denise said, "Two more weeks a year? I'm sorry, Reid. That's not enough for me."

"Maybe we could try that this Thanksgiving and see—"

"I love her." Denise's tone slipped to... if he didn't know her better, he'd say reverent. "I know I've done a lousy job showing it, but I love her, and I want her."

"She's not a shiny new car, Denise. She's a human being. A sweet little girl. You can't just—"

"I can. I'm sorry, but I can."

The line went dead.

CHAPTER ELEVEN

Jacqui woke to the sound of pounding.

She opened her eyes in the dim morning light. She rarely slept past seven. Being at home in her own bed again after so many months, she should have fallen right to sleep. Instead, she'd stared at the ceiling half the night. The heat outside and lack of breeze had her throwing off all but her sheet. The nights were so much cooler in the New Hampshire mountains than here in the city. And she was no longer accustomed to the noises—car engines and slamming doors and chatting people on the sidewalk one story below. She'd considered going up to the third floor, but it was even hotter up there. The window in the room Annie was using stuck. It was uncomfortable enough that Jacqui had told Annie to feel free to sleep in her bed on hot nights.

But it wasn't the heat that kept her awake, not really. Mostly, she'd been thinking about Don and the lab and Reid's fears and how safe her house really was.

It was ridiculous. Don wouldn't hurt her. Sure, in a fit of grief-induced rage, he'd destroyed her lab. But those feelings had surely faded by now. He was probably embarrassed about his behavior. The man she'd known most of her life was a gentle, kind man.

He wasn't a monster.

Only after she'd told herself that and then started praying for him had she fallen asleep.

The noise came again. Fully awake, she realized it wasn't pounding, it was knocking, the sound coming both through her open doorway and the open window overlooking the street below.

She peered out the window but couldn't see her stoop from this angle. She called, "Just a minute," and the knocking stopped. She pulled on a pair of shorts and a T-shirt.

Was it Reid? Why would he be here? She'd told him she'd pick him up, and they'd drive to Cambridge together for their last couple of appointments. While she brushed her teeth, she checked her phone for missed calls and texts. None.

Reid would have let her know he was on his way, right?

She brushed her hair, threw it in a ponytail, and hurried down the stairs. It was probably one of the house sitter's friends, unaware that she'd gone home for the weekend.

Jacqui started to unbolt the door, but the thought of Reid and the concerned look on his face the evening before stopped her.

She took her hand off the deadbolt and called, "Who is it?"

The windows were down and locked on this floor. To leave them open would invite intruders, and though she didn't consider herself fearful, she wasn't stupid. Though the door was thick, she was confident that whoever was on the other side had heard her.

"It's me." The voice had her stomach swooping. "It's Don. I just want to talk."

Heart pounding, she reached for her pockets, but these shorts had none. She'd left her phone upstairs. Even if she had it, what would she do? Call 911? The man wasn't breaking any laws, and, as far as they could prove, hadn't done anything wrong. Should she call Reid? He was across town. How could he help?

"Please, Jacqui. I know I don't have the right to ask anything of you."

She settled her forehead against the door. This man, this old man who'd been nothing but good to her for so long, who'd been like a loving, caring grandfather, sounded broken. How could she refuse him?

But... "How did you know I was here?"

"I was walking the neighborhood, and I saw your car."

She thought back to where they'd parked the night before on the next block over. Not exactly close to Don's place. And since when did Don walk?

She didn't ask the question, but they'd worked together so long, he must've guessed her thoughts. "I walk every day now. My therapist..." The words trailed. "Look, I'll explain everything if you'll just open the door."

"You could have called."

"I know. I know, I should have. Like I said, I saw your car and came over on a whim. But you're right. I'm sorry. I'll just go."

He should go. After what he did to their lab, to her, she owed him nothing.

But he sounded despondent, despairing. And... she owed him everything.

She swung the door open.

Don was already on the sidewalk, walking away. At the sound of the door, he swiveled his head, eyes wide and questioning. Slowly, he turned around and nodded to the steps leading to her property. "Is it okay if I come up?"

She should say no, it wasn't okay. But, as wounded as he'd sounded, he looked worse. His once salt-and-pepper hair was thinner and all gray now. His bright gray eyes had dulled and sunk into thick bags beneath them, the eyebrows above like overgrown shrubs. Lola would've taken the tweezers to them, but Lola was gone.

Don had once stood over six feet tall, but he seemed to have shrunk since his wife's death. The belly he'd had for years was gone. His shoulders were hunched.

As frightened as she'd been of him, he seemed harmless and scared. How could she turn him away? "I don't have long."

"This'll only take a minute."

She half expected him to hobble toward her like an old man, but his movements were quick as he climbed the steps.

He waited until she'd gone inside, then paused on the stoop. "I can stay out here, if you'd prefer."

She held the heavy door open. "It's okay. Come on in."

He did, pausing in the foyer.

She swung the door closed and nodded to the living room. "Have a seat. I don't have any coffee made, but I can—"

"It's okay. I'm off coffee. And alcohol, and sugar." He didn't move into the living room. "Could I maybe use the bathroom?"

"Sure."

After he stepped into the half bath on this floor, she went to the kitchen, turned on her single-cup coffee maker, and fixed two glasses of water. Once her coffee was finished, she carried all three drinks to the living room on a tray and set them on the coffee table.

He still wasn't out of the bathroom.

Taking the opportunity, she hurried up the stairs and snatched her phone. She sent a quick text to Reid. *Don's here. We're talking. Probably nothing to worry about.*

She didn't wait for a response but kept the phone with her as she returned downstairs.

Don had settled into one of the side chairs, and she took the one opposite. The table guarded the space between them. Not that she was afraid of Don, but she wasn't sorry the front door was close and unlocked, which should allow her to make a hasty exit, if the need arose.

Which it wouldn't. She shouldn't have let the detective back in March—and Reid in the last couple of days—convince her Don was dangerous. This man would never hurt her.

Still, her heart pounded, and not from the rush up and down the stairs. She hoped her subconscious wasn't seeing something she'd missed.

He rested his palms on his knees and took a few breaths. Was he nervous?

She decided to start the conversation with a neutral topic. "Walking and eating right? Is this a new and improved Don?"

"Maybe. I hope so." His lips, pressed together, lifted in an almost-smile. "I've been seeing a therapist. He's helped me figure some things out since the... since I..." He swallowed, massaged his knees. She'd seen him do that exact thing before. Once when they had to fire an employee. Another time when he'd caught her in a mistake. This was his tell that he was trying to say something he didn't want to say. She wasn't great at reading people, but she could read something that obvious. Finally, he seemed to force the words out. "What I did was inexcusable."

"So you admit it."

His eyebrow quirked. "No. And this next statement in no way relates to the previous one, just an offhand remark—I'd prefer not to go to prison."

"Even if you deserve it?"

"Even if I deserve it."

It was as much of an admission as she was going to get. She could call the detective and tell him what Don had said, but Don would only deny it, and then whatever tenuous link existed between them now would be severed.

Did she want that? Did she want to sever ties with Don?

She didn't know yet. Again, there was that pull between the love she felt for the man she'd known for years and the dislike she felt for the man who'd threatened her and ruined her lab.

At this moment, the dislike was winning. "Was that supposed to be an apology?"

"No. This is." He leaned his elbows on his knees and held her eye contact. "I am very, very sorry for the way I treated you. Lola would be..." He shook his head, but his eyes got watery and turned red around the edges. "I can hear her voice in my head, lecturing me about my inexcusable behavior. You loved her. I know that. Even if I don't agree with what you did, I know your heart was in the right place."

Jacqui's eyes teared up. "I did love her. I only wanted what was best for her."

"I know. I still believe that, if she'd only fought harder, she might still be here."

Jacqui didn't argue with him. He was wrong. Lola's cancer had spread throughout her body. There was no way she would have survived apart from a miracle. God could have performed that miracle if He'd chosen to. He hadn't. Jacqui wouldn't question Him about that. Maybe, if not for Lola's terminal diagnosis, she never would have surrendered to Jesus. Maybe Lola's death would ultimately lead Don and his kids to the Lord. Maybe there was another reason for Lola's death that Jacqui could never and would never understand. What Jacqui knew was that God could heal but didn't always, and that God was good. And even when she didn't understand what He was doing, she trusted Him.

But she'd said all of that to Don in different ways and at different times during Lola's long illness. There was no sense rehashing it today.

"And for the other thing." Don sat back in the chair, rubbed his hands down his thighs. "I channeled all my feelings—sadness, despair, grief—into rage, and then I directed that rage at you. It was unacceptable, inexcusable. I can only say that I am truly, truly sorry. Whatever the insurance doesn't cover, I'll pay for."

"But you won't confess?"

"I'm too old for prison, Jacqui. Please don't ask that of me. Please just forgive me."

She could do that. But she wasn't going to make any promises about the rest of it. Her insurance company might have something to say about her withholding this confession. She'd need to pray and seek counsel—she could guess what Reid would say—before she decided what to do.

Now, it was her turn to lean forward. She folded her hands and held Don's eye contact. "I forgive you because I've been forgiven. I forgive you because I have a Savior who died—"

"Don't start with that stuff today. Please."

"I want you to be with Lola again, and Lola is with Jesus."

"Jesus, Jesus, Jesus." He shook his head, smirk in place. "How can someone so smart be so deluded?"

She sat back and sighed. Only God could soften Don's heart, and it appeared, despite the grief and the apology and the remorse, that his heart was still hard as New Hampshire granite.

She pushed herself to her feet. "If that's all—"

"Actually, I wanted to talk about the deal I put together."

Slowly, she sat back down. "Is this a new deal, Don? Or are you still—?"

"I never took you for a racist."

The very word had her heart pounding once again. "You know better than that."

"You don't want to work with them because they're an Asian company. What else can I conclude?"

"There are ten Asian companies I can name off the top of my head that I'd consider working with. Just not that one, and you know why."

"Nobody's going to offer us anywhere near—"

"I'm not selling my invention to a group of people who have a greater interest in ensuring nothing is ever invented than they do in saving lives. That's not going to happen." She stood again. "I have an appointment. I need—"

"In Cambridge. I know." He got to his feet. "At least two, if I'm not mistaken."

Surprise kept her mouth shut, but he must've seen it in her expression.

"I know a lot of people in the industry, Jacqui. People you've never met. People who are loyal to me."

"So you knew I was in town."

He shrugged.

"That bit about seeing my car—"

"I did see it."

"You were looking for it because you knew I was here." He'd

lied to her. She couldn't believe she'd been so foolish. She started for the door. "It's time for you to go."

The pounding of his footsteps was the only warning before he grabbed her shoulder and whipped her around to face him. "We need to talk about this."

"There's nothing to talk about." She tried to step back, but he held firm, his grip surprisingly strong. "That company is out of the question."

"So you're going to throw it away?" His voice was loud, and spittle collected in the corners of his lips. "All our work, all our research, and you're just going to let some penny ante upstart like Boylston botch it and do nothing with it."

He'd heard about her meeting yesterday. Maybe he'd heard about them all. She glared at the hand on her shoulder. When he let go, she said, "You can't possibly think that of me. I'm doing my best." She took a deep breath. She didn't need to defend or explain her actions. "This is none of your business, Don. When you sold me your shares, you forfeited your authority. BNB is my company now."

"Do you forget who the Burgess is in *Burgess* and Beal?"

"I remember he washed his hands of the business."

He stepped closer until less than a foot separated them.

Her heart raced with fear. She barely kept herself from moving back and revealing it. *Never back down from a fight*—another lesson her father had taught her. *Bullies always give up when you refuse to give in.*

"I was scared." Don's admission was delivered in a voice filled with malice. "Scared and desperate, trying to keep Lola alive after you gave her a reason to quit fighting, and you took advantage of that. You stole my shares, and now you're trying to steal my profits."

What? He'd begged her to buy his shares. With tears in his eyes, he'd literally begged her. She'd offered to loan him the money he needed, but he'd refused. To now claim she'd *stolen* from him?

The man was insane.

"It's time for you to leave." She turned for the door.

He grabbed her wrist, whirled her around, and pressed her against the wall. His face was red and contorted into an expression so hate-filled, the sight of it shocked her almost as much as his violent actions. "It's time for you to listen to reason."

CHAPTER TWELVE

Reid couldn't shake off the nightmare.

He'd had them every night for months after Ella's abduction. As Ella had told him more about what happened to her, the details in his nightmares had become more vivid. In his dreams, he could see the cave where she'd been kept. He could hear the bear that ambled in one night, the bear that could've killed her with a swipe of its paw. He could imagine the man chaining her, threatening her. The man who'd been responsible for the deaths of two other little girls, one of whom was the sister of Reid's best friend.

As Ella had trusted Reid with her memories of that harrowing experience, Reid had taken them on. He'd carried them for her. Each one, he'd hefted to the foot of the throne of God and tried to leave there.

But at night, when he slept, the images came alive in his dreams.

Time hadn't healed those wounds, not for Ella or for him. But God had healed and was still healing. Things were better, had been for a long time. Now, the nightmares came rarely.

But last night's was different. The cave had turned into a back-yard pool.

The abductor's face had morphed into Denise's.

And Ella hadn't been afraid. She'd been drowning in the clear blue waters, giggling all the way down, her sweet little voice—*you're the best mommy*—fading as her life slipped away.

He'd gasped awake, heart pounding, Denise's words thrumming in his head like a mantra. *It's not enough for me. I love her, and I want her.*

Reid had given up on sleep at just after five a.m. Showered and packed, he headed to the coffee shop in the lobby with his laptop and worked, nibbling a cinnamon roll, until the sun came up.

Now, he was walking the streets of Boston, dragging his overnight bag behind him and dodging people as they rushed to their jobs or breakfast dates or gyms or wherever city people went this early in the morning.

So different from Coventry, where half the population was on vacation in the summertime. More than half, probably. And the folks who lived there were rarely in any hurry.

He loved small-town life.

Not that the city wasn't impressive. The old buildings lining the road dripped with character. The scent of the flowers blooming in pots and the tiny front yards competed with the stink of exhaust, and even the exhaust seemed to be carried away on the breeze coming from the Charles River. The rush of people and cars and buses distracted him from the worry that rolled through as regularly as the green-line train that rumbled beneath him, its occupants crushed together like fish in a net.

Reid was surprised to find that he didn't hate the city. He wouldn't want to live there, but he didn't hate it. It was new and interesting. Different from Coventry, but he figured each neighborhood had its own character. Maybe the neighborhoods here were like small towns. Maybe the people knew each other and shouted hellos when friends walked by. Maybe there were neighborhood restaurants like The Patriot, where people recognized each other and got to know the servers and bartenders. Maybe it wasn't so different.

But, as he walked past shops and converted brownstones filled with residents, he didn't hear a single person shout a single hello to a passerby.

If they had lived here, who would have cared when Ella went missing? Would anybody in this city have helped him search as the people of Coventry had?

Would they rally around him, bring him meals, pray with him and for her?

He didn't know. He only knew that, lovely as Boston was, it wasn't home.

But, really, he wasn't homesick for his house or his town or his friends. He missed Ella.

He needed his baby girl.

He couldn't lose her. He wouldn't lose her.

He'd left a message at his attorney's office the night before. He needed a plan, and he needed one quickly if he was going to thwart whatever Denise was cooking up. Because there was no way on the planet he was giving up his daughter without a fight. How could he protect her if she was in California? And how could he trust his ex, a woman who'd abandoned them both, to make sure Ella was safe?

Denise might want to win this battle today. She might think right now that she wanted Ella to be with her, but he knew how fickle she was. Once she got what she wanted, she'd move on to the next new thing.

Reid couldn't trust Denise with Ella. She'd proved over and over she wasn't trustworthy.

And anyway, he was lost without his daughter.

But maybe it wasn't only Ella whom Reid was missing.

As he took in his surroundings, leaving the congestion and weaving along smaller streets, he admitted the truth.

Somehow, though he'd just met her and had only gotten to know her in the last few days, he missed Jacqui. Which explained why he was just a few blocks from her house a solid hour before she was supposed to pick him up.

Maybe they could have breakfast together. If nothing else, he could save her the need to drive to his hotel.

He pulled his phone from his jeans pocket to let her know he was on his way and saw that he'd missed a message. From her.

Don's here. We're talking. Probably nothing to worry about.

Probably?

He increased his pace. He should respond, but he was pulling his suitcase, and he wasn't one of those text-one-handed people.

He'd been closing in on her place but not following the map exactly, not in any hurry. Now, as he weaved around the city folks who suddenly seemed slow as sludge, he studied the directions on his screen.

He walked two blocks, made a couple of turns, and finally saw her place up ahead. Door was closed. No activity as he neared. Maybe everything was fine. Maybe he was worried for nothing.

He wasn't about to risk Jacqui's life or safety on a *maybe*.

He took the steps two at a time and banged on the door. "Jacqui!"

"Reid!"

The single syllable dripped with fear.

He tried the door, expecting it to be locked, but it swung open.

He stepped inside and found Jacqui gripping the stair rail, one hand on her chest and breathing hard. Eyes wide and flicking from him to...

An old man. He was standing a few feet away, hands up as if in surrender, looking at her. "You know I would never hurt you."

"Get out," she said. "Get out and don't come back. Ever."

"Look, I'm just... I get it." The old man's words were rushed, pleading. "You don't like that company. Let me help find—"

"Get. Out."

"You can't do this without me, Jacqui."

Reid marched across the floor, grabbed Don's upper arm, and manhandled him to the door. He shoved him onto the stoop and down the stairs.

Don didn't struggle or argue. He wasn't stupid. And, from

what Reid could tell, he wasn't done. Jacqui might have won this battle—because Reid had shown up—but the war raged on.

On the sidewalk, Reid jerked the old man around to face him. "If I catch you within fifty feet of her, you'll have to deal with me. And I won't be so gentle next time."

He let go, and Don rubbed the spot Reid had gripped. He glanced at the house, where Jacqui was surely standing, then leaned in and whispered, "You're in way over your head, Reid Cote. Walk away before it's too late."

AFTER DON TURNED THE CORNER, Reid climbed the steps.

Jacqui was standing in the doorway but stepped aside as he approached. She said nothing, but her eyes were round, her bottom lip trembling.

He grabbed his suitcase and passed her, dumping it in the foyer. He was so angry, he could hardly speak, hardly look at her.

She said, "Are you—?"

"Call the police." He yanked his phone from his pocket and held it out to her.

She didn't reach for it.

"Call the police, Jacqui. You need to tell them what happened. You can't let him get away with—"

"I'm not." Her voice was shaky. She was shaky as she slammed and locked the door.

When she faced him again, he saw the terror in her eyes.

He breathed through his fury and held his arms open.

She stepped into them, all but collapsing against his chest.

"It's okay. You're safe now." He rubbed her back and repeated the words. If this were Ella, he'd swing her into his arms and settle her on his lap and bathe her in kisses and pray aloud for both of them.

Well, he couldn't do all of that, but he could do the most important thing.

"Father, bring Your peace right now. Guide us to the next thing, and the next after that. I pray a hedge of protection around Jacqui, her home, her company, her employees, and her invention. You have good plans for all of it, and we believe You will bring those plans to pass. Right now, help us both to feel Your peace. In Jesus' name—"

"And Don," Jacqui said. "We pray You'll soften his heart. Save him, Lord. He needs You."

Reid wasn't proud of the surge of anger at her prayer. After the fear he'd seen in Jacqui's eyes, he had a lot of feelings regarding Donald Burgess, none of them charitable. But Jacqui was right—the man needed God desperately.

When she said nothing else, Reid ended the prayer.

Jacqui seemed calmer. He expected her to back out of his embrace, but she didn't move.

He didn't either.

The moment shifted from comfort to something else. Something that sent his blood rushing for an entirely different reason.

He backed up just enough to look at her.

Her gaze flicked from his eyes to his lips, and he felt the invitation. How easy it would be to lower his head and take the kiss he'd hardly allowed himself to think about.

But the memory of what he'd arrived to find nudged its way in.

He couldn't get involved with this woman. He couldn't get involved with someone shrouded in danger, someone who wasn't wise enough not to let her enemy into her house.

She must have seen the shift in his thinking because she blinked and stepped back. "I'm sorry."

The two words had his ire firing like an engine. He started to say what he was thinking—that she should be sorry, that she was a fool—but her pale skin and trembling lips shut him up. He pointed to the living room. "Sit and call the police."

"I'm not a puppy. You're not welcome to talk to me that way." The words came out breathy and weak.

"Fine." He unlocked his phone. "Stand there and pass out while I do it."

She moved to the couch.

He grabbed a glass of water from a tray on the coffee table and handed it to her. "Drink this. Are you cold?"

"What? No. Just... It all happened so fast, and I haven't eaten or had coffee and..." She swallowed a sip of water. "I'm fine. Really."

Her color was returning. She wasn't shivering. She seemed coherent. So she wasn't in shock. That was good.

He said, "Are you calling or—?"

"I'll do it."

She dialed the police. While she was on the phone explaining what had happened, he went to her kitchen and snooped until he found the bread and butter. He fixed her a couple of pieces of toast and poured a glass of orange juice. The simple task helped him focus, figure out why he was angry, figure out what to do with it.

He was just setting the toast on the table when she stepped in. "They're on their way."

"Good." He pointed to the food. "Eat." At her smirk, he realized how rude he sounded. "Please eat, Jacqui. You've already had a hard day, and it's not even"—he glanced at the clock on the oven —"seven thirty."

She slid into the chair. "Did you make yourself some?"

He leaned against the counter and crossed his arms. "I ate at the hotel."

She lifted the toast and took a bite. Swallowed and took another.

After a couple of bites, she rubbed her temples and headed for the cabinets. She opened one and peered at the top shelf.

"What do you need?"

"I think I have a bottle of Tylenol up there. I'll need the step stool." She turned and probably would have scooted to wherever she kept it, but he was right behind her.

He reached over her head and snatched the red-and-white bottle.

"I can't believe you can reach that." She seemed to be trying for levity. When he said nothing, she twisted off the cap and shook two tablets into her palm. Leaving the bottle on the counter, she returned to her seat and downed the pills.

"Monkey arms," he said.

She set down her juice, eyebrows lifted.

"When I was a kid, they called me monkey arms." Lifting his overlong arms, he stretched to show off his ridiculous wingspan. "The kids used to make fun of me—until I learned to dunk a basketball before anybody else on the team."

"I never noticed, but they are rather long."

"I try to keep from dragging my knuckles."

She almost smiled as she nibbled a few more bites of food. Her trembling seemed to subside. The toast helped.

He was right about the food. He was right about more than just the food.

When she'd polished off the first piece and taken a few sips of the juice, she sat back. "What is it you're dying to say?"

"What are you sorry for?"

Those pretty eyes squinted. "What do you—?"

"Before"—he pointed toward the foyer—"after..." After he'd held her close. After he'd almost kissed her. "After Donald left. You said you were sorry. What for?"

"Oh. I don't know. It just seemed—"

"Because you should be sorry."

Her jaw dropped. "Should I? Why is that exactly?"

"You let that man into your house."

She glared at him. "It is *my* house, after all. I'm allowed to—"

"You put yourself in danger. What would have happened if I hadn't come when I did?"

She broke eye contact. "I'm sure he would have left. He was just trying to talk me into his plan." She rubbed her forearm, probably not even aware she was doing it.

He crossed the space and took her arm in his hand.

Gently, he turned it over, sickened at the marks on her pale skin. Red now, but they'd be bruises by lunchtime.

Fury colored everything in the room. He let the anger rise and fall.

He'd been to this place before. This place of rage at a person not in the room, forced to hide it to protect the person who was.

"When Ella was kidnapped..." He let go of Jacqui's arm and paced away. Turning his back to her, he gripped the countertop, letting the stone cool his temper. He needed to calm down. He had no right to be angry. He had no connection with Jacqui beyond friendship. She owed him nothing.

Jacqui remained quiet while he fought to bring his racing thoughts under control. He didn't turn to look at her, didn't know if she was glaring at him again or looking at him with the compassion so many people had in their eyes when he mentioned Ella's abduction.

He hated that compassion. He didn't deserve it. If he'd been a better father, he'd have protected her. A few cameras installed in her grandparents' yards and his own and they'd have known immediately who'd taken her.

Probably, the existence of those cameras would have discouraged the kidnapper.

There were simple and affordable steps he could have taken, steps he'd never considered and hadn't bothered with. His daughter had nearly been stolen away forever because of his negligence. Eventually, her captor, in his madness, would have murdered her.

Reid didn't turn. Didn't want to see Jacqui's anger or her compassion. "Ella was only five years old. She knew the man who took her. She trusted him. She had no reason to believe he was a threat."

With effort, he made himself face Jacqui.

He saw neither pity nor anger. Wariness filled her expression. "Okay."

"You're a grown woman. An intelligent... No, a brilliant woman. Yet you let that man into your house. That man who—"

"I know what happened, Reid."

"There's no excuse."

"Good thing I don't have to explain myself to you then."

"Right. I'm just the business consultant. You owe me nothing." Hadn't he had the same thought? But they were more than business associates. If he were honest, he'd admit they were more than friends. He cared for her, too much.

"That's not what I meant." Her words fell between them like bricks.

Before either of them could figure out how to navigate the obstacles, a knock sounded from the other room. He was halfway down the hall before he heard the scrape of her chair. He pulled the door open and let the uniformed police officer in.

Chubby cheeks and skin as smooth as Ella's. Did they make teenagers cops in this city?

Where was his adult supervision?

"Officer Bridgeman," the kid said.

Was this really the person the local police trusted with Jacqui's safety?

Reid led the man to the kitchen. While Jacqui explained to the pubescent officer what had happened, Reid leaned against the doorjamb, arms crossed and fighting the anger, admitting to himself that it was fueled by fear and nothing else. Apparently, Don had started their conversation with an apology, and she'd believed him sincere.

Was she really so gullible?

When she said that Don had admitted to breaking into her lab in March, Bridgeman asked the name of the detective involved in that case and promised to get in touch with him.

So that was something. It seemed the kid might know what he was doing.

Bridgeman turned his attention to Reid. "What did you witness when you arrived?"

Reid recounted the scene while the cop took notes. A few more questions, a few more marks in his notebook, and he stood to leave.

Rising, Jacqui said, "Thank you for coming."

At the same time, Reid said, "Are you going to arrest him?"

Bridgeman focused on Jacqui. "You're sure you want to press charges?"

"The man assaulted her." Reid pushed himself away from the wall. "That's why she called—"

The look Jacqui flashed him had him clamping his mouth shut.

Fine, then. He'd be quiet. But...

But nothing. Jacqui wasn't a child. She was an adult who didn't need his help.

Certainly not as much as he needed to offer it, to do something to keep her safe.

The cop kept his focus on Jacqui, his tone even. "I'll open an investigation. A detective will be in touch. Be aware that, if we arrest and charge Burgess, he'll most likely get out on bail within a couple of hours. If you think this man is a threat to you, then you'll need to take measures to protect yourself."

Jacqui massaged her temples. "I can't believe it's come to this."

Reid was careful to keep his tone even when he said, "Maybe you should get a restraining order."

"Unfortunately," Bridgeman said, "you can only file a restraining order against a member of the family or someone with whom you have an intimate relationship. Unless—"

"Not intimate," Jacqui said. "Just business partners."

Reid turned on the cop. "There has to be something she can do."

"You could get a harassment protection order if you could prove that Burgess was the one who broke into your lab. If his confession is believed, he'll be charged for that, and that, plus today's incident..." The cop shook his head. "I don't think that would do it, either. You'd have to show three things he's done in order to qualify for the protection order. Is there anything else you can think of?"

"No, there's nothing—"

"After the funeral," Reid said. "He threatened you, right?"

"Yeah, sort of. Not really, though. He was angry, but I doubt it qualifies."

"Not illegal to be angry," Bridgeman said.

"And I was at his house," Jacqui added.

Reid dug his hands into his hair. Neither of them was taking this seriously enough. Burgess had strong-armed her. The assault charge might stick—might. But he'd probably get off without spending a minute in jail.

Reid had hoped Don's erratic behavior was about getting his hands on Jacqui's invention, but the man's behavior that day confirmed what he'd believed since he'd seen those photos of her wrecked lab—that it wasn't just the artificial neuron that needed to be protected.

CHAPTER THIRTEEN

J acqui settled in the driver's seat an hour later. They'd rescheduled their first meeting for that afternoon, and she'd hoped the extra time would help her regroup after the unsettling morning.

She was showered and dressed and looked prepared to meet with the Cambridge-based company interested in her artificial neuron. But she felt wobbly, like gelatin just released from a mold.

Beside her, Reid said, "Are you sure you don't want me to drive?"

"I'm fine." She didn't want Reid's help. She needed it, but at that moment, she wished she didn't. Reid had been rude and angry and demanding. She didn't appreciate the way he'd spoken to her as if she were a child, as if she'd done something wrong.

She eased away from the curb and turned at the corner toward Beacon Street. Traffic was heavy, drivers focused straight ahead, determined to get where they needed to go without a care for the others on the road. The tension outside, though, was a summer breeze compared to that in the car.

She was turning onto Mass Avenue, which would take them over the Charles River and into Cambridge, when Reid finally spoke. "I'm sorry." He stared forward, lips pressed as if he were trying to keep something in.

"For what exactly?"

A deep breath and a long exhale. "I was angry because you put yourself at risk by inviting Burgess into your house."

"It seemed like the right thing to do. I've known him all my life. I never thought he'd hurt me. And he didn't, not really." She turned her wrist to expose the red marks there.

"That didn't hurt?" She would have expected Reid to sound angry when he voiced the question, but his tone was curious.

She shrugged. At the time, she'd been more shocked than anything. The sharp pain had dulled to a low throbbing.

"How do you feel about the situation now?" Reid asked. "Are you still willing to give him the benefit of the doubt?"

They were about halfway over the bridge when the traffic stopped. Stately brick buildings lined the riverfront. The water shimmered in blue, reflecting the clear skies. Sailboats skimmed the surface, and a team of rowers were fading into the distance toward the harbor.

Along the river's north shore, people walked and rode bicycles, some out for recreation, others hurrying to wherever they were going that morning. If school were in session, there'd be people everywhere, but many of the students abandoned the city in the summertime. From here, the scene looked idyllic, far from the chaotic thoughts churning in her mind.

"Because of my long relationship with Don," she said, "because of his relationship with my parents, I chose to believe he came this morning to apologize. Now I realize he was only trying to get me to change my mind about Tarim."

"What did he say exactly?"

She'd skimmed over the details when she'd recounted the conversation to the police officer, mostly because much of what they'd said to each other was confidential information she didn't want ending up in a police report. "He told me Tarim is prepared to transfer the funds for the patent license as soon as I turn over the device and research. That, as far as they're concerned, it's a done deal. They upped their price, and they believe their offer has been accepted."

"Why would they believe that? Did Don tell them that?"

"That's my assumption."

"You didn't ask?"

"I was preoccupied." Don had seemed so bent and frail standing on the sidewalk. He'd felt anything but in her house as he'd grabbed her and shoved her into the wall, lording his superior size over her. She'd hardly been able to conjure a coherent thought.

Reid's gaze flicked to her wrist, which she was still massaging. She moved her hand away, and Reid faced forward again.

Traffic inched forward before it stopped again.

"Why do you think Don is being so forceful?" Reid asked. "You've made your opinion clear on the matter, and he has no right to dictate to you. Why won't he move on? Why hurt you?"

"I can only assume he thinks he can change my mind."

"Would you say, in the past, you've been one whose mind changed easily?"

"Are you asking if I'm fickle?" She peered at Reid, thinking he might smile at the question, but no amusement graced his face. "I can be pretty stubborn if I need to be. I used to defer to Don in business matters, so I can see why he believes he can convince me. What are you getting at?"

"How did he know my name?"

She'd started to inch forward with the traffic but hit the brake to look at him. The hard edges around his mouth were the only indication that he was frustrated. Or maybe the right term was angry.

She asked, "When did—?"

"When I escorted him out, he called me by name."

Nearly dragged him down the stairs, more like. She'd been equally relieved Reid was protecting her and worried he'd hurt the old man she'd once considered a friend. "What exactly did he say?"

"That I was in over my head. The point is, how did he know my name? Did you tell him?"

"I didn't mention you."

"Did you tell your assistant about me?"

She thought back over her conversations with Braden. "I didn't tell Braden your name. And even if I had, he wouldn't have shared it with Don."

"But you told the police officer that Burgess knew you were in town and knew who you'd visited yesterday. How would he have found that out if not for Braden?"

Traffic moved again, and she made it to the light and turned.

Reid's question was a good one. "I'd hate to think Braden is talking to him behind my back."

"You'd also hate to think that Don might be dangerous." He left the rest of his thought unspoken, but she heard it nonetheless. The ache in her arm wouldn't let her forget.

"I'll call Braden and find out."

"You think he'll tell you the truth?"

"How could I know that?" She couldn't help the rise of frustration in her voice. "I can ask and see what he says. That's all I know to do."

Reid was quiet as she navigated the busy streets. When they were parked in a paid lot, Reid took her hand, and she turned to face him. She thought maybe he was going to say something kind to her, something to make up for his rudeness that morning, something to explain his temper.

"Why don't you call him from the car, so I can listen in on Bluetooth? Maybe I'll be able to pick up something in his tone that you miss."

Because obviously she wasn't intuitive enough to do that on her own. What irritated her most was that Reid was right.

They had a few minutes to spare before their appointment, so she pulled her hand away from Reid's and dialed Braden's number.

It rang four times before it went to voice mail. She left a message asking him to call her back and ended the call.

"Interesting he didn't answer," Reid said.

"He's probably busy."

"Or he's avoiding you."

She didn't want to consider that her loyal assistant wasn't so loyal after all. But the man she'd considered a mentor and friend had turned against her, and Reid, whom she'd hoped would help her, the man she'd been falling for, was abrasive and angry. If she'd ever thought herself a good judge of character, today's events were proving those thoughts wrong.

She opened her door and climbed from the car before Reid could come around.

THE FIRST TWO appointments felt different than those they'd had the day before, though Jacqui couldn't put her finger on why. The people they met seemed curious. They asked questions and engaged in conversation. They expressed interest and requested that she send more details.

But something didn't feel right.

She wished she and Reid had time to discuss it, but they ran long in the second meeting and barely made it to the front door of their third on time. They were still adjusting to the dim light in the small brick-walled lobby when a man approached.

As he neared, she recognized him and felt the first genuine smile all day long. "Mack. How are you?"

He dodged her outstretched hand and pulled her into a hug, lifting her off her two-inch heels. "Jacqui O, elegant as always."

She laughed at the old nickname. She'd been described as a lot of things, but *elegant* was never one of them. When he set her back down on the tile floor, she straightened her suit and regarded the man who'd been a short, skinny eighteen-year-old kid when she'd first met him. Back then, his head had seemed too big for his scrawny body, his long curly hair always a mess. Somewhere between freshman year and graduation, he'd gained about four inches and now stood nearly as tall as Reid. Mack had filled out enough that his head fit very nicely on his wide shoulders. His unruly hair was pulled back into a ponytail. The one thing that hadn't changed about Mack was the mischievous gleam in his eyes.

She shook her head, feigning disappointment. "Charming as ever."

He backed up and puffed out his chest. "Charm comes naturally. I can't help myself." He turned to Reid and stuck out his hand. "Eugene McDonald, Mack to my friends."

"Reid Cote." The men shook hands. "What's the O stand for?"

Before she could answer, Mack said, "Jacqueline O-so-much-smarter-than-me Beal."

"Than I," she said, just to irritate.

Mack rolled his eyes. "See what I mean?"

She turned to Reid. "Ignore him. The O stands for whatever he wants in the moment."

Reid's smile seemed tight at the corners, like he was worried about something. Or maybe... No, not jealous. The thought proved how bad she was at reading people. "How do you two know each other?" Reid directed the question at Mack.

"We were at MIT together. Undergrad," Mack added. "She hung around here while I traded up and got my doctorate at RPI."

"Traded up." Jacqui snorted, then slapped a hand over her mouth, which made the men laugh and caused her cheeks to burn.

"Jacqui Overwhelmingly-classy Beal never ceases to amaze," Mack said.

She focused on Reid. "I spent four years of college perfecting the art of ignoring this guy."

He nudged her shoulder. "I'm unignorable and you know it."

"Like a bad rash."

He chuckled, but his expression grew serious. "Listen, I'm supposed to feel you out about coming to work for us. Unofficially, of course. You'd like working here, and I'd enjoy working at your side, together instead of in competition for a change. Mostly because you always won."

"I'm happy where I am, but—"

"I know, I know." Mack waved her words off as if they were irrelevant. "The money is excellent. The owners are supportive and give us a lot of freedom. More than that, you'd have a stake in anything you developed. You can make a killing here and have job security to boot. I heard about the vandalism at BNB, and I know you haven't started rebuilding yet. It's a shaky business you're in. Just think about it."

She wouldn't, but she appreciated the offer. "You've done your unofficial job."

He didn't try to hide his disappointment, gesturing past a gathering of chairs and the receptionist's desk to the elevator on the far end of the narrow room. "Officially, I've been sent to escort you up."

On the ride to the top floor, Mack looked past Jacqui and spoke to Reid. His tone was all business when he said, "You're Jacqui's assistant?"

"Business consultant," Reid said.

Mack nodded once. "I assume you've been to visit a number of device manufacturers in the last couple of days. IntraHeart is different. We're a boutique developer. We're small, and we have very few products on the market, but each one is the best of its kind. As you might guess from our name, we specialize in pacemakers and other heart-related products. We've branched out, but devices for the heart remain our main focus."

"And you have the capital to invest?" Reid asked.

"Absolutely. I've heard enough about what our brilliant Jacqui O has designed to know that IntraHeart would be a great home for it." He turned to Jacqui, that spark of mischief back. "And I hope the fact that I'm your oldest and dearest friend doesn't affect your impartiality *too* much."

"Oldest and dearest rival, more like."

Mack shook his head. "I wish. You're the reason I bailed on this city. Had to go somewhere I wasn't overshadowed by a gorgeous redhead."

Before she could come up with a suitable response, the elevator dinged, and Mack led them across a hallway covered in plush carpet to darkly stained double doors. He opened them and escorted Jacqui and Reid into an outer office. A young man sitting behind a desk looked up when they walked in. "I'll let them know you're here."

After he stepped away, Mack turned to face Jacqui and Reid, lowering his voice. "Keep it short and straightforward. Mr. Keeler has no time for wasted words."

Jacqui asked, "Have you ever known me to prattle on?"

"Never, but"—he nodded toward Reid—"just thought the warning might help."

"I think I can handle it," Reid said. If she'd expected a hint of humor in his voice, she'd have been disappointed.

Mack turned as the receptionist stepped back in.

"They're ready for you," the man said.

The conference room was long and narrow, its exterior wall brick and glass. After introductions to the four men positioned at the table, Jacqui took the seat offered at the end. Reid handed out the brochures he'd had printed, and she began the spiel she'd given enough times to know by heart.

Reid was focused on the room and, as he'd done so often in previous meetings, clued her in when she got too technical and lost people.

She thought the meeting went well. And, as she had at the other meetings that morning, she felt something was off when Mr. Keeler, the balding fifty-something CEO, stood and thanked them for their time with a terse, "We'll be in touch."

Just like that, they were dismissed. Jacqui should have felt relieved to have the sales appointments over with, but unease prickled the back of her neck.

Something wasn't right.

CHAPTER FOURTEEN

R eid stood straight against the back elevator wall as Mack pushed the button to the lobby.

After the doors closed, Jacqui turned to Mack. "What's going on?"

At least Reid hadn't imagined the tension in the conference room that morning. He'd picked up the same tension in their other two meetings. The reason seemed obvious to him, but he waited to hear what Mack would say.

Mack wasn't saying much, though. "I'm not sure."

Standing behind Mack, Reid couldn't see his face, couldn't hear anything but confusion in his voice.

"Best guess," Reid said.

The elevator dinged. Mack stepped off the lift, crossed the lobby, and pushed out the doors into the sweltering June heat. He turned to face them. "When I told Keeler a couple of days ago that Jacqui had requested this meeting, he was enthusiastic." He directed the next words at Reid. "I don't know how much you know about the medical research industry in Boston, but it's a pretty small community."

Reid had gathered that in the two days they'd been there.

"Rumors about Jacqui's neuron have been circulating for

months. When Keeler found out we might have the opportunity for exclusive rights"—he focused on Jacqui—"he was downright jubilant. For him, anyway. Which means he almost smiled."

"He didn't seem exactly jubilant today," Jacqui said.

"Far from it," Reid added.

Mack ran a hand over his head. "Something changed. I don't know what."

"Can you find out?" Reid asked. "And tell us?"

"I'll find out for sure. Tell you?" His gaze flicked between them and settled on Jacqui. "My loyalty is to the company that pays my rent."

"Of course," she said. "But if you have any insight for us—"

"I'll pass along whatever I can. Now, I gotta run. I'll try to let you know what I learn." He kissed Jacqui's cheek, and the jealousy Reid had been fighting ever since Mack had pulled her into a hug tried to nudge its way into his thoughts. Stupid. Jacqui wasn't Reid's girlfriend. He had no claim on her. And anyway, she obviously wasn't Mack's girlfriend either. That thought cheered him a little.

"Whatever happens," Mack said to Jacqui, "I'm proud of you. Proud to know you."

She backed up, cheeks turning pink. "It's mutual."

He shook his head and went back inside.

Jacqui watched him leave, a wistful look on her face, which had Reid tamping down irritation. "After you."

She started down the sidewalk, pulling her phone from her pocket. "I have a couple of missed calls."

"Anyone we know?" Had her assistant called her back? Reid was eager to hear what the man had to say.

Jacqui raised the phone to her ear, listened, then tapped the screen and did it again before she shoved her phone into her laptop case. "Two of the companies we spoke to yesterday want to meet with us again."

It was good news. "Any chance we can set that up for today?"

She glanced up at him. "Best bet will be tomorrow. I'd planned to go back to Coventry and then return for the conference Friday, but it looks like I'll need to stay here."

It was only Tuesday. "Do you mean stay tonight or—?"

"I see no point in going back to New Hampshire tomorrow only to come back down the following evening, and the conference starts first thing Friday. I'm sure Bree can manage the ice cream shop without me. If you need to get back, we can rent you a car. BNB will pay for it."

He stopped and took her hand, giving her little choice but to stop as well. She looked up at him with a question in her eyes.

This woman. He'd only begun to get to know her, but he found almost everything about her to be beyond impressive. She was gorgeous and smart and competent. She was kind and forgiving—too much so, in his opinion. Maybe, this instant, she was also a little dense if she thought he was eager to leave her side. "I don't need to get back to Coventry."

"I see. You just looked... I don't know."

"Worried?"

She shrugged, her gaze slipping to somewhere around his chin. "I've never been good at guessing what people are thinking. I missed nonverbal communication one-oh-one."

How could she be so smart and so clueless at the same time? The urge to kiss her came again, a desire warmer than the June breeze. How easy it would be to tip her chin up and press his lips to hers. How wonderful it would feel.

And how wrong. Because he had Ella, and Ella had to come first. He couldn't let himself fall for a woman whose life was in Boston, a woman whose life might be in danger.

He squeezed her hand. "I'm worried about you. I want you out of this city and away from the man who hurt you today. That's what you saw on my face."

"Oh. I didn't..." She blinked, confusion filling her light brown eyes. "Okay."

How could she not pick up on what he was feeling?

It was better she didn't. Better they kept it casual.

The longer he spent with her, the harder it was to pretend.

~

"I'm not happy about this."

Jacqui's words had no effect on Reid as he leaned against the wall in her foyer. She was glowering down at him from the landing halfway to the second floor. "You're a grown woman," he said. "You can do what you want." If she opted to stay at her house, he'd be sleeping in her car at the curb. No way was he leaving her alone there again.

She took the final few steps to join him, suitcase in hand. "I really think it would be fine."

"You also thought it would be fine to let Don in your house this morning."

Anger flashed in her eyes—the look gone within seconds. "I won't make that mistake again."

Reid had hoped it wouldn't be an issue, that Don would be in police custody. But a detective had called Jacqui and explained that the DA had decided not to pursue criminal charges against Don. Jacqui had put the call on speaker so Reid could listen in, though she'd asked him to keep quiet.

It hadn't been easy as the detective had explained their reasoning. Apparently, Jacqui hadn't been injured enough to warrant an arrest. The fact that she'd willingly let him in the house proved she hadn't feared him. And Don was an old, grieving man. Not only that, but Don had claimed that Jacqui had tripped, and he'd only grabbed her to keep her from falling.

The courts were too backed up to take on "frivolous cases," the detective had said.

Reid had barely kept his mouth shut. His words hadn't been necessary, though, as Jacqui had calmly but sternly told the detective exactly what she thought of his opinion.

She'd finished with, "How much damage does Don need to do to me before you take it seriously?"

The call hadn't ended on a pleasant note.

Reid said as calmly as he could manage, "Don's behavior is reckless and desperate." They'd gone over this more than once, but Reid would continue to press his case until Jacqui agreed with him or ordered him out of her house. He held out his hand for her suitcase. "You've already rented the room."

It seemed a monumental feat when she relinquished her grip on her overnight bag and let him take it.

"Did you contact your house sitter?" he asked.

"I told her not to come back. If it's not safe for me, it's not safe for her."

"Just until this is over."

When Jacqui looked up at him, he caught the sheen of tears in her eyes. "Will it ever be over?"

The sympathy he felt came with a generous portion of affection that could easily turn into something else. He hugged her to his side with his free hand—a nice, safe hug. "It will. I promise."

Thirty minutes later, they were checked in at the place he'd left that morning, a luxury hotel on Huntington Avenue. After they stowed their things in adjoining rooms, they met back in the hallway. She'd pulled her hair into a ponytail and changed out of the business suit and into a green T-shirt, ankle-length jeans, and flip flops. She looked like the ice cream shop manager he'd first come to know.

"You hungry?" he asked.

"Maybe for a snack."

They'd eaten a late lunch. Exhausted from the day's events, they'd spoken about the promising appointments the next day. Jacqui had spent much of their lunch on the phone with contacts at the businesses they'd visited, but she'd learned nothing about why their management had seemed so reticent to get involved with her.

Now, he took her hand and led her to the elevator, which took them to the roof. They left the cool elevator car for the warm air scented by the pool that filled much of the space. Music was playing, but Reid couldn't make out the song over the hum of conversation coming from the bar. Men and women were crowded around it and the small tables nearby, clinking glasses and laughing and flirting. It wasn't his scene, but he could understand the appeal of the rooftop bar, so different from the establishments on the street level. It felt upscale and classy.

She paused and gazed around. "I've never been up here."

"I checked it out last night. The view, not the bar." He led her the opposite direction from the partyers to the railing.

The sun was low in the western sky, the buildings alight with a golden glow in its reflection. She gazed at the skyline. "It's lovely."

The view was something, but the woman beside him put the glory of the city to shame.

"I'll be right back." He left her at the railing and ordered them two iced teas and a couple of appetizers, ignoring the crowd of revelers and the scent of alcohol that permeated this end of the rooftop. Cold drinks in hand, he returned to Jacqui, who'd settled on the end of a lounge chair.

Nobody was in the pool at this hour. Nobody would bother them over here.

He sat in the lounge chair beside hers and handed her the drink. "Hope this is all right."

She squeezed her lemon into the liquid and sipped. "Perfect choice for a warm evening."

It had been a long and difficult day. He needed a moment to regroup, to consider all that had happened, and to figure out what to do about it. He was convinced that the strange reception they'd received in their meetings that day was linked to Don. The man had learned about those meetings, and he'd somehow sabotaged them. But how?

"This was never my scene."

Jacqui's voice cut into his musings. He turned her direction to find her staring at the crowded bar.

"How about you?" she asked.

"In college, yeah. I mean, not like that." He nodded to the

upscale crowd. "There's no place like this at Plymouth State, but I did my share of drinking in college."

"I never tried it."

He caught the wistful tone and turned to see a similar look on her face. "You're not missing anything."

"Oh, I know." Laughter carried over the sparkling water. "It sounds like they're having fun, though."

"I can get you a drink, if you want."

"No. That's not..." She shook her head.

Ah. It wasn't the alcohol she was craving but the camaraderie. He shifted in his chair to face her. "What you're seeing over there —it's not companionship. At least, not for most of them. It's a bunch of business people, maybe some older college students, searching for something meaningful. They're trying to fill an empty space in their hearts with fun and friendship. They'll find fleeting enjoyment, but not joy. They'll find comfort in the arms of a lover—or a stranger, maybe—but not love. It's an illusion."

Finally, she faced him. "You're very wise, Reid Cote."

He shrugged. "I learned the hard way. I mean, Denise and I were together all through college, so at least I didn't make *that* mistake, but we did our share of drinking and partying, always searching for the next high. What I've learned is that true joy comes not from fleeting moments, vacations or unique experiences —though some can be wonderful. But true joy comes from the Lord, and it comes from the pursuit of the calling He placed on your heart. For me, that's found in worship, in my work, and in my relationships. For me, true joy is found in being Ella's father." The thought of his daughter started a knot in his stomach. He wasn't going to worry about Denise's threats. His lawyer was on it. God was on it. "For you," he continued, "I suspect that joy is found in your research."

"That's true." But her voice still carried that wistful tone.

He reached across the space and took her hand. "But we all need friends. Companionship. There's nothing wrong with craving that."

"I've never been very good at friendship." She kept her face tilted down but looked up at him, shyness filling her gaze.

He swallowed hard. This woman, this gorgeous woman, looking at him like that...

He thought of all the reasons why he'd wanted to keep this casual, but they were carried away in the summer breeze.

The sound of footsteps had him clearing his throat and turning. A server approached carrying two dishes. "Where do you want these?"

Reid dropped his feet to either side of his lounge chair and scooted back. "Just set 'em—"

"Gotcha." The guy put the food down, handed Reid two rolled silverware-and-napkin bundles, and hurried away.

"Calamari. My favorite." Jacqui dipped a fried morsel into the marinara sauce and popped it in her mouth.

"I'm glad I guessed right." Reid took a nacho from the heaping plate. The chip was crunchy, the cheese creamy, and the chicken spicy. He chewed and swallowed. "I figured you'd like one or the other."

"Or both," she said, choosing a nacho.

They ate and sipped their teas and chatted about nothing important for a couple of minutes, but the unspoken conversations hovered like the scent of their dinner. Much as Reid craved the conversation they'd been having—and the closeness they'd experienced—he figured it was time to get back to business.

"What do you think happened today?"

She wiped her fingers and sipped her tea. "I'm thinking that, when Don found out what we were up to, he started making calls."

"That's my assumption too. The question is, what did he say?"

"Something to either cast doubt on the neuron—"

"I don't think he'd do that," Reid said. "He needs people to know that it works. He has a vested interest in people believing it's as good as you're saying it is."

"I agree. So he must be casting doubt on me, or maybe on our company."

"You hear anything from Mack?"

"Nothing."

"How about Braden?"

She blinked, checked her phone. "Nothing from him either." Before Reid could articulate his suspicions about the man, she added, "It doesn't mean anything."

Except somebody had told Don about the meetings—and about Reid. If not Braden, then who?

She must've seen something in his expression, because she dialed her phone and put it on speaker. A moment later, Braden answered. "Hey, Jacqui. Sorry I didn't get back to you. I was in the middle of a job, and then I forgot. What's up?"

"We had an interesting day."

After a short pause, he asked, "What does that mean?"

Jacqui explained about their meetings the day before and that day, giving him more information than Reid would have liked. If Braden was against them, then they'd just confirmed that his scheme was working. Jacqui trusted him, though. Reid would try to do the same unless he had a good reason not to.

"Can I ask you a question?" Jacqui sounded almost nervous. "I'm not going to be angry, but I do need you to be honest with me."

"Of course." The man sounded irritated, adding, "When have I ever not been?"

"I know. I just..." Jacqui looked at Reid, and he nodded to encourage her to continue. "Don showed up at my place this morning. Did you tell him I was in town?"

"After what he did to our lab? Why would I?"

"Well, I know you and he talked about the Tarim deal, so I wasn't sure—"

"Look, Jacqui. I work for you. I definitely *don't* work for Don. Yeah, I thought the deal sounded good, but when you explained your reasons for rejecting it, I accepted them. I trust you. I would never betray you."

Jacqui lifted her gaze from the phone to Reid. She seemed to be seeking some reassurance that her assistant was being honest. As far as Reid could tell, Braden sounded sincere, but he'd never met the man, and he couldn't exactly read his body language on the phone. He shrugged, and Jacqui dropped her gaze again.

"I'm sorry to ask," she said. "Somehow, he learned of our plans. We're pretty sure he's the reason today's appointments didn't go as well as yesterday's. I made some calls earlier, but I'm not getting anywhere with my contacts. Do you think you could reach out to yours? See if you can find out if Don's been in touch and, if so, what he said?"

"I'll do it and let you know what I learn."

After she hung up, she dropped her phone into her small purse. "It wasn't him."

She was probably right, but... "We don't know anything for sure yet."

She glanced at the remaining food on the end of his chair. "I'm finished."

He snatched another nacho, popped it into his mouth, and then carried the dirty plates to an empty table nearer the bar. When he returned, Jacqui was standing at the railing, gazing at the skyline. The sun had set, and night was creeping over the city.

When he joined her, she said, "It's funny how it all looks so shiny and clean from up here. But when you get down into it, it's messy and complicated."

He turned and leaned against the railing, seeing the crowd at the bar the same way. "Everything is messy and complicated when you get involved. The people who choose to remain above it all might miss the complicated parts, but they miss the good parts too."

"I guess I've always been more comfortable with books and facts than I have with people and relationships. But I'm coming to understand what that's cost me."

"Meaning?"

She shifted to face him. "Don's so good with people. Right now, he's using that against me, and I have no idea how to combat it. All my knowledge, this invention—it'll mean nothing if I can't sell it." She tilted her head down, a defeated posture if he'd ever seen one. "Alone, without someone to manage the people part for me, I'm useless."

With a knuckle beneath her chin, he lifted her face so he could meet her eyes. "None of us can do this life thing alone. We all have different gifts and talents. We all need each other. I'm just sorry that a person you relied on, a man you thought you could trust, betrayed you. That doesn't make you less-than, though. To rely on others, to admit when we need help—that makes us stronger, not weaker." He leaned close enough to catch her unique floral scent. "And you're not alone."

She blinked, her wide eyes filling with wonder. Wonder, as if his closeness, his desire, surprised her. As if she weren't the most desirable creature on the planet.

All his reasons for keeping his distance dissipated in the warm air. He slid his hands down her arms and laced his fingers with hers. "Jacqui..." But whatever words he might've said were lost in the tide of his emotions. He leaned down and pressed a simple kiss to her lips.

And the world exploded in color and beauty. He went back for more, and she opened up to him. Opened her lips and her heart, and he dove in and tasted the goodness and light he'd seen in her eyes and felt on her skin.

His hands slid to her hips, up her back, and drew her close.

Hers caressed his chest and wound around his neck, her fingers digging into the hair at his nape. And all thoughts about inventions and daughters and lawyers were swallowed up in need for this amazing woman.

He didn't know how many minutes passed before his mind and body started scheming and the thought of their adjoining bedrooms had him ending the kiss.

She rested her cheek against his chest.

He held her close, rubbing her back and trying to calm his racing heart, knowing she'd feel it thumping through his thin T-shirt.

He could stay like this, just like this, for the rest of the night.

At the feel of her sigh, he forced himself to lean back. She looked up at him, and after one gaze at her shy expression, he almost kissed her again.

He didn't know what to say. He feared he'd scare her away if he said what was on his mind—that he'd never felt anything like that before, that he never wanted to let her go.

She seemed just as confused, just as... blown away? He hoped so. He hoped he wasn't the only one trying to get his legs under him.

"I think," she said, "that was the very best part of this day."

He chuckled. "That's not saying much."

"I can't imagine any event on any day overshadowing that."

Oh, man. He was done for.

He rested his forehead against hers. "What are we supposed to do with this?"

"How would I know? You're the expert in these things, right? I'm following your lead."

"Then we're in deep trouble."

CHAPTER FIFTEEN

Jacqui wasn't ready for the night to end. After that kiss, she might never be ready.

She'd been kissed before. She'd had boyfriends—a couple, anyway. She'd felt a man's lips against her own. But she'd never felt... that.

She didn't even know how to define it. It was like an electromagnetic pull. No, a gravitational pull. She felt as if her entire being wanted to orient itself around Reid. It was a delirious feeling. A dangerous feeling.

She'd read plenty of novels that contained love and romance, but this was the first time she'd ever understood. This was the first time her body had responded to a man's touch. This was the first time she'd craved more.

She didn't understand it and couldn't define it and was terrified of it.

And she didn't want it to end.

They'd turned back to face the view, and the city lights that had only been lights ten minutes earlier now seemed like a million sparkling stars.

She tried to shake off the ridiculous tween-girl romantic thoughts, but they wouldn't dislodge.

Reid slid his hand across her back, hooked it on her hip, and drew her close, and all thoughts of trying to rid herself of these emotions dissolved in some bizarre hormonal solution.

She leaned her head against his chest and stopped fighting.

This man. Oh, this man. He'd awakened in her something she hadn't known herself capable of. He could be boorish and demanding when he was angry. But even that came from a desire to protect. He made her feel safe and comfortable and wanted.

Not for her mind. Not for what she knew or could create, but for herself. Her being. Her spirit.

What was this feeling she had for him? Affection didn't cover it, but it was too soon for love, wasn't it?

Was it?

She didn't know.

And usually, when she didn't know something, she felt it her job to find out. To solve the problem. To come up with an ordered solution, and maybe even to improve it, whatever *it* was. But this thing she was feeling?

How could it be improved?

Did it need to be defined?

Was there a solution?

She dearly hoped not.

She glanced at him, hoping to see the contentment on his face that she felt in her heart. She was disappointed. His lips were pressed together, his eyes, stormy. "What's wrong?"

"What? Oh, nothing."

"Something."

He blew out a long breath. "I'm just trying to figure out..."

What? Was he thinking about their meetings, or their kiss, or something else? "How's Ella?"

"She's having a blast."

Jacqui decided she'd better not tease him about his unhappiness at that fact. "Did I miss something?"

"Denise is demanding more visitation."

"Oh. What are you going to do?"

He lifted his broad shoulders, dropped them. "I hope we can come to an agreement without going to court, but Denise is demanding too much." He explained a conversation he'd had with his ex the night before.

Jacqui was trying to catch up. "She told you all of this last night?"

"She called when I was on my way to the hotel."

"I'm sorry I didn't ask earlier. This must have been weighing on your mind all day."

"I was distracted." His lips quirked up at one corner. "You're a good diversion."

"Me and all my problems, which are insignificant compared to what you're going through."

"No, they're not. And anyway, I'm not going through anything yet. My lawyer's handling it. All I can do right now is pray or worry. I'm trying to pray and leave it in God's hands."

"Very mature."

He chuckled, but the sound died fast. "Ella needs me. Her mother is"—he shook his head—"not fit."

"Not that I'm disagreeing, but based on what?"

"She abandoned her. She left us both."

"Which is awful and might even be unforgivable. But you're a Christian, so—"

"I forgave her." Reid shifted away, dropping the arm that had held Jacqui so close. "That doesn't make her a fit mother."

"Of course not. But maybe she's matured. Maybe she's—"

"She's a narcissist."

"Literally? Like, diagnosed, or—?"

"I was married to her. I know how she is."

"Okay." Jacqui still felt one step behind in this conversation. Denise was Ella's mother, right? And his ex-wife. Surely she had some good qualities. "You loved her. There must have been something lovable—"

"Why are you taking her side?" Reid stepped back, placing a

foot or more between them. "You don't even know her, and you're taking her side."

"I'm not taking sides. I'm trying to understand."

"You won't be able to understand. If you're not a parent, if you've never been in this situation—"

"I've been in a family. I've had a mother. I couldn't have survived without mine."

"Well, then." His smile was tight. "I stand corrected. You understand everything there is to know."

Tears stung her eyes. His sarcasm hurt, but he was right. She didn't understand anything. Human relationships couldn't be figured like math problems. Her mother wasn't Ella's mother, her father wasn't Reid.

But she wanted to understand. She wanted more than anything to comprehend what Reid was going through, to help him as he'd helped her. Obviously, he didn't want her help or her opinion or anything.

For her to rely on him was mature, or so he'd said, but for him to rely on her, apparently ridiculous.

Maybe she had nothing to offer.

Reid certainly seemed to believe that.

She blinked tears back. "It's getting late."

"Look, I'm—"

"It's fine." She walked toward the exit, snatching her purse from the lounge chair on the way. "I need to get some rest."

She was nearly to the elevator when Reid took her hand and tugged. She stopped and looked at him, fully prepared to see that angry expression again. But his face held only kindness. "I'm sorry. I was rude."

"You were. It's..." It wasn't fine. And to say it was wouldn't help. Instead, she said, "I forgive you." Which sounded formal and rather stupid but was true. She added, "I'm only trying to understand. And please don't be angry with me for saying this, but from what I can see, it seems maybe Denise is trying hard to make up for her past wrongs. What happened last summer, maybe it was a wakeup call. Maybe she wants to be a better mother. And maybe she can be, if she's given a chance."

"She doesn't deserve a chance."

Jacqui nodded slowly, letting those words gather their meaning. She thought of something Braden had said to her about mercy way back in the spring. "That's a pretty loaded word, 'deserve.' Do you want her to get what she deserves?" Before Reid could answer, she added, "Do you want to get what *you* deserve?"

His jaw snapped shut, remained clenched for a few seconds before he ground out, "I understand what you're saying. Mercy and grace. I get it."

"Okay."

"I have to do what's right for Ella. Not me, and not Denise. Ella is paramount here."

"Okay." Except Denise was Ella's mother. Denise had rights as her mother, and Ella had a right to have a relationship with her. This felt like a clear issue of right and wrong—mother loving her daughter, daughter loving her mother, and father standing in the way.

Jacqui felt nothing but affection for that overprotective, loving father. But it was possible he was wrong.

Reid's voice was fully confident when he added, "And what's right for Ella is to be with me, not her narcissistic, movie star mother." He nodded as if he'd made his point.

Jacqui didn't *okay* that statement. Because Reid, for all his good qualities—and they were myriad—wasn't seeing this rationally. For his sake, Jacqui prayed Denise wouldn't press for custody, because she feared that, no matter what Reid believed was best for Ella, a judge might see the situation very differently.

When they arrived at Boylston the next morning, the CEO didn't greet them in the lobby as she had before.

They were ushered to the same conference room they'd met in

two days prior, a long, gloomy, and windowless room with a dark cherry table surrounded by the same kinds of padded chairs that surrounded every dark cherry conference table they'd seen since they'd begun this venture.

This time, however, the room was empty. No managers with pens poised to take notes. No eager CEO with a list of questions.

Jacqui rounded the table and sat facing the door.

Reid settled in beside her. "I feel like we've been sent to the principal's office."

She knew exactly what he meant. It wasn't anything anybody had said, but the few people who'd looked at them as they'd been escorted to this space had worn looks of disapproval.

Jacqui didn't understand but hoped that, by the time this meeting was over, she would.

Finally, Doreen Nadler stepped in, a bespectacled man Jacqui remembered as the corporate attorney on her heels. Doreen took the seat at the end of the table, and the man settled beside her and across from Jacqui. "You remember Mr. Conneally."

He pulled his phone from his breast pocket, tapped the screen, and said, "I hope you don't mind. I'll be recording this conversation."

Jacqui glanced at Reid, who shrugged. She turned back to Doreen. "I have nothing to hide."

The woman nodded once. "We were very eager to hear more about your artificial neuron."

Jacqui didn't miss the use of past tense. Her stomach swooped as if she'd stumbled on the woman's cold words. "But something happened to change your mind," she said. "May I ask what?"

"I called an old friend of mine. I'd call him a mutual friend, but I'm not sure that term applies to you anymore."

"Donald Burgess, I presume."

"Don tells us that you don't have the legal right to license the neuron."

Jacqui absorbed that blow. At least now she knew who'd tipped Don off about her appointments in town. After he'd heard from

Doreen, he must have spread his lies among his contacts at the other medical R and D companies. The man was thorough, she had to give him that.

"Don is wrong." Jacqui tried to sound confident, but her voice shook with anger and betrayal. "He sold me all but ten percent of his shares in BNB. I have the legal documents to prove it. I am the managing partner, and all patents belong to me."

"I've known Don Burgess for thirty years." Doreen's voice took on a lecturing tone, as if she were speaking to an errant child. "He mentored me. He got me my first job, and he's been a faithful friend throughout my career. And who are you?" Doreen leaned forward, her expression slipping into a sneer. "An untested, unknown, obscure researcher who happens to share her father's name and family's fortune. A woman nobody's ever heard about. A woman taking credit for somebody else's work. From where I sit, Ms. Beal, you look like a lying, conniving little thief." Doreen's words rose to a shout, her skin turning a deep red.

The attorney cleared his throat and pushed his glasses higher on his nose. "According to Mr. Burgess, his shares were coerced from him during a time of great suffering." He peered at Jacqui over the top of his glasses, the look of censure clear on his face. "Mr. Burgess informed us that he is pursuing legal action against you."

"He begged me to buy his shares. I offered to loan—"

"Jacqui." Reid's voice was calm but commanding.

When she turned his direction, he shook his head, pushed back in his chair, and stood. He addressed Doreen. "Mr. Burgess has no legitimate claim, which will be evident *if* he brings legal action. We can assure you that he has done no such thing. Ms. Beal has not been informed of any lawsuit. At this point, we can only assume that Mr. Burgess, in his grief, is confused and perhaps misremembering the events that took place before his wife passed away. Fortunately"—now, he directed his attention to the attorney—"there were lawyers representing both sides involved in the transaction. If you would like more information about this matter, we will happily put you in touch with our legal team."

"We're not interested in getting into a legal battle with Mr. Burgess," the attorney said.

Reid ignored the man as he pulled Jacqui's chair out and helped her up.

Too stunned to speak, she focused on keeping her shoulders back and started for the door. She was nearly there when Reid spoke again.

"I can assure you, Ms. Nadler, that Ms. Beal owns the patent on the artificial neuron she herself invented, and we will continue seeking a partner to trust with exclusive rights to that patent." He was still standing where Jacqui had left him, looking down at the two still seated at the table. He looked as calm and collected as ever. "If you'd like to be among the companies we consider, please send your proposal right away. If you have any more questions, feel free to call. Good day."

He joined Jacqui, settled a hand on her back, and led her down the long hallway toward the front door. Only his strong touch kept her moving. She swallowed the nausea that tried to rise, forcing herself to look confident despite the thoughts swirling inside.

By the time they reached the sidewalk, her stomach was roiling, her heart thumping as if she were being chased. Out of sight of the glass doors with the words *Boylston Tech* emblazoned proudly, she bent at the waist, barely keeping herself up. "I think I'm going to be sick."

His arm slid around her and supported her as he ushered her forward. She couldn't focus on anything but the sidewalk beneath her feet as she stumbled beside him.

They hadn't gone far when Reid stopped, pulled open a door, and led her into a chilled space and to a table. A restaurant of some kind, if the scents of coffee and donuts were any indication. She slid into the booth and set her forehead on the cool laminated table, breathing deeply.

"What can I do?" Reid asked.

She swallowed, shook her head, prayed the nausea would pass. Unfortunately, even when it did, the nightmare wouldn't be over.

Apparently, it was just getting started.

~

JACQUI PICKED at the sandwich Reid insisted she try to eat. After their disastrous meeting that morning, her nausea had passed, and she'd pulled herself together. The second meeting mirrored the first—though the CEO had been apologetic, not accusatory, when he explained why he wouldn't be seeking exclusive rights. At least Jacqui had been prepared.

There were no more meetings that day. No calls. No interest whatsoever in the invention people had called groundbreaking and world-altering just one day before.

She lifted her sandwich, took a small bite, and tried to enjoy the creamy chicken salad. She should be thankful for the warm summer breeze that tried to whisk her napkin away, but it irritated more than refreshed.

"All is not lost." Reid studied her from across the bistro table on the Newbury Street restaurant's patio.

This upscale shopping district was only a couple of blocks from their last meeting but might as well have been in a different universe from the world of medical research they'd just left. Here, shoppers clad in overpriced clothes and carrying designer bags wandered past, chatting and laughing as if all were well, as if their money could solve their problems. If only Jacqui had the kinds of problems that could be solved with the swipe of a credit card or the writing of a check. Even then, she'd be sunk. BNB had little cash and no assets, thanks to Don's temper tantrum. She'd spent all her savings buying him out. And she'd sworn she wouldn't dip into her trust fund for any reason.

"My reputation is ruined." She dropped the sandwich back onto her plate. What would her father say? Maybe she should have told him and Mom about the rift between her and Don. She'd avoided bringing them into it, hoping it would work itself out. She hated feeling like she needed her parents' help. Her goal had always been to make her own way in the world, to achieve her dreams without relying on anybody. That was what Dad had done, after all.

Now, Dad would hear the rumors, probably sooner rather than later. What a disappointment she was turning out to be. All she'd wanted was to make him proud, and instead, she'd managed to drag their family name into the mud. No, she couldn't face Dad yet. "In this business, a person's reputation is everything. He's destroyed me."

"He's *trying* to destroy you, but he'll only succeed if you let him."

"Everybody in this industry knows Don. Everybody respects him. You think Doreen Nadler is alone?" Those last few words had come out nearly shrill. She lowered the pitch and started over. "Do you have any idea how many people Don has helped during his long career in this city? I'd guess fifty or a hundred or more. I'm not the latest or the youngest, just one of a huge crowd. And the rest of this crowd thinks Donald Burgess walks on water."

"But you have the truth—"

"What good is that going to do me?" Her words had been loud enough that the people at the neighboring table turned to look. Again, Jacqui tempered her tone. "The truth is irrelevant, and Don knows it. He doesn't have to file suit against me. He only has to say he's thinking about it, spread his rumors and lies. If he chooses not to file suit, he'll tell people it's not worth it, that he doesn't want to hurt me, and people will see him as the kind, benevolent mentor he's always made himself out to be. If people consider working with me despite the rumors, then he will file suit, keep the neuron tied up in court for years. By the time it's over, there won't be anything left worth fighting for."

"The artificial neuron is worth it."

"If nobody wants it, then it isn't worth a dime."

Reid leaned forward and lowered his voice, though the words

were vehement. "The devices that could be developed with it... We're talking about millions of dollars' worth of profit here, not to mention the opportunity to change lives. To *save* lives. Will people really pass on it and all the good it can do because of rumors?"

"If they end up in court on charges of patent infringement, the legal fees could destroy a small company like Boylston. Could put a huge dent in the profits of a larger one like IntraHeart. And if they lose? No, nobody will take the chance."

Reid sat back, shaking his head. "Why is he doing this? What does he hope to gain?"

"He's trying to box me into a corner, and he's succeeding. If I want to keep BNB afloat, I'll have no choice but to go with Tarim."

Or lose the company that had made her father so proud. How could she ever face him again?

When she'd told her father she was going into business with Don instead of taking one of the many opportunities Dad had gotten for her, he'd been disappointed. But when they'd done so well, he'd started to trust her judgment. If it all fell apart now...

"You've made it clear Tarim isn't an option," Reid said. "What happens when you refuse to sell them exclusive rights?"

"BNB doesn't get the cash it needs to reopen. My business will go belly-up, and I'll be left with nothing."

Reid had no answer to that. He focused on his lunch, and Jacqui tried to do the same. Though she'd skipped breakfast, she couldn't force down more than a few bites.

It felt like lunch on the *Titanic*, the water rising to their ankles, the band playing in the background as if all were well.

And now, even Reid had quit trying to find solutions, which proved that all was indeed lost. She had no idea what to do next. No idea how to fight Don. No idea how to get her invention into the hands of people who could do something useful with it.

Reid sipped his drink, then set it on the table with too much force. "We have to quit reacting and go on offense."

She was so tired. She didn't have any idea what he was talking about. "How, exactly?"

"Call your lawyer. We need to see him right away."

She barely stifled the sigh. Sweet Reid wouldn't give up fighting for her, even when the cause was lost. "For what purpose?"

"You need to warn them about Don's threats and find out what legal action you can take against him. And you—"

"*Me* take against *him*? What do you mean?"

"Slander is illegal in this country, Jacqui. He's trying to ruin you. I'm not sure of the best option right now, but we need to figure it out. You get on the phone with your lawyer, and I'm going to find you a publicist. We're going to attack this thing head-on."

"That sort of thing isn't really done in—"

"And you need to knock it off." His tone was anything but kind as he tossed his napkin on his plate. "Stop acting like you've already lost. You can't walk into a battle wearing that hang-dog, woe-is-me look. This is a fight for your reputation, but it's more than that. We're fighting for all the people your invention is someday going to save. Quit acting like the war is over. It's just getting started."

CHAPTER SIXTEEN

Reid wasn't sure if his forceful speech at lunch had done more harm than good as he and Jacqui said good-bye to the publicist and headed for the door. He'd gotten Martha Leyton's name from the CEO of the company he'd worked for. Chelsea Hamilton knew people everywhere and in every industry. She'd made some calls and directed Reid and Jacqui here. It wasn't the largest firm in Boston, but it had an excellent reputation for managing media relations in a crisis. Reid thought the appointment had gone well, but Jacqui still looked as defeated as she had when they'd left Boylston that morning.

He stopped on the sidewalk outside the modern office building, slipped off his suit jacket, and folded it over his arm.

Jacqui, in her sleeveless dress belted at the waist, seemed perfectly comfortable. And perfectly beautiful, despite the worry lines on her forehead.

He said, "I'll get a Lyft." Because of the traffic and the lack of parking, they'd left the car at the hotel and walked from one appointment to the next that day.

"It's not that far." She started off.

Apparently, her pretty sandals with the high heels were more comfortable than they looked.

He fell into step beside her. He'd planned to return to Coventry after a couple of days, but there was no reason he needed to. He'd been managing his workload in the mornings before they left and keeping up with emails during breaks. Business was slow—as slow as it'd been since he'd hung out his virtual shingle that spring. Maybe that was a harbinger of things to come, but he didn't think so, and he refused to let himself worry. He believed the Lord was keeping his workload light so he could focus on helping Jacqui navigate her troubles.

God knew what he needed, and he knew what Jacqui needed. He saw what was happening, saw the injustice being done to her. God was with them, and Reid refused to be discouraged, despite the despair wafting off the woman walking beside him like the stench of yesterday's fish.

"What did you think?" he asked. "Did you like her?"

Jacqui's shoulders lifted and fell.

"Are you relieved she recommended we not bring legal action against Don for slander?"

Again, Jacqui shrugged.

The PR specialist hadn't been what he'd expected. Her old-fashioned name had conjured the image of a grandmotherly sort, but Martha was young—maybe mid-thirties—tall, slender, and dressed in a slim-fitting suit and stilettos. Being in the clothing industry, he knew enough about women's fashion to know that her outfit—shoes to suit to high-priced bag resting on her desk—cost upwards of a thousand dollars. If she'd been trying to convey her success, she'd done her job well.

Reid nudged Jacqui's shoulder. "No thoughts at all?"

"She seemed competent. I suppose we'll have to evaluate her ideas before we can make a final judgment." Jacqui seemed far from convinced.

"If you didn't like her, we can find another firm—"

"No." The word was harsh and delivered with a glare.

He barely kept himself from lifting his hands in surrender. "Okay."

He allowed her to go ahead of him, and they maneuvered past a crowd of tourists following the red bricks that led the way on the Freedom Trail, which snaked through the city past historical sites. Reid had walked it when he was in high school during a field trip. Back then, he should have been focused on the revolutionary-era buildings, but he'd spent much of the day goofing off. Today, like then, he barely glanced at the three-hundred-year-old cemetery. They crossed a street and walked parallel to the Boston Common. Or maybe the Public Gardens. Both big parks—who could keep them straight?

With the bulk of the crowd behind them, Reid stepped to Jacqui's side and took her hand.

Her quick glance was enough for him to pick up the concern in her pinched expression. "I'm sorry. I'm being difficult."

"Only a little."

Her lips quirked at the corners. He hoped that, given a little more encouragement, he might be able to coax a full smile out of her before the night's end.

"I'm too tired to think about it anymore."

"Then let's not. You want to get something to eat?"

"You can, and I'll meet you back at the hotel. I'm not hungry."

How could that be? Reid was starving. Not that it'd been that long since lunch, but the lunch had been pretty paltry. Who put avocado and kale on a sandwich? "You haven't eaten all day."

"I ate at the café."

"You nibbled the bread like a mouse watching for the cat."

Still no smile. "Maybe later."

The park was filled with people, some enjoying the warm evening, others hurrying from one side to the other on their way somewhere. Flowers bloomed, their scents overwhelmed by exhaust coming from the cars backed up at the traffic light. A horn blared, engines hummed, and Jacqui moved forward, seemingly oblivious to it all.

Thanks to the walking they'd done in the previous few days, he'd managed to construct a crude map of the city in his head. He was happy to let her lead the way, but when he glanced at her, she seemed anything but content. The fear in her expression was unmistakable. She'd said she didn't want to think about what was going on with her business, but it was clear she could think of little else.

Sure enough, not five minutes had passed when she said, "I just can't believe it's come to this. A publicist." She said the word like one might say *pimp* or *politician*.

"It's not as if you've hired a fixer to take out your enemy and make it look like an accident."

Still no smile. "You don't understand. My reputation..." She shook her head. "I come from a well-known family."

"I managed to put that together all by myself."

She continued as if he hadn't spoken. "My great-grandfather was one of the founders of two of the specialty hospitals in this city. My grandmother started a nursing school. My grandfather was a diagnostic genius. People used to come from all over the world to see him. My dad is a pioneer, a researcher and surgeon. He's traveled the globe and tried things other doctors could hardly conceive of, and he's saved countless lives. For generations, my family has made a difference in the world. All of them contributed to the family's wealth rather than drawing from it. After college and med school, Dad never took anything from his parents. He never needed to lean on their money to survive. And he never needed to defend his reputation." She sighed, the sound heavy with burden. "All I ever wanted was to live up to their expectations."

"Jacqui, I can't imagine that any of them are disappointed in you. How could they be?"

Jacqui led him around a corner and along a narrow road. Perhaps it was a shortcut. Reid wasn't that familiar with Boston, but this didn't feel like the way back to the hotel.

There were fewer people on this street, though, so he wasn't complaining. Boston was a beautiful city, but he'd like it better if not for all the people and cars and noise.

"I don't know if he's disappointed," she said, picking up on his last comment. Though he'd spoken of her family in general, it seemed Jacqui was focused on her father.

"What does he think about what's going on with Don? They were friends, right?"

"I haven't told him."

Reid stopped. "Why not?"

Jacqui faced him, shrugging one shoulder. "He's going to find out now."

"You haven't done anything wrong, Jacqui."

"I know. I just feel like Dad would never have gotten himself into this mess. If I'd been smarter—"

"You trusted Don. Your father did, too, right? Surely he won't blame you."

Jacqui walked on, and Reid walked beside her, taking her hand in his. Less than a block later, she stopped and looked at the building across the street. Only then did Reid realize where they were. Back at Jacqui's brownstone. She didn't make a move toward the door, just stared up at the stately five-story building.

Reid let go of her hand and pulled her against his side. "Do you want to go inside?"

"No."

He put together everything she'd told him, and something became clear. "You're willing to live here because your father did. He made that concession with his family's money, so you make it too."

"Maybe." When she looked up at Reid, there was a vulnerability in her expression he'd never seen before. Not just fear of Don and fear for her reputation. This seemed like something more, something soul-deep. As if she felt her entire worth were at stake, and she was losing the wager. "Living here reminds me of my family, my heritage. It reminds me that my life isn't all about me, that I was created to make the world a better place. That's my family's legacy—the understanding that we're all meant to achieve something meaningful and important."

Ah. But who defined what was meaningful? Who got to decide

what was important? "I love what your family has taught you. We're all made for a purpose—no doubt about it. Let me ask you this. Do you think your mother has done something meaningful and important with her life?"

"Of course." Surprise filled Jacqui's features. "Mom isn't like Dad. Though she's well educated, she had no desire to go out and change the world. But she's involved in charities. She raises money for good causes and teaches Bible studies."

"She raised you and did a fine job of it."

Jacqui nearly smiled at that. "I don't think she takes credit for how I turned out, but she should, for the good things, anyway. I get my intellect and my ambition from my father, but"—she tapped her heart—"most of what I know about love, I learned from Mom. She's an amazing mother."

"Despite that some might say she's been more of a consumer than a contributor in your family, it sounds like your mother does what the Lord puts on her heart to do. And your mother is infinitely valuable, regardless of what she does with her life."

"I agree, obviously."

"I guess what I'm saying is that your worth isn't wrapped up in your invention or even in what you contribute. God has a plan for you, and your job is to walk in it. You're successful to the degree that you walk the path He's laid out for you. But your worth has nothing to do with that. You are priceless, regardless of what you do."

Jacqui turned back to the house across the street. "I know. I mean, in my head, I know. But there are expectations I have to live up to."

"Only the Lord's expectations matter."

He studied the brownstone, the old red brick and stately front porch with its wrought iron railing, at the intricate trim and leaded glass windows. It was beautiful, but it was nothing compared to the woman who dwelled there.

"I live here because of Dad."

He turned her direction, but she didn't take her gaze from the building.

"Surrounded by his things, knowing he lived here when he was my age, it reminds me of him. That he wanted me to live here reminds me that he loves me, that I'm important to him." Her gaze, when she turned it on him, seemed filled with insecurity. "It's stupid. Of course I know my father loves me."

"I'm sure he does." Reid squeezed her to his side, trying to convey his own affection, which would never make up for her father's. "Even if he didn't, though"—he leaned away so he could face her, wrapping his arms around her back—"that would be a reflection of him, not you. You are a precious, beautiful, and brilliant person. I'm sure your father sees that, even if he's not good at showing you." Which he obviously wasn't, if Jacqui felt so insecure about it. "But whether he loves you or understands you or values you or not, that makes no difference to your worth. You are a masterpiece, crafted by the hands of your Heavenly Father, and valuable beyond expression."

Tears filled her eyes. She pressed her forehead against Reid's chest, and he held her close. If only she could see herself as he saw her.

If only she could see herself as God saw her.

She met his eyes. "You always know the right thing to say."

"I have a daughter who has the same questions about her mother, a daughter who is herself a masterpiece, whether Denise understands that or not."

"You've had practice with that little speech, I gather."

"Not exactly. I try to convey those truths to Ella, but she's a bit young to comprehend the words. Whether I've said it or not, I feel it. I believe it. I'll be praying that you understand your worth as well."

Jacqui turned back to the brownstone. "I do love living here."

"I can see why."

"Honestly, the place is one headache after another. Ancient pipes, and the electrical system needs to be updated, again. But it reminds me of the family I come from. It reminds me that I have to do something that matters."

"And you are. But even if you didn't, *you* would matter. Just by following God's plan for your life, you're living a life that matters. Whether that results in fortune or fame—those things are irrelevant."

"It's not about fortune or fame."

Her words carried no weight, no conviction. They weren't true, and on some level, she knew that. For Jacqui, her ambitions seemed to be about impressing a father who either didn't love and value his daughter or didn't know how to show her he did.

Jacqui was trying to fulfill God's plan for her life and fulfill her father's expectations. Reid wasn't sure she'd be able to do both, and he feared the attempt was tearing her apart.

REID'S STOMACH growled loudly enough that Jacqui looked at him, eyebrows lifted.

They'd resumed the walk back to the hotel. Jacqui hadn't needed anything from the brownstone. She'd just needed to be there, to see it. He suspected maybe the old place and its heritage were more burden than blessing, but he didn't say so.

"I suppose we should eat," she said.

He chuckled. "I could force myself. You want to go back to the rooftop?"

"I'm not in the mood for anything that fancy." She tugged his hand. "A few more blocks, and we'll be at Northeastern. Surely there's a pizza place near campus."

Ten minutes later, they ordered a medium pepperoni at the counter of the first pizza place they came across and found a seat in a booth. The joint looked as if it'd been there for generations, which was a good sign. The imitation leather on the bench was torn in a couple of places, and the laminate floors probably hadn't been replaced since the Bush administration—the first Bush.

He started with, "Let's talk about the meeting with the publicist. I thought it went well, didn't you?"

"I suppose."

"Martha has good contacts at some major media outlets. If she can get a buzz going about the invention, that can only be a good thing." When Jacqui said nothing, Reid added, "And there are plenty of device manufacturers in this country and abroad. The rumors about you seem to be localized right now, as is Don's influence. There's no reason a company outside of Boston won't be interested."

Jacqui sipped her soda. "That makes sense." But there was no conviction in her words. No enthusiasm.

Reid tried again. "I liked her idea to coordinate the media releases with the conference this weekend."

"I'd rather skip the conference." Her lips pressed together and tipped down at the corners. "I suppose I need to be there."

"If you aren't, people are going to think you're afraid to show your face." The publicist had said the same, but Reid suspected that Jacqui had missed most of Martha's words. She'd been too distracted and discouraged to pay attention. "That'll only add to the speculation that you've done something wrong."

Jacqui sighed. "I don't know if I have it in me."

"You're starting to get on my nerves." He hoped the statement would perk her up, and the way her eyes widened gave him hope.

"Sorry I'm not more chipper as my life falls apart."

"If your life falls apart, you'll have only yourself to blame."

Her shoulders hunched as if the world rested on them.

He hated to sound cruel, but if she wanted to save her business and her invention, she was going to need a new attitude, and fast. "Look, Jacqui, Don's a step ahead of us, but not for long. The publicist—"

"What can she do if I'm embroiled in a legal battle?"

"You're not going to be. I've been thinking about this all day. Don is desperate, right? That means he's out of money, or almost out of money. How can he afford to sue you if he doesn't have cash?"

Her expression brightened for the first time in hours. For such a brilliant woman, she could be rather dense. "That's a good point."

"He has very shallow pockets, but yours are pretty deep."

"I'm not going to use family money to rescue my business." Her tone bordered on angry.

He lifted his hands, palms out. "I'm not saying you should. I'm only saying you *could*. And everybody knows it, including Don."

"Don knows how I feel about my trust fund. Dad never dipped into his, and he managed to build quite a career, quite a fortune, actually. I intend to do the same."

"I understand that, but what good does that money do sitting in a bank. It's just gathering interest, making you wealthier every day. Is that your goal, to amass as much wealth—?"

"Of course not!" The fire in her eyes was a welcome sight, even if it was directed at him.

"Really? Because by hoarding it, all you're doing is making yourself richer. It makes me think of the parable of the talents. You've been given a gift, and you've just buried it in the ground."

Her mouth opened, snapped shut. Maybe he was getting through to her.

"What better way to use it than to get your invention into the hands of people who can save lives? What better way—"

"I'm not dipping into my trust fund." Her words, measured and delivered with conviction, told him she wasn't about to budge on this. He'd let it go for now.

"The thing is, Don doesn't know *for sure* that you won't use your trust fund to fight him in court. He can hope, he can guess, but he can't be certain. Do you think he's willing to risk whatever money he has left on a court battle he's almost sure to lose? And for what purpose? If he loses, he gets nothing, right? You own the patent. If he wins, years have passed, and very likely someone else has come along with a new invention that can do something similar to yours. Would he really sue you just to ruin you, with no financial incentive?"

"If he sues me, it'll be because he believes he can win." At least her voice had lost the anger. Now, she sounded confused. "We need to talk to the lawyer. Maybe I'm missing something."

"It's possible. But I don't think he plans to sue. If that were the plan, what is he waiting for? The sooner he starts the process, the sooner it'll be over. No, I think Don believes that he can get what he wants by ruining your reputation. He believes he can corner you. He's the business guy, right? So he must figure you're in over your head. You'll eventually give up and give in and sell the exclusive rights to Tarim."

"Even if I were to do that, he can't think I'm going to give him any of the profits at this point over and above the ten percent he'll receive in dividends as part owner of BNB. I'm willing to forgive a lot, but he's gone too far." She ran her hand over her head, but it got caught on the bun she'd worn all day. She yanked the clips out and let the beautiful red hair fall over her shoulders. Reid could easily allow himself to be distracted by the sight, by her beauty, but her words pulled him back into the conversation. "Not that I won't forgive him. I know that's the right thing to do. But what he's doing is so wrong. I just can't imagine how he can justify it."

"Right and wrong don't seem to matter to him at this point."

"Of course they matter." She sounded shocked that he might not agree. "He must believe, deep in his heart, that I've betrayed him. Maybe he does believe that I coerced the shares from him. Maybe he truly doesn't remember how that came about. He must not. Otherwise, he wouldn't be doing this. He's a good man, and good people try to do the right thing."

Reid wasn't sure how to respond to that. He tried to make sense of her words, but they didn't track with what he'd experienced in his life. There were lost people and saved people, but good and bad? Even the best people could do the wrong thing sometimes. He remembered the moment he'd punched his best friend just a year before. He'd been certain James had wronged him—certain, but way off target. Reid wanted to be a good person, but sometimes he did bad things. Wasn't that true of all people?

"Maybe he's lost his perspective. Maybe he's losing his grip on reality."

"You think he's insane?" She seemed almost encouraged by the thought, as if that would explain everything.

Reid didn't think Jacqui would appreciate what he really thought, that Don was a selfish conniving jerk who wanted to steal Jacqui's invention and make himself rich. "I think he's not behaving sanely right now."

"That would explain it. Because what he's doing simply isn't right."

There was that concept of *right* again. Reid loved how Jacqui assumed people always wanted to do the right thing, but *right* seemed to have nothing to do with Don's motives. "Whatever he's thinking, we have to stop him."

The pizza was delivered, along with paper plates and napkins. The top of the pie glistened with hot oil. Delicious.

Speaking of right and wrong, taking a napkin to the top of that pizza was most definitely wrong, but Reid didn't stop Jacqui as she sopped up all that delicious grease. He waited until she'd chosen a piece, then grabbed one for himself, folded it, and took a bite.

Perfect.

He'd eaten half when he set the slice down. "It's delicious."

"These places usually are." For the first time all day, Jacqui was eating a normal meal. Until Ella was kidnapped, he'd never comprehended people who didn't eat when they were stressed or worried. Before Ella's abduction, Reid had never had any trouble shoveling food into his mouth.

Now he understood. He was gratified to know that Jacqui felt secure enough to eat. Or at least hungry enough. "You made a good point earlier. One we need to explore."

"What was that?" She set her slice down and wiped her fingers on her napkin, leaning forward as if ready to get back to business.

"He can't expect that you'll be giving him anything from the sale to Tarim, even if you go that way. Why do this, if that's the case?"

"Yeah. Now that I think about it, I can only assume they've offered him a financial incentive to get me to sell the rights to them."

"Must be some incentive."

She looked beyond Reid for a moment, then shrugged. "He still owns ten percent of BNB, so he will share in the profits to a degree, but not like he would have. I think that, after he destroyed my lab, he figured he'd be receiving nothing beyond what he was owed. At this point, whatever he squeezes from Tarim will be more than he'd get otherwise. And that company has deep pockets. I suspect they've offered him quite a finder's fee to get me on board."

"We're going to make sure he earns none of that fee."

They finished their pizza and sodas, chatting about Ella and the ice cream shop and nothing important for the remainder of the meal. It was good to think about something besides the invention for a few minutes.

They were walking back to the hotel when Reid's phone rang. He pulled it from his pocket and glanced at the screen, heart pounding when he saw the name. "It's my lawyer. I have to—"

"Go ahead."

He swiped to connect. For the man to call him after business hours... "What happened?"

"Denise is asking for joint custody."

He froze. "Joint as in, she wants Ella *half* the time?"

"That's what she's demanding."

"Is she crazy?" He looked around, trying to find someplace off the sidewalk for this conversation.

Jacqui pointed ahead, and he saw the doors to the hotel. He nodded, and she led the way while he focused on his call. "How does she think Ella can manage school from California?"

"Apparently," the attorney said, "Denise is suggesting you enroll her in an online school. Her lawyer sent a number of options with the suggestion that you look through them and choose your top three."

Online school. His friendly, vivacious daughter, stuck in front of a screen all day long so her selfish mother could get her fifty percent. He swallowed his rage and barely kept himself from punching the glass as he walked into the lobby.

He sent Jacqui a look he hoped conveyed apology before stalking to an empty set of chairs across the spacious room. "We have to fight this, fight hard. What can we do?"

"Our first move is to try to get the jurisdiction moved to New Hampshire. She filed in California. I think she'll have a better shot of winning there than she would with a local judge."

"Can we do that? How does it work?"

"Technically, her lawyer should have filed in New Hampshire because that's where Ella has lived the majority of the last six months. However, since you and Denise don't have a legal arrangement, it's going to be tricky. She's claiming that you've refused her desire to see Ella and—"

"That's a lie. I've never refused—"

"Calm down, Reid. I understand. She's building a case. Our job is to knock her points down, one by one. I think we have a good shot of moving the jurisdiction to New Hampshire. But that's not the biggest problem."

"Okay." He was afraid to ask, afraid of the man's next words.

"The biggest issue we have," his attorney said, "is also the simplest. Denise is Ella's mother, and she has rights. If you want to keep full custody of your daughter, you're going to have to prove she's an unfit mother."

"She *is* unfit! She barely knows Ella."

"That doesn't make her unfit."

"She's a movie star. She's always off on location or... I don't even know what she does with her time."

"Movie stars have children. Her profession doesn't make her—"

"Her daughter was kidnapped!" His voice was too loud in the

quiet space. A woman walking toward the doors glanced his way. The clerk behind the counter gave him a scathing look.

On the far side of the lobby near the elevators, Jacqui sat on a bench, head bowed. If she'd heard him yell, she didn't react.

Reid lowered his voice. "Her daughter was kidnapped, and she didn't care enough to show up."

"That's definitely an issue." The lawyer's bland tone made Reid want to reach through the phone and strangle him.

He took a deep breath, then another. At least the lawyer was thinking clearly, something Reid felt incapable of doing. "What should we do?"

"What Denise is asking for is unreasonable. I *think* a judge will take into account the fact that Ella has lived in New Hampshire all her life. She goes to school there and has friends there and family there. A judge will also take into account the fact that you've been her sole caregiver since she was a few months old. Denise's abandonment, her absence when Ella was kidnapped—those things are going to work in your favor. But don't be deceived, Reid. Denise is Ella's mother, and she has rights. The truth is, a judge can do anything. Some judges think girls belong with their mother. Others think the ability to raise a child is directly affected by a person's income. Heck, the judge might be president of your wife's fan club. I'm just saying—"

"Anything can happen."

"Whenever human beings are involved, even judges, anything can happen. I want you to start a list of the different things that you think make Denise an unfit mother, and I'll get things going on the change of venue. But Reid?"

"Yeah."

"You should try to keep this out of court. See if you can work out a fair agreement with Denise. That's your best option right now."

CHAPTER SEVENTEEN

Exhausted as she was, Jacqui poured everything she had into praying for Reid and Ella while Reid was on the phone. And as often happened, the less she had to offer, the more the Spirit got involved.

When a hand settled on her shoulder, she finished her prayer, wiped her eyes on the tissues she'd dug from her purse, and looked up.

"Hey, what is it?" Reid's voice was soft, concerned.

"Nothing." She sniffed and balled the tissue in her hand. "I don't know why I always end up bawling like a baby when I pray like that."

When she stood, he slid his hand behind her back and pulled her close. "You have a lot going on right now. I'm not surprised that you're feeling emotional."

She leaned back to look at him. "You have a lot going on too. What did your lawyer say?"

"Denise is suing for joint custody."

"Oh no. I'm sorry."

Reid's jaw clenched. "I'm going to fight her with everything I have in me. There's no way she's taking my daughter from me."

Their daughter. It wasn't as if Denise were demanding full custody. Joint—that was a lot to ask, but if Jacqui had to guess, the woman was asking for more than she expected to get. "Does your lawyer think you can win?"

"He wants us to work it out, but I can't imagine how we're going to do that."

"Start with prayer. God can do the impossible, even change hearts."

Reid's expression didn't soften at all. "Yeah. I'll do that."

"I'll be praying for all of you. There must be a solution. I'll pray you and Denise can find it without involving a judge."

Reid said nothing, just stared straight ahead. Beyond the glass doors, the sun had gone down. Though it was barely nine o'clock, Jacqui felt too exhausted to think any more that night, to do anything but crawl into bed.

Reid must've agreed, because he nodded toward the elevators. "Everything will look better in the morning, for both of us."

She took his outstretched hand. "I hope you're right."

On their floor, they walked to her door. She unlocked it and stuck her foot in the opening to keep it from closing. "I'd say it's been fun, but..."

He chuckled. "I'll give you this, Jacqui Beal. You're anything but boring."

"Oh, I'm plenty boring most of the time."

He ran his hand down her hair, gently tugging a lock. "I doubt that. Everything about you excites me." His hand slipped from her hair to her neck, its warmth seeping into her skin and traveling to every cell in her body.

He dipped his head and brushed a kiss on her lips, stirring sparks from the embers that'd been smoldering since the night before.

When his kiss turned from gentle to eager, she dropped her bag and slid her hands up his chest and over his strong, broad shoulders. When he tugged her nearer, she went willingly, shifting her feet and angling her body.

The door closed with a snick.

Reid ended the kiss with a groan. "I think you'd better get in there and lock the door."

"I'm not afraid of you, Reid Cote."

He kissed her cheek and stepped back. "I'm afraid of you, Jacqui Beal. I'm afraid that, a few more minutes in your presence, and I might forget my vow."

"Vow?"

"Oh, you know." His close-mouthed smile seemed shy. "This feels sort of tween girlish to say, but a purity vow. To not make the same mistakes with anyone else that I made with Denise. Not that you..." He shook his head, the smile widening and showing all his teeth. "I really should shut up."

She nearly giggled, stifling the sound before it escaped. "I really should go inside."

He took another step back. "Yes. Good idea."

She had zero desire to step into her room and leave Reid in the hallway, which was exactly why she needed to do it. Because she knew how he felt. No man had ever made her long to go further than a kiss before, and the more she knew him, the more she longed for him.

Whatever this was between them, it wasn't nothing. And it wasn't going to go away. Which opened up a whole new set of problems.

She was falling in love with this man. This man who had a daughter and a life far from the city where she lived.

How could this end with anything but two broken hearts?

HER RINGING PHONE yanked Jacqui from sleep. She snatched the cell from her nightstand. She didn't recognize the number but swiped to answer anyway. "Hello?"

A man whose voice she didn't recognize said, "Is this Jacqueline Beal?"

She sat up in the bed, heart pounding as if it knew something she didn't. "Yes."

"This is Terry from SecureNet. There's an alarm going off at your house. Are you at home?"

She shook her head to rid it of sleep's confusion. "The burglar alarm?"

"Yes, ma'am." The man's tone was no-nonsense. "Are you there, or is anybody staying on the property?"

"No. No. It should be empty."

"Okay. We're dispatching the authorities. Since you're not at the house, I assume you're out of town. Is there anybody you can have meet them at the property?"

"I can be there. I'm in the city."

Jacqui hung up and climbed out of bed. She needed help. She needed Reid. She yanked open the door adjoining their rooms and banged on the one that opened into his space. They hadn't unlocked these doors once since they'd checked in. With all the attraction between them, adjoining rooms maybe hadn't been the best idea.

She was thankful for them now.

There was no sound from Reid's room, and she was about to knock again. But thanks to her jumping out of bed moments after waking, she felt dizzy. The dark room seemed to get darker, her legs weaker.

She was sinking when a hand gripped her arm. "Whoa." Reid supported her as she settled on the floor, leaning her head against the doorjamb between their rooms.

"What's going on?" he asked. "Are you sick?"

She felt his presence in front of her but couldn't make herself focus. It was all she could do not to fall on her face.

"Jacqui, what is it?" The fear in his voice registered just as her vision and strength started to come back.

"I got out of bed too fast."

He was kneeling in front of her, eyes wide in the dim light

coming from behind him. He'd had the wisdom to flip the lamp on before answering the door. She hadn't been thinking so clearly.

"What happened?" he asked again.

"There's an alarm going off at the brownstone. I need to get over there."

"Okay. I just need to get dressed." He stood and held out his hand to help her up. Only then did she really see him. His short hair was messy. He wore nothing but blue plaid sleeping pants. His bare chest was muscled and mesmerizing. When she didn't move, he cleared his throat. "Are you okay? You seem a little—"

"I'm fine." She forced her gaze away from that beautiful chest, took his hand, and stood. "I'll need a couple of minutes."

"I'll meet you in the hallway in five."

It was closer to seven minutes later by the time she stepped out of her room, embarrassed about her behavior. That her first thought had been to wake Reid from a sound sleep was bad enough. That she'd been in such a hurry to reach him that she'd nearly passed out was worse. And that she'd done all of that while wearing nothing more than the flimsy thigh-length baby doll nightgown...

She had to force herself to meet his eyes. When she did, she saw concern there and nothing else. "Are you up for this? If you're sick—"

"I'm not. I probably needed to process the call a little before I knocked on your door."

He studied her another minute, then took her hand. Together, they hurried to the elevator.

The lack of traffic at four in the morning meant they were able to navigate the streets in record time, getting them to her home less than thirty minutes after the security company's call.

She'd expected a single cruiser, maybe two.

She definitely hadn't expected multiple police cars.

And two fire trucks.

And the scent of smoke.

She was reaching for the door before Reid stopped the car. He grabbed her hand, held her in place until he parked.

She didn't wait for him, just bolted up the sidewalk toward her family's home. The rare and beautiful treasure.

Passing beneath one of the many trees planted in the sidewalk, she got a glimpse of the front of her place.

Smoke gushed from the second-story window.

Firemen streamed in the front door, carrying a hose.

Confused, determined, she started to follow them. This was her house. She had to do something.

But a hand gripped her upper arm from behind just as a police officer approached from in front.

"Ma'am, you'll need to—"

"This is my home. I live here."

"I understand, ma'am." He pointed to a spot on the narrow street on the opposite side of the parked cars. "Wait there. I'll get the officer in charge."

"But I have to—"

"Jacqui, sweetheart, breathe." Reid's voice in her ear calmed her. "There's nothing in that building that's worth more than your life."

Reluctantly, she walked with him to the spot that the policeman had indicated. While she stared up at her burning building, Reid wrapped his arms around her from behind and held her close. He was quietly praying, his voice no more than a murmur above the shouts and sounds of the firefighters and cops. She tried to join his prayer, but words were so small in the face of the fire. Words felt irrelevant and inconsequential. All she could think was *no, please no.*

Spectators were streaming from nearby buildings, watching the scene. Jacqui could see them out of the corner of her eye, staring, wondering what happened, and probably thanking God it wasn't their house on fire. Wasn't their tragedy.

Their lives probably weren't perfect. Certainly, they had trials.

But nobody had broken into their homes that night and set them ablaze.

Nobody was trying to steal their life's work.

Nobody was trying to ruin their reputations.

Standing in the middle of the road, Jacqui felt raw, exposed, and vulnerable as she never had before. Nothing was sacred. Nothing was safe. Not her research. Not her invention. Not her home.

Not her life.

"You're safe, sweetheart. It's going to be all right."

Only at Reid's tender words did Jacqui realize she was sobbing. Soul-deep sobs that seemed to pull all her strength, all her resolve.

Would it be all right? Would it be all right if the home her family had entrusted to her was destroyed? Would it be all right if the invention she'd risked everything for was sold to a company that would bury it to protect their profits?

How would any of this be all right?

The flames on the second floor dissipated, but smoke continued to pour from the window.

She watched the horror scene, wishing she could have the numb feeling so many talked about. Wishing she didn't feel the depth of destruction.

Wishing she'd never fought Don. She should have just done what he'd suggested. Sold the invention to Tarim. Taken the money. Was any of this worth what it was costing?

Reid turned her around and pulled her to his chest. Maybe he'd sensed her thoughts. Maybe he just knew her well enough to know she couldn't watch anymore.

He rubbed her back and spoke more prayers and held her close. She allowed herself to feel the comfort of his arms, but the moment didn't last.

"Ms. Beal?"

She spun at her name.

An older police officer walked toward her, his gray hair alternatively blue and red in the lights coming from the emergency vehicles. He was not quite as tall as she, but what he lacked in height, he made up for in girth. He stopped in front of her and tugged on his low-slung belt. "Officer Almeida."

She held out her hand. "Jacqui Beal." Her voice sounded normal, even if nothing else was. "This is my home. Do you know what happened?"

"Too soon to know how the fires started, but it doesn't take a genius to know they were started intentionally."

"*Fires?* There was more than one?"

"Two. One on the second floor, the other in the basement."

Her hand rose to her mouth. "My lab."

His brows lowered over narrowed eyes. "What kind of lab, ma'am?" His voice was filled with concern. "Anything I need to tell the—?"

"Computer equipment. Nothing combustible."

His expression returned to the kind one he'd worn before. "Hate to lose good men because we don't have all the information. Where were you?"

"Staying in a hotel."

The officer's gaze flicked to Reid, a knowing look that made her temper rise.

"My business associate is in town for a few days," she said. "We're working on a project."

But of course, the man had seen Reid holding her. He said nothing, but his conclusions were clear.

Oh, what did it matter what this man thought? Her reputation was taking so many hits already. What was one more?

"Why not stay here?" he asked. Jacqui guessed the tone was suspicion. It seemed she'd guessed wrong about the man's assumptions. He wasn't judging her for staying at a hotel with a man not her husband. He was suspecting her of arson.

Reid squeezed her hand, perhaps to impart courage. Perhaps to get her to speak past the shock of it all.

"Two days ago, my former business partner, Donald Burgess, came here to my home. Though we'd had some disagreements in the past, he convinced me he'd come to apologize, and I let him in. His apology quickly turned into demands that I do what he wished. When I refused, he grabbed me and threatened me. The DA decided not to pursue assault charges. Since the man is loose in the city, I didn't feel safe here and rented a room at the hotel."

The officer wrote a few things on a little notebook. When he looked up again, she thought maybe the suspicion was gone from his gaze. "This Donald Burgess fellow, he lives nearby? Is there anything he'd have to gain by burning your house down?"

"I can see him breaking in to steal from me, but to burn it down?" She swallowed and looked at the second-story window. "That's my bedroom. There's nothing in there. I can't imagine..."

Her words trailed as the truth of it settled inside her.

It seemed Reid and the police officer were coming to the same conclusion.

"Jacqui?" Reid's voice was low, rough. He cleared it, turned to face her, and started over. "Who inherits the business if you die?"

She didn't want to answer the question. To answer the question would make it too real. She swallowed against the knowledge, trying to ignore the knowing look the police officer was giving her. Trying to ignore the man beside her. She wasn't good at reading facial expressions, but she could feel the fury wafting off Reid as thick as the smoke still pouring from her home.

"Ms. Beal?" the officer said.

"Don." She swallowed again. "I never... When we first set up the partnership, that was our agreement. One of us dies, the other gets everything. It made sense at the time. BNB was only worth what the two of us had put into it. It was only worth our minds, our inventions. It never occurred to me. He's so much older than I am. I always figured he'd go first. And he only owns a fraction now. And..."

Reid pulled her back to his side and held her close. "It's okay. He's showed his hand. Now we know."

That Don wanted her dead. That if she'd been sleeping in her bedroom, she would have burned to death. Or died of smoke inhalation.

Her invention would be Don's. Everything she'd invented would be his.

It was bad enough her father would discover his family home had burned. If she'd been there...

Her parents would've had to bury their only child.

The police officer asked Reid where they were staying, and he offered the information. Jacqui was too stunned to think about anything.

Don had tried to murder her.

CHAPTER EIGHTEEN

The police officer released them, asking them to come to the station later to give their statements.

When it was all over, numbness finally set in. Jacqui let Reid support her as they parked in the garage beneath the hotel and made their way to the lobby. She expected him to direct her straight to the elevator, but he stopped in the grand space. The scent of coffee wafted from the restaurant. Beyond the glass doors, the world was turning from black to gray. Within minutes, the sun would be up, and a new day would begin.

A relatively normal day for everyone else, everyone whose houses hadn't burned overnight. Everyone who'd not discovered someone was trying to kill them.

Reid took her hands. "We have two hours before we're supposed to be at the police station. What do you want to do?"

She wanted to curl up in her bed and sleep until this was all over. A lovely fantasy, but avoiding the problem wouldn't make it go away. And it wasn't as if she'd be able to sleep.

What she really wanted to do was curl up beside Reid, let him soothe all her fears away.

Another bad idea. Very bad.

"Do you think you can sleep?" he asked.

When she shook her head, he said, "Me, either." He looked over her head and blew out a breath. "Let's get cleaned up and go for a walk."

She didn't want to walk. She didn't want to shower. She didn't want to do anything. But she said, "Okay," and allowed him to lead her to the elevators.

Less than an hour later, Reid stood outside her bedroom door, two cups of coffee in hand. She took one of the cups, then swallowed a sip. She had another as they walked to the elevator. The coffee was hot and bitter and exactly what she needed to jumpstart her brain, which seemed to have shut down at some point since they'd left the smoldering brownstone. She couldn't concentrate, couldn't think past the fact that a man she'd trusted, a man she'd thought of as a grandfather, wanted her dead.

She'd dressed for the day in a sleeveless shift dress, adding a short-sleeved jacket, which she'd wear until it warmed up. She wore heels again, a bit shorter than the ones the day before. She *looked* ready for the meeting at the police station and then with her lawyers. She didn't feel ready, but maybe she never would.

When they stepped onto the sidewalk into the warm summer air, Reid turned right on the busy street, toward the shops and the craziness of Copley Square. She didn't argue, though it wasn't the direction she'd have chosen. This way was all traffic and crosswalks, construction and crowds. But she said nothing, sipping her coffee and allowing him to lead her. She barely looked up, just concentrated on putting one foot in front of the other, on not tripping and falling, on not thinking about anything.

A few minutes later, she found herself walking on red bricks. Only then did she look up and realize where they were.

Trinity Church. In all the years she'd lived in Boston, she'd never been inside, though she'd walked by it countless times. It'd been built in the eighteenth century. She'd always loved the way the mirrored John Hancock tower reflected the rustic beauty of the historical place.

Reid directed her up the steps. He took her coffee and set both their cups in the corner against the building. "We're probably not allowed to take those."

"We're going in? Is it even open?"

He pulled the door. "After you."

Stepping inside was like stepping back in time.

No. It was like stepping into another realm.

The sounds of engines and horns and construction faded, replaced by the solemn silence of a sanctuary.

The scents of exhaust and humanity were replaced by those of incense and worship.

The sight of modern buildings was replaced by old-world architecture.

She took in the stained-glass windows and the paintings depicting Christ in different scenes. Her gaze continued to the pink marble altar and, above it, the intricate gilded cross suspended on the far wall.

Their footsteps sounded in the quiet as they walked down the central aisle. She thought to slip into a pew and sit, but her feet brought her forward. She stopped at the edge of the raised chancel and dropped to her knees.

Reid kneeled beside her, saying nothing. Just being there. For her.

She bowed her head and considered the beauty and majesty, not of this church, which was a pale comparison of the One it was built to honor, but of her God, who sat on His throne. Who saw everything and knew everything. He was still in control. He'd never taken His eyes off her. And He never would.

Her problems shrank as her God took His place in her thoughts and considerations. This situation wasn't about her. It wasn't about her or proving herself or achieving anything. Her invention, her company, the trials she was facing—they were all about bringing glory and honor to the One who'd saved her, who'd given her talents and abilities and intellect.

She was reminded of the truth. That God had allowed her to

be pulled into this difficult situation, and He would assuredly lead her back out.

~

JACQUI SETTLED in a chair across from the detective's desk at Boston Police headquarters, a newer structure fancy enough that it had probably been photographed for some architectural magazine at some point. Though it didn't fit her stereotype of what a place like this would be, she wasn't soothed by the environment. Surrounded by cops and chaos, she was fighting hard to keep hold of the peace she'd found at the church.

Beside her, Reid scooted his chair a little closer, his presence a reminder that she wasn't alone. Thank God he was there. She didn't know how she'd have done any of this on her own.

On the opposite side of the desk, Detective Klein studied a laptop screen. She hadn't seen him since the day her lab was broken into, though they'd spoken on the phone many times. He had skin dark enough to be called black, though his hair was straight and his eyes were blue. She wouldn't even try to guess his heritage, though she assumed he got the blue eyes from the same ancestor who'd given him the name Klein. She couldn't guess his age, either. Maybe forties, maybe fifties.

"Looks like you've had an eventful couple of days." Klein shifted to her. "After Burgess showed up at your house, Officer Bridgeman contacted me, and I followed up with the detective assigned to the case."

"Who decided not to pursue it," Reid said.

Jacqui gave Reid a look, a reminder of the conversation they'd had on the way over. She appreciated Reid's help, but she could speak for herself.

"Sorry." He looked chagrined. It seemed that, when he was riled up and protective, he had a hard time keeping his mouth shut.

"Technically," Klein said, "the DA decided not to pursue it. I disagreed, and so did Bridgeman, but we don't get to make the final determination. It was your word against his. The way these things work, it was unlikely he'd have spent a minute behind bars. It would have been pled down so much." He shrugged. "Anyway, that's out of our hands, but this—" The phone on his desk rang. He picked it up, said, "Klein." And then, "Give that to Smith. I'm working on something else." He hung up and offered Jacqui an apologetic look. "Sorry. I hope we can get through this with minimal interruptions."

"If you're not the detective assigned to the case," Jacqui asked, "then who is? And—don't take this the wrong way—but why are we talking to you?"

"At this point, arson and homicide detectives have been pulled into the case. We're all working together. Since it started with the break-in, and since you and I have already met, I'll be your contact. They might get in touch with you directly, but at this point, you're stuck with me."

"I'm glad," she said. "You've been straight with me from the start."

He slid his laptop out of the way and rested his forearms on his desk. "Here's what we know. The burglar alarm went off at three forty-six. Your security company called it in at three fifty. Officers arrived on scene at just after four and reported the smell of smoke. The fire department arrived within minutes. There were two fires burning in the house. One in a storeroom in the basement, the other—"

"In the storeroom?" she said. "Not in the lab itself?"

He glanced at the computer's screen. "A storeroom filled with files, they said. Though the fire investigation isn't finished, preliminary reports tell us no accelerant was used there. They were able to get that fire out quickly."

"Maybe some of the equipment was spared," Jacqui said. "That would be a blessing."

Klein shrugged. "No idea, but they fought the fire with water, and water damages."

Just like that, the spark of hope was extinguished.

Reid cleared his throat. He seemed to be asking permission to speak. He looked so eager to say something, as if the words were dying to get out of his mouth. It was almost amusing.

"Go ahead," she said.

"Why set the storeroom on fire? Wasn't it just old notebooks?"

"It was." She considered the question but had no answer.

"Do you think he stole the notes related to the artificial neuron?"

"Even if he did, those notes wouldn't be useful to anybody but me. They're not organized, and I only write about half of what I'm thinking, and my handwriting is terrible, and I have a sort of code."

Reid's eyebrows lifted. Klein seemed just as confused.

She blew out a breath. "Once, when I was in college, a fellow student stole my notes and my ideas. When the professor thought our solutions to a problem were too similar, we were both questioned about it. Since I was able to explain precisely what I'd been thinking and how I'd come up with the idea—and since I had the better grades and reputation—they believed the idea had been mine. Ever since then, I've been careful to be more cryptic in my note-taking. I guess it's just become a habit."

"So those notebooks wouldn't be worth anything," Klein said. "Would Burgess know that?"

"Definitely. He used to grab my notebooks and try to read them aloud. That always got a laugh from the techs."

Reid said, "Maybe he wants to keep you from being able to prove the idea was yours."

"I have all the research, though. He doesn't have access to it."

"Is it personalized?" Reid asked. "Is it clearly a Jacqui Beal idea, or could anybody claim it?"

"Oh. I see what you're saying. But it still doesn't matter. I have it, and he doesn't."

Reid squinted, processing that. "But he was involved in the development of the neuron. He might not have done the nitty-gritty, but maybe he could get somebody to recreate what you did.

And maybe he thinks he can decipher your notes or knows somebody who can."

"I still own the patent."

"The *provisional* patent," Reid said.

True, but that was just a formality. "I'll ask the lawyer when we meet with him where we are in the process of getting the permanent patent."

By the distant look on Reid's face, there was more on his mind, something he was still thinking through.

Jacqui and the detective waited.

Finally, Reid said, "Would an American patent keep a foreign company from stealing your invention?"

"I see what you're saying. Most foreign companies respect—"

"Tarim, though. Would they respect the American patent?"

She didn't like the answer that came to mind. Before she could speak, Reid continued.

"You assumed that Tarim wanted to buy the exclusive rights to your neuron in order to bury it, to keep anything from being developed. Maybe that was their first goal. But maybe they're hedging their bets. Maybe, if you remain unwilling to sell them those rights, they've decided to compete with you, to develop something themselves. Either way, they win."

Klein had pulled his laptop in front of him again. "Tarim's the company Burgess wanted to sell your invention to, right? But it might not be them. I mean, if this neuron thing you made is that great, there's no telling how many people want to get their hands on it."

Reid said, "But Burgess is the only one who was there during its development. To everybody else, it's just a theory. Without the research, they can do nothing with it. But maybe Burgess could recreate it."

Jacqui hated the thought that occurred to her, but she swallowed the reluctance and forced herself to say it anyway. "Braden was there. Braden worked with me, hand in hand, throughout the development."

Reid's eyebrows shot up on his forehead. "I thought you trusted him."

"I do. I did. But I trusted Don too."

Klein tapped on his laptop again. "Braden Reilly. He's the guy who was in the lab with you the day of the break-in."

"I can't imagine he would..." She rubbed her temples, trying to work it out. Could Braden be working against her?

Maybe Braden and Don were in this together. Except, Braden had seemed so sincere.

So had Don when he'd apologized, just minutes before he'd grabbed her and demanded she do as he wished.

She didn't know. She didn't know what was going on. She didn't know what to do about it.

While Klein took another phone call, Jacqui tried to work out what it all meant.

Across the desk, Klein returned the desk phone to its cradle. "They finally let my guys into your place. Looks like the basement lab was thoroughly searched before it was set on fire." He clicked a few buttons on his laptop. "Forensics sent me a couple of photographs." He turned the screen toward Jacqui. One file cabinet had been opened and emptied, the papers strewn across the laminate floor. Every drawer and cabinet was open. Debris was everywhere, much of it visibly wet.

Reid wrapped his arm around her back. "I'm sorry, sweetie."

She swallowed the rise of nausea. "I thought it had been destroyed in the fire, so"—she waved at the computer—"that's not as bad as I'd imagined."

"I don't understand," Reid said. "The burglar alarm went off, you guys were called right away, and the fire was raging when you arrived. How did the intruder have time to search?"

"Good point. Hmm." Klein turned his attention back to the laptop. "Okay, according to this, it looks like the intruder came in through an unlocked window on the back of the property. The window was wide open, and there are signs someone—"

"That can't be," Jacqui said. "I never unlock the first-floor windows. And anyway, even if it were unlocked, if it was raised, the alarm would go off."

"Maybe not if it was already cracked," Klein said. "If the connection was already broken—"

"But I wouldn't have opened it."

Reid said, "Maybe Annie—"

"No." Her voice was too loud, and she worked to temper it. "No. You and I checked all the windows when we searched the other night."

Both Reid and Klein were watching her. Klein was nodding in that way that people did when they accepted what you were saying but thought you were wrong.

But Reid said, "Any chance Don could've opened it when he was there?"

"What? No. I never..." But she had left him alone. "He used the rest room. I ran upstairs to get my phone. It's possible he unlocked it then."

Klein made a note on his notepad. "I'll have forensics look for his fingerprints."

"Good, good, Reid said. "But then, why did the alarm go off? If not when he went through the window, then—"

"The back door was open. We assume the man ran out after he set the fire, and that's when the alarm went off."

Made sense.

Reid faced her. "The neuron and research are in a safe deposit box, right? So they're safe."

"Yes, and I have the key. Don doesn't know that though. Maybe he thought they were in my house."

Klein pushed his laptop aside again. "Okay. A lot to deal with there. You two think it through, let me know if you come up with anything that might be helpful. I'll interview Braden and look into what he's been up to." He blew out a long breath. "You'll be able to go over there and see for yourself how much of it was damaged and if anything is missing. The bigger issue is the fire in the bedroom."

The mention of it had Jacqui's stomach dipping.

"They believe that an accelerant was used in that fire. Again, the investigation isn't complete, but right now, they're thinking gasoline on the bed."

On the bed. Talk about a personal attack.

"How much damage was there?" Reid asked.

"Fire department was on the scene very quickly. From the reports, it seems they were able to put out the blaze before it did any structural damage. They're still investigating, but when they're done, you should be able to go in and see for yourself."

It sounded like it wasn't as bad as it had looked that morning. The house was still standing. It would take some work to clean it up, she knew, but it could have been so much worse. She'd put it off too long already. She'd call her father as soon as they were finished.

"So," she said, feeling better than she'd felt in hours, "it wasn't an attempt to kill me. Maybe they were just trying to scare me or send me a message. Because obviously, if they got close enough to pour gas on the bed, then they had to know I wasn't there."

Klein was watching her carefully, and she realized there was more to the story. She swallowed the fear rising in her throat. "What?"

"There was somebody there."

"What? No. The house was empty." Even as she said the words, she started to tremble, her stomach roiling. She was afraid to ask what he meant. Afraid to know.

"A woman. She left her purse in the kitchen, so we were able to get an ID." Klein glanced at his screen again. "Name of Annette Griffiths."

"No, she was... Is she all right? Did she get out?" How had Jacqui not seen her that morning, if she'd been at the house? "Was she injured? Oh, my gosh, where is she?"

Klein's lips were pressed together, and he watched her, waiting, it seemed, for her to put it together. But... "She shouldn't have been there. If she was hurt... I told her..." She couldn't finish her thought. Didn't want to hear the words Klein was speaking.

Why couldn't people close their ears as easily as they could close their eyes?

Despite how little she wanted them to, Klein's words penetrated.

...found the body on the bed.

...never had a chance.

Jacqui crossed her arms and bent over. This couldn't be happening. What had Annie been doing there?

Reid scooted closer and settled his hand on Jacqui's back, but his comforting touch didn't help this time. He spoke to Klein. "She's Jacqui's house sitter." And then, "Was, I guess. She *was* Jacqui's house sitter."

"I see," the detective said.

Annie was dead.

Dead.

Jacqui'd hardly known her. They'd only met in person once, but she was kind, generous, and funny.

She was a beautiful young woman, a student working on her Master's degree, working to become a social worker, to do good in the world.

She had a family and friends. A future.

She hadn't done anything wrong.

Why, why had she been there?

Jacqui wiped the tears spilling from her eyes and looked at Klein. "She wasn't supposed to come back." Her voice was shaking, but she couldn't get it under control. "I told her not to, that I wouldn't need her. I knew it might not be safe. After Don... I should have told her it wasn't safe, but... I just... I don't know why." She looked at Reid. "Why didn't I tell her it wasn't safe?"

"Because you didn't know you needed to," he said, his tone soothing. "What did she say when you talked to her?"

Jacqui thought back to the short conversation. "She said... she said was happy to be home with her family." She faced the detective again. "She said she'd stay in Connecticut for the weekend and come back Sunday unless she heard differently from me." That was it. That was all.

Annie had changed her mind. A decision that cost her life. And it was Jacqui's fault.

Klein was studying her.

She had no idea what the man was thinking and didn't care. "Have you told her family?"

"We had a local officer tell them in person. They're here, in the building."

She started to push to her feet. "I need to see them. I need to tell them I'm sorry." Reid's grip held her in place.

Klein nodded slowly. "Maybe another time. Today, they have enough to deal with."

That made sense. It wasn't as if Jacqui could do anything to lessen their loss. There was nothing she could do to fix this. She settled back in her chair.

Klein continued. "According to Annie's parents, she returned to Boston last night because she had a date. She figured you wouldn't mind if she crashed there. She texted her parents when she got to your place late last night and said she left you a note in the kitchen." He pulled a plastic bag from a desk drawer and set it in front of Jacqui.

I needed somewhere to crash. It's after two, and you're not here, so I'm betting you won't be home tonight. Since it's about a bazillion degrees on the third floor, I'll be in your bed. If you get home, kick me out, and I'll go upstairs. Hopefully, you won't see this note, and you'll never know I was here. (Except the bed will have fresh sheets. Promise.)

The words were followed by a smiley face and Annie's signature.

Lighthearted, funny, and confident. Jacqui could practically hear the younger woman's voice in the written words.

"It wasn't your fault." Reid's arm slid around her shoulders, and he pulled her close. His other hand found hers and held on.

"You didn't start the fire, Jacqui. The person to blame for Annie's death is the person who did."

"Where were you at four o'clock this morning," Klein asked.

His question jolted Jacqui back to the moment. She met his eyes and held the contact. Beside her, Reid said, "She was..." but Jacqui squeezed his hand, and he quieted.

"I was at the hotel. I got the call from the security company and immediately woke Reid."

"What time did you get back to the hotel last night?"

"About nine," she said. "We were in the lobby for a few minutes while Reid took a call, then went up to our rooms."

"Rooms? Plural?"

"Plural." Reid's single word held a hint of irritation.

The detective ignored him, keeping his focus on Jacqui. "Did you leave the hotel at any point after you went up to your room at nine and before you got the call."

"No."

"Not even to get ice or soda? Not once?"

"Not once."

Klein shifted to Reid. "What time did she call you this morning?"

"She didn't call, she knocked. It was around three forty-five, three fifty. We left about ten minutes later for her house."

"Did anybody see you leave?"

Jacqui had no idea, but Reid said, "There was a clerk behind the counter when we walked through the lobby. I don't know if she saw us. Asian-American, long black hair."

Klein said, "What hotel?"

Reid gave him the name and their room numbers, and Klein wrote the information down. When he looked up, his expression had softened. "Okay. Those questions are standard procedure. I'll have someone talk to the clerk, see if she can corroborate your story. If we need to, we can always look at security footage. At this point, you're not suspects."

"Have you questioned Burgess yet?" Reid asked.

"I called him this morning. He's on the Cape."

The news had Jacqui sitting back. "That can't be." She tried to make sense of it.

"Maybe he hired somebody to do it," Reid said. "Or maybe he drove up in the middle of the night, started the fire, and drove back down.

Or maybe Braden had done it, but neither of the men suggested that. Good thing, because her mind couldn't wrap itself around the idea.

"Why are you so certain it was Burgess?" Klein asked. "Take me through it all again."

Though she'd already done so, months before, and though she was exhausted and heartbroken and overwhelmed, she explained again about her invention and Don's desire to sell the exclusive rights to Tarim. "I realized this morning that the partnership is still structured in such a way that, if one of us were to die, the other would inherit everything. If I were to die, then instead of making ten percent of what we earn for the invention—the percentage he owns of BNB—he'd make ten times that."

"More than that, really," Reid said. "Because in that case, he'd also get to decide who to sell to, and from what we've seen, he'd make that decision based solely on income."

Klein jotted a few things on his pad, nodding as he did. "Okay. But if he thought he was going to kill you, why waste his time destroying your notes?"

Jacqui shrugged, looking at Reid.

Reid said, "He might've taken the notes related to the neuron. Maybe he burned the others so nobody would know what was missing."

"There's a thought," Klein said. "Another theory—maybe it wasn't Burgess."

"Who, then?" Reid asked. "I can see why someone might want to get their hands on Jacqui's notes or even the neuron, if she were dumb enough to leave it there, but Burgess is the only one with a clear motive to kill her."

Klein snapped his laptop shut. "All questions we're going to find the answers to. This is a good start." He sat back and stretched as if he'd already had a long day, though it was still just mid-morning. "If you have any questions or think of anything else, call me, and I'll get you in touch with the right person."

Jacqui started to stand, but Reid didn't budge.

"What do you think, though?" Reid asked. "Do you agree that Burgess was behind the fires? That Jacqui's life is in danger?"

Klein glanced at Reid before holding Jacqui's eye contact. "There's no question about it now. If I were you, I'd get out of Dodge, find someplace to hole up until the guy who did this is behind bars."

"We should go back to New Hampshire." Reid squeezed her hand. "Nothing is more important than your safety."

She patted his arm and slipped her hand away, facing him. "I can't do that," she said. "I'm not going to do that. You said it yourself. If I don't show my face at the conference tomorrow, everybody will believe the rumors about me, and my reputation will be ruined. Nobody will want the neuron, at least not if it comes from me. And all those lives it could save." She shook her head. "No. I'm not hiding. I'm not giving up. I'm going to fight this, fight him."

Reid swallowed the retort she could practically see forming in his head. "Then I'm not leaving your side." He turned to Klein. "And I expect you'll be working hard on your end."

"Obviously, but it's going to take time to put this all together. Whoever did this has shown his hand. He wants you dead, Miss Beal. Be careful."

~

Jacqui felt blindsided, confused, as they stepped out of the police headquarters and into the sunshine.

"Jacqueline!"

She turned at the voice, barely registering who'd called out before she was wrapped in her father's strong, strong arms. She took in the scent of his cologne, his strength, his comfort.

He held her close, held her as he hadn't since she was a little girl, and all the emotions she'd been battling flooded out.

"Thank God." His voice cracked. "Thank God you're all right."

The composure she'd felt just minutes before melted away, and she wept against his chest, fighting to get herself under control. But he spoke tenderly in her ear. "It's okay, sweetheart. You're safe now."

Finally, she pushed against his chest and leaned away to face him. He wore a Harvard T-shirt and jeans, so different from the trademark suit and tie he wore almost every time he left the house. His hair was white, his skin clear and tanned. His eyes were crinkled and narrowed, studying her as if searching for wounds.

They were there, scars on her heart, but he wouldn't be able to see them. All the things that'd happened that week, all the things that'd happened since Don first confronted her after his wife's funeral in the spring, they flooded back, closed in. Everything was a mess. The home her family had owned for generations, burned. Her business, on the brink of bankruptcy. Her house sitter, murdered.

It was too much. Staring into the eyes of the man whose respect she craved more than anything, shame prickled her skin like the sweat gathering on her brow. "I'm sorry, Dad." Her voice pitched high, but she couldn't control it. "About the brownstone, and about..." But she couldn't finish the statement. Didn't know how she'd meant to end it.

"You're sorry?" His eyes narrowed. "For what?"

"It all fell apart. BNB. I didn't know how to tell you. Don—"

"Burgess? What does he have to do with this?"

She was so tired. She didn't have the energy to explain it again. She hardly had the energy to keep standing there.

"Come on." Dad took her hand and started toward the corner.

"Wait." She stopped and turned to where Reid was standing under the overhanging structure of the building. "Sorry, uh—"

Reid lifted his hand, dangling her keys. He'd asked if he could drive after they visited the church that morning, and she'd gladly let him, her thoughts too scattered to focus on the road. Now, he said, "I'll wait in the car."

She should insist on introducing him to her father, but she didn't have it in her. She gave him a smile she hoped conveyed her gratitude and walked around the corner with her father.

He led her past the police headquarters and into a small park.

Little kids, younger even than Ella, ran in a field not far away, all chasing a soccer ball. The shrill of a coach's whistle carried on the wind. The sounds of summer accompanied the hum of car engines, the nearly constant background noise of the city.

They found a bench under a tree and sat.

Dad angled to face her. "What's going on?"

For the second time in just a few minutes, she recounted the events that had led her there. She hated to tell her father about Don's behavior—they'd been friends since Jacqui was a little girl—but she couldn't hide the truth from Dad any longer. She hoped, prayed, he'd see her side of it. That he'd believe her and understand why she'd done all she'd done.

But as she spoke, his face filled with fury until the look in his eyes was hotter than the blazing sun.

She didn't have the emotional energy to hide her feelings, which spilled out of her eyes and set her jaw to trembling. "I'm so sorry, Dad. About the house and BNB and—"

"You're sorry?" He stood, paced away. He took a few breaths before he turned and walked back. "Why are you...?" He pulled her up and wrapped her in his arms. "Oh, sweetheart. *I'm* sorry. I'm sorry you didn't know you could come to me with this. I'm sorry I wasn't here for you."

His words processed in her mind, and she felt, despite everything that had happened that day, as if she could breathe, really breathe, for the first time in months.

He set her back and met her eyes. "Jacqui, I love you with every cell in my body. The moment the nurse set you in my arms, I fell hopelessly in love with you, and there hasn't been a single day, a single moment, when I haven't been completely, head-over-heels in love with you." His eyes turned red around the edges. "I wish I were better at showing that. I know I wasn't a great father, always off saving the world, one procedure at a time. But you have never been far from my thoughts. I'm good at a lot of things, but being a father..." He swallowed hard. "My failures as a father are no reflection on you."

She sniffed, swiped her leaking eyes. "You're a great father."

"If you didn't know you could come to me with this back when Don first threatened you, if you thought I'd be disappointed in you because your business was having trouble... If you ever thought I'd take Don's side over yours..." He shook his head, then gripped her shoulders and crouched to look into her eyes. "You are my baby girl. I will always, always choose you."

She stepped into his embrace and let the words wash over her like a cool, healing balm.

After a few moments, Daddy led her to the bench again. "Do you have—?"

"—What are you...?"

He nodded to her, and she started again. "What are you doing here?"

"The police called me first thing this morning. Since the brownstone belongs to me, they asked me to fly in. I was in New York, consulting on a case. I've been trying to call you, but you haven't been answering."

"Oh?" She checked her bag, but her phone wasn't there. She tried to remember if she'd ever grabbed it off the night stand, but the morning felt like a blur. "I must've left it in the hotel." Or the car, maybe? She had no idea.

"I knew you were all right," Dad said. "The detective assured me that you hadn't been in the house. But I was still frantic. I flew in this morning and came to the station to give my statement. I've been loitering outside, waiting for you. When I heard about the woman in the house..." He blinked back tears. "I'm sorry for her family, but I don't know what I would have done if it'd been you."

She leaned against him, allowed herself to soak up his strength.

"What are you planning to do now?"

She filled him in on the conference, and his expression darkened. "I think you should get out of town."

"I can't. My reputation, the neuron—"

"Aren't as important as your life."

Was he right? Were Klein and Reid right? Should she run away, save herself?

And sacrifice the neuron she'd poured her heart and soul into for years? Sacrifice the people it could save to protect herself?

"I can't, Dad. This is bigger than just me and my career. I have to see this through."

He pressed his lips together. "Okay, then. I want you to hire a bodyguard. No sense borrowing trouble. I'll make some calls right away, get someone who can keep you safe."

The last thing she wanted was to be followed around by a bodyguard everywhere she went. And then she thought of Annie and the horrible way she'd met her end and realized a bodyguard wouldn't be so bad. "Okay. Thank you."

They stared out at the park, the tall trees and green grass and preschoolers attempting to learn the game of soccer not far away. A few moments passed before he said, "So who's the guy?"

She angled to look at him and found his eyebrows raised as if he were trying to be funny. But she heard the seriousness in his tone.

Standing, she held out her hand. "Come on. I'll introduce you."

CHAPTER NINETEEN

While Jacqui was with her father, Reid sat in the passenger seat of her Audi with the AC on high, making a list of all the reasons he believed Denise was an unfit mother. He'd written the most important things—she'd abandoned Ella when she was just a few months old and hadn't bothered to see her again for years.

And she hadn't flown in when Ella was kidnapped. No mother who cared about her daughter would be able to stay away.

He believed Denise's travel for her job and her Hollywood lifestyle were unsuitable for raising a child. The numerous rumors about her and various men, who might not be safe for Ella to be around, also went on the list. But deep down, he was convinced that the first two should be enough. More than enough.

Unfortunately, he feared a judge would disagree.

What Reid could prove was that Denise *had been* an unfit mother.

Not that she was now.

When his phone rang, showing Denise's number on the screen, the anger that simmered whenever he thought of his ex came to a boil.

But it was only ten o'clock in Boston, which made it seven in

Los Angeles. Denise had always slept well past sunrise. Ella was like Reid, an early riser. Maybe this was his precious daughter. He hoped so as he swiped to connect.

"Hello."

"It's me," Denise said. "I wanted to call while Ella wasn't listening."

He should've let it go to voice mail. "Is she still asleep? How late are you letting her—?"

"Don't start with me. I took her to a movie premiere last night." Before he could ask, she added, "A Disney movie—rated G. She loved it, by the way."

A premiere. He could imagine her all dolled up in a pretty dress, hair done. Had she met the actors? She'd have reveled in the experience.

That was the kind of event that was commonplace in Denise's life. So unlike the normal, healthy life Ella lived in Coventry. He didn't say any of that, though. Instead, remembering the conversation with his lawyer the night before, he took a deep breath, prayed for patience and wisdom, and said, "I heard about the petition."

He expected Denise to make some snide or cutting remark, but she only sighed. "I don't want to do it that way, Reid. I understand everything you've done. Ella needs you. If not for you…"

Her voice trailed, but he waited, let her finish the sentence.

"If not for you, I don't know where she'd be. Or where *I'd* be. Knowing you were taking care of her, knowing my daughter was in good hands, allowed me to pursue my dreams. I wouldn't have been content staying in Coventry. But if I hadn't known you were taking good care of her, I never would have left."

As if Reid's being a good father had given Denise the freedom to abandon their child.

He didn't even know how to process that.

"I was selfish," she said. "I know that. I know that she was—she still is—my responsibility. We created her."

"God created her. He trusted us with her care."

Another long pause had Reid wondering what happened to the impulsive, short-tempered woman he'd married.

"You're right," she said. "Looking at Ella... I've spent a lot of time debating in my head—and with others—the existence of God. But one look at her precious face, and it leaves no doubt. There is a God, and He is so good."

A week earlier, even a few days earlier, Reid would have assumed Denise was playing a role, trying to manipulate him. But the woman on the other end of the phone sounded so sincere, so like the girl he'd fallen in love with back in high school.

Maybe Denise was maturing. Maybe.

The thought didn't bring peace, but fear. A selfish, manipulative woman he could handle. That woman, he could fight.

How could he fight this one?

"I'd like to talk, in person," she said. "I was thinking it could wait until I brought Ella home to you at the end of the month, but"—she sighed, the sound heavy on the phone—"to be honest, she needs to see you. She's having fun, but after last summer, she seems more fearful of new places. Seeing you would do her good."

It'd been nine days since Ella left for California with her mother, six days short of her normal two-week visit. But nothing was normal since the kidnapping.

"You don't mind?" he asked. In a similar circumstance, if Reid only had his daughter for snippets of time, and if she'd asked to spend some of that time with Denise...? He hated to think how he might react.

"This is the bed I've made, Reid. I'm not going to punish Ella for my shortcomings."

The fear pulsed loudly in his ears. Who was this woman? This wise, mature woman.

No. This was Denise. Nobody could change *that* much.

"When?" he asked.

"If it's all right with you, we're going to catch a flight to Manchester. I'd rather not go all the way to Coventry if I could avoid it, so maybe you could meet us there?"

Yup, there was the Denise he knew, the one who'd get to within an hour of her parents and not bother to call. "I'm in Boston on business. Why don't you fly in here?"

"Even better. I'll let you know our arrival time. With the time change, it'll probably be late. Can we meet tomorrow?"

"What are you thinking exactly? It's not like we can talk about custody with Ella present."

"I hired a nanny who can stay with her."

"A nanny? Ella's six, a little old for that."

"The woman's former special forces. She's a nanny, but she's also a bodyguard. A bodyguard who loves kids. Ella thinks she's her new best friend."

A bodyguard. If Reid could afford a bodyguard, he'd hire one himself.

"She can stay with Ella while you and I talk," Denise said, "and then you can take Ella for a couple of hours. I really want..." Her voice cracked, but she cleared her throat to cover it. "I intend for us to finish our month-long visit. If she wants to see you again during her visit, I can fly you out to L.A."

"I don't need you to pay my way. I can afford my own ticket."

A long pause was followed by an irritated, "Whatever." Then she added, in a kinder tone, "Whatever works for you, Reid. I'm trying my best here."

He could see that. He could see that Denise was doing everything in her power to prove she was a fit mother. Not just fit but able, loving, and kind.

If she didn't show a crack in that veneer, how was he ever going to defeat her?

AFTER HE ENDED the call with Denise, Reid jotted a few more items on his list. So many actors used drugs and alcohol, and from some of the snapshots he'd seen of her, photos in which her eyes had been bloodshot and puffy, he'd suspected she might be addicted to something. Though he hated to spend the money, he would talk to his lawyer about the possibility of hiring a private investigator to look into her daily routine. His friend Dylan back in Coventry was a PI. Maybe he could recommend somebody. It was possible a PI could uncover something that would convince a judge of what Reid already knew—that there was no way Denise was capable of raising a child.

He'd run out of ideas by the time he spotted Jacqui and her father coming from around the corner. Reid climbed from the Audi as they crossed the street. Despite the difficult morning and the terrible news, she looked better than she had in a couple of days. He didn't know what her father had said, but apparently, it'd been the right thing.

"Reid," Jacqui said as she approached. "Thanks for waiting."

"Of course."

Jacqui turned to her father. "This is Reid Cote. He's been helping me with... well, everything, I guess."

Reid grasped the man's hand. "Nice to meet you, Dr. Beal."

The man held onto his hand a moment longer, regarding him through narrowed eyes. It was a moment before he stepped back. "It's Nathanial. Nice to meet you."

Feeling like maybe he'd passed some sort of test, Reid said, "Did you fly in from South Carolina?"

"New York."

"That explains how you got here so fast."

"How exactly have you been helping, Reid?"

Before he could respond, Jacqui said, "Actually, Reid's been advising me on the business end of things. Don always took care of that stuff. Reid helped me craft my sales pitch, put together some paperwork to give potential buyers, that sort of thing."

Nathaniel nodded, though by the smirk of his mouth, he wasn't impressed.

Reid wasn't a doctor or a research scientist. He didn't have a genius IQ and hadn't gone to Harvard or MIT. But he knew who he was. He was good at what he did, and his worth wasn't wrapped up in diplomas or titles or net worth. He met the man's stare with one of his own.

Jacqui, seeming unaware of her father's attitude, said in a light-hearted tone, "His superpower is protectiveness."

Superpower? Talk about overselling it.

But Nathaniel glanced at her. "Oh, yeah?"

"If not for him, I'd have been at the brownstone last night. He's the one who insisted I rent a room at the hotel."

Reid didn't think he'd ever seen an expression shift as quickly as Nathaniel's did in that moment. The condescension was replaced as his eyes softened. He pressed his lips together and swallowed. He clasped Reid on the shoulder and squeezed. "It seems I owe you... everything."

"Not at all." Reid expected Jacqui would be looking at her father. But she was watching him, tenderness in her gaze. "Hers is a life worth protecting."

Her father nodded a few times, stepping back. Either he couldn't think of what to say or couldn't say it without betraying his emotions.

"I'm sure Jacqui will be glad to have your help." Reid glanced at his watch. "We have that meeting with your lawyer—"

"Oh, right." She turned to her father. "I'd love it if you'd come with us. I could use your insight."

He took her hands and held them to his chest. "I wish I could, sweetie. But I'm supposed to meet the insurance adjuster at the house. I need to get started on the repairs right away. Obviously, you can stay in the hotel as long as you want, but I'm sure you're eager to get home. With a bodyguard, you'll be safe there."

Bodyguard? That was a good idea, but Jacqui staying in Boston? The words yanked the bottom out of Reid's stomach. He wasn't ready for that.

Jacqui glanced his way. "I have to go back to Coventry Sunday. I told Fred I'd manage the shop until he returned."

Reid knew the owner of the ice cream shop. The man was

planning to be gone until August, which gave Reid another month with Jacqui. He planned to make the very best of that time.

But her father said, "I'll take care of Fred. I'm sure he can find somebody else to manage the place. You need to stay here, get your business up and running. With a bodyguard to keep you safe, there's no reason for you to wait to rebuild. You've got the money."

"You think I should dip into my trust fund?"

His brows lowered, a look of confusion. "Of course."

"But you never did. You were able to do everything you've done without ever taking money from yours."

"I'm a medical doctor, sweetie. I started making a good salary right out of college. And my parents let me live in the brownstone for free. What did I need the trust fund for? Once you were born, your mom and I decided to save it for you."

Jacqui blinked as if this were new and shocking information.

"Besides," Nathaniel said, "I didn't start my own business. What you've created, that artificial neuron, you need to get it out there. If that means using your trust fund, then I say use it. Empty it, if you have to. What could be more important?" He said the words as if they were the most obvious thing in the world.

Jacqui's eyes filled, and she stepped into her father's arms.

Nathaniel looked at Reid over her head, confusion in his gaze.

Maybe, someday, Reid and the man could have a heart-to-heart about what that conversation had meant to her. Because it was as obvious as the red in the man's eyes that he adored his little girl. And yet, somehow, she hadn't known that.

Reid thought of one of the beliefs he'd adopted after Ella's birth. Children spell love T-I-M-E.

That was what was missing in Nathaniel's relationship with Jacqui. The lack of time spent with her had kept her wondering, all her life, if he loved her.

Thoughts of Denise intruded. Denise wanted more time with Ella, and Ella needed to know her mother loved her.

No. In that case, more time would probably only convince Ella her mother *didn't*.

Jacqui stepped back from her dad. "Maybe we could have lunch, or—"

"I wish we could," he said. "I have to catch a flight back to New York ASAP. They rescheduled that surgery I was consulting on for this afternoon. I think the surgeon can handle the procedure, but he wants me there."

"I understand. Thanks for coming."

Her father placed his hands on her face. "Call me anytime. I'll come back if you need me."

"Okay."

He turned to Reid. "You too. I'm going to hire her a bodyguard, but if you think of anything else I can do or if I need to be here, don't hesitate." He riffled through his wallet and pulled out a business card, which he held out to Reid. "Whatever you have to do, you keep my baby safe."

"You have my word."

He shook Reid's hand, hugged Jacqui one last time, and walked away.

She sniffed, and Reid pulled her to his side, whispering in her ear, "Your father adores you."

She nodded against his chest. "He'd stay if he could. His work is important."

It was. But being a father was important too.

Reid respected the man for all he'd done for the world of medicine, for all the lives he'd changed.

But Reid vowed his daughter would never, ever wonder about his love. If he ever had the choice between changing the world and loving his daughter, Ella would win every single time.

CHAPTER TWENTY

Jacqui and Reid sat side-by-side on a Victorian-era replica couch in the office of BNB's attorney. Ira Myers, a nearly bald octogenarian with piercing blue eyes, was seated on the fancy armchair catty-corner to them. His desk on the far side of the room was covered with so many files and folders, just a glance at it made her stomach hurt.

Glancing at a stack of papers in his lap from time to time, Mr. Myers explained that the deal she and Don had made for her to buy his shares—a deal put together with Myers and Don's personal attorney—was ironclad, and the value they'd assigned the shares was more than generous. "I can't believe Don would try to convince anybody you'd coerced the shares out of him. Golly, I remember how grateful he was when you signed those papers. He was practically in tears."

She remembered too. Don had pressed her hands between his own and held on for a long time. "Thank you," he'd said. "This might just save her life."

Jacqui had known then that no amount of money was going to save Lola, but she'd given up trying to convince Don. If subjecting Lola to more treatment would make Don feel like he'd done everything he could, if it would help him feel at peace after Lola's death, then Jacqui had thought it would be worth it in the end.

Her intentions had been honorable. Now, she was simply grateful the man no longer held control over their business.

That the lawyer had seen, that he knew how badly Don had wanted the money, and that he seemed to be on her side, comforted her, considering he'd been Don's business attorney since before Jacqui was born.

Myers also confirmed that, if one of the partners were to die, ownership would automatically transfer to the surviving partner. "If I remember correctly, you were both adamant that the business stay in your control."

They'd done that because neither of them wanted Don's kids to have any voice in running the company. Even Don had agreed that his adult son and daughter, who were both struggling financially and, as far as Jacqui knew, in every other area of their lives, had no business getting involved in BNB. Bankruptcy, legal battles, multiple spouses producing multiple children. They were a mess. Don had spent his life mentoring young protégés, but he'd somehow neglected to raise his own kids well.

That wasn't fair, though. Maybe Don had done his best. Kids had free will, after all.

Reid asked, "Is there no provision that the surviving partner pay the other partner's family for the value of the shares?"

Jacqui hadn't thought of that, though she was sure both the lawyer and Don had when they'd first written up the contract.

Myers's eyes sparkled. "An excellent question, young man. The way they set it up, the surviving partner would receive all the shares and would have three years to pay the other partner's family for the value. Meanwhile, both the partner and the deceased's estate would receive profits from the business."

Reid nodded, taking that information in. "So, if something were to happen to Jacqui, Don would have three years to pay the value of her ninety percent to her family, and he'd maintain control of BNB that entire time."

"Correct." Myers seemed pleased, as if a prized student had just worked out a difficult problem.

"Can you change that?" Reid asked, "Make it so the shares automatically go to the partner's estate?"

Myers focused on Jacqui. "If that's what you want. I'll need to look into it, see how it's structured. It's been a coon's age since we set it up." He checked the time on his watch. "I'm in meetings all day, so I won't be able to get that taken care of until Monday."

"What about tomorrow?" Reid asked.

"I haven't worked a Friday in a decade." He rubbed his bald head. "My wife's been on me to retire, but I've never been much for fishing." He winked. "Sunburns the scalp."

"It's vital it gets done ASAP," Reid said.

Jacqui was tempted to tell him to tone down the attitude with the old man. But Reid's next words shut her up.

"Someone tried to kill Jacqui last night."

The attorney's expression shifted from amusement to concern as he pressed his back against the chair. He focused on her. "Were you injured? Are you all right?"

"Someone set my home on fire," she said. "I was staying in a hotel, but a woman was killed. My house sitter."

Color drained from the old man's face. "God rest her soul. But Don couldn't have done that. I've known the man most of my life. He would never do such a thing."

Jacqui glanced at Reid, happy to let him field that.

"The police are investigating, but you can see why Jacqui would want to eliminate any incentive to end her life."

"Yes, well." Myers seemed flustered. "Of course. I'll get on it as soon as possible. But I assure you, Miss Beal, the man I knew wouldn't hurt a fly."

Jacqui rubbed her bruised arm. She hated to say anything against their mutual friend, but Mr. Myers needed to understand. "Unfortunately, the man we both knew hasn't been the same since his wife died. I'm not saying he's the one who tried to kill me. But his behavior these last few months... He's changed."

"That much?" the lawyer asked.

"I think so, yes."

"Okay." He swallowed hard, nodding. "I'll get on it right away."

"Please, don't let Don know we talked," Jacqui added. "Not until it's done."

"Since you're the managing partner—and he was adamant than he wanted no role in running the business—you can make whatever changes you wish, but we will be required to notify him."

"Of course," she said. "Just not until it's signed."

The lawyer set his papers aside. "If there's nothing else—"

"One more thing," she said. "Where does the artificial neuron stand on getting the official patent?"

"Right, yes." He sat up straight, shook his head as if to shake off the unpleasant topic and shift to a new one. "After you called yesterday, I got in touch with the IP specialist in our office. She said Don told her back in March to hold off on filing the patent application. She never heard differently."

Jacqui leaned forward. "You're saying she hasn't even filed it?"

"She was told not to. Shall I tell her to file the patent immediately?"

"Yes." She felt breathless, shocked. Thank God she'd asked about that. If the provisional patent had expired, then anybody with access to her technology could steal it. "Yes, right away. Today, if she can."

"We'll get it done."

A few minutes later, Jacqui had just started her Audi, Reid in the passenger seat, when her phone rang. She answered, and the publicist's voice came through the speakers. "Have you had a chance to look over what I sent?"

Jacqui had gotten an email from the woman that morning, and she and Reid had studied it as they'd waited to meet with the attorney. Before she'd seen her father, she'd decided not to hire the woman. But Dad had helped her understand what Reid had been saying all along—that her invention was worth fighting for, not just for her sake but for the sake of all the people it would help.

She wasn't going to give in to Don's attacks on her reputation. She was going to fight with everything she had.

"We did," Jacqui said, "and it looks great."

"No changes? No suggestions?"

Beside her, Reid shrugged.

Jacqui couldn't think of anything to add to what Martha had put together. "You're the professional. We trust your judgment."

"Excellent. I'll get started on those press releases right away. I'll send you an invoice for the first payment this afternoon."

Jacqui would have to figure out how to access the money in her trust fund to pay the hefty fee. The thought of it sent a twinge of reluctance, but she remembered her father's words that day and brushed the worries aside.

What better way would she have to spend the money her family had given her? "I'll get it paid right away. The conference starts first thing tomorrow."

"I'll put a rush on the literature and have it delivered to your hotel by the end of the day."

Jacqui thanked her and hung up.

"Good decision," Reid said.

"I hope you're right."

She started the car and headed for the hotel.

"What are you going to do about Braden?"

They hadn't talked about her assistant since they'd left the police station earlier. She still couldn't believe that he could be working against her, that he might've tried to kill her. Or maybe she just didn't want to believe it.

"He's planning to be at the conference tomorrow. I suppose I could tell him he's not needed."

A block or two passed before Reid said, "I don't think that's the best play. I think he should come. I want to meet him, get a feel for him. If he's working against you, maybe he'll show his hand."

"I really hope he's not." Jacqui thought of the younger man

who'd worked at her side. "He claims to be a Christian. And he seems so sincere. So wise, honestly. I'd hate to think he's been lying to me all along about his faith. Or worse, that he sacrificed it on the altar of profit."

"That's what we need to figure out. Let's just be careful not to give away our suspicions."

"It won't be easy. I hate not knowing who I can trust." Cars were moving slowly at that hour in downtown Boston. She inched forward toward a stoplight. "Speaking of, I have an email from Mack at IntraHeart. They've sent a proposal." She'd glanced at the messages when Reid had bought them a couple of cups of coffee after they'd left the police station, though she hadn't had a chance to study the proposal yet. She'd been meaning to bring it up, but there were so many spinning plates, she'd nearly forgotten about it. "Despite the rumors, his boss is eager to work with us."

"That's great news. If you and he can come to an agreement, then the rest of this stuff will take care of itself, right? Once those exclusive rights are licensed—"

"I don't know if we should go with IntraHeart."

"Why not? We did our homework. They were your first choice. It's a solid company. Your friend works there, and he only had—"

"I did an internet search before bed last night."

"Nice bedtime reading?" His smile was a welcome sight, but she knew it wouldn't last.

"One of their artificial limbs malfunctioned, causing a man injury. Rather than making it right, they're fighting back." She shook her head. "I don't understand how a company could make that choice. The guy was seriously hurt."

"Maybe it wasn't the device's fault," Reid said. "Maybe the guy was using it wrong. Maybe he damaged it."

"Or maybe IntraHeart and their investors would rather fight it than fix it."

"What does Mack say?"

"I haven't talked to him, but he's loyal to them. He's going to take their side."

"These things aren't always so cut-and-dried, Jacqui. Before you cross them off your list, you might want to get more information."

"What else is there to know?" Why was Reid arguing with her? Did he really expect her to trust her invention to an unethical company? "They don't stand behind their work."

"Have there been other suits regarding that product?"

When it was finally her turn to go, she hit the gas, and the car lurched forward. "How would I know?"

He blew out a long breath. "Jacqui, you're going to have to give up some of the control here. You're going to have to trust God with this."

"You think, because I'm not willing to let my invention go to any Tom, Dick, or Harry who wants it, that I'm not trusting God? I'm trying to be a good steward of what He gave me."

"Okay." His tone was placating, and her pulse raced faster. "But if you're seeking perfection, you're never going to find it."

"Not perfection. Just a company that behaves morally." She braked hard at the next light. "And one that has the resources to develop the products. Those two requirements don't seem too much to ask."

"The sooner you make this decision, the sooner Don will back off. The sooner you'll be out of danger. The longer you put it off—"

"So this is my fault?"

"That's not what I'm saying." Reid was quiet as Jacqui pulled into the dark garage beneath their hotel. She parked and started to reach for the handle, but Reid stopped her with a palm on her forearm. "I talked to Denise this morning."

"Oh?" The sudden shift threw her, and she forced herself to let go of her irritation. For the moment. "What did she—?"

"I'll tell you all about it. But one thing she said feels like it applies here. She said that Ella was our responsibility because we created her. I reminded her that God created our daughter and entrusted her to us. I know it's not the same thing, but the neuron—

it's not yours, it's His. Rather than try to figure out the best place for it, maybe you need to trust Him—"

"I am trusting Him, Reid. He gave me a brain, and I'm using it."

His hand slipped away. "If you say so."

She climbed from the car and slammed the door behind her.

The sound reverberated in the dark, concrete space. She inhaled the cool underground air, exhaled her annoyance. She was overwhelmed and afraid and taking it out on Reid.

He walked around the car and leaned against it. "I'm sorry if I overstepped."

"I'm sorry I'm being so defensive. I welcome your opinion. And you're right. I'll pray about IntraHeart's proposal. I won't reject anybody out of hand."

"Except Tarim."

"That's different." She turned to face him. "Their record is—"

"I know." He brushed her hair away from her face, his touch soothing and gentle. "They've built their business on unethical behavior. But IntraHeart and the other companies we researched aren't the same. God has a good plan for your invention, Jacqui. I'm just saying, let's seek Him first."

On the far side of the garage, the heavy door leading to the stairwell slammed, and footsteps echoed in the space.

Jacqui's heart pounded. What were they doing, standing there? No witnesses, practically trapped in the soundproof space.

Reid's mind seemed to go to the same place. He grabbed her hand and pulled her behind a cement pillar, blocking her with his body.

She peeked around him, watching as a man walked past and climbed into an SUV parked a few spaces beyond theirs. He started the vehicle, backed out of the spot, and maneuvered through the narrow space toward the exit.

She exhaled. They were safe, for now.

Reid spun and pulled her against his chest. "I'm sorry. I should have gotten you out of here. That was stupid."

"We're okay," she said. "It was nothing. I didn't think of it either."

He straightened, his lips tipping up at the corners. "But I'm the one who's supposed to be the protective superhero, remember?"

"Even superheroes make mistakes sometimes."

They gathered their things from the car and hurried to the door that would take them to the hotel lobby. Reid may not be a superhero, and they may not agree on everything, but she felt safe with him at her side. Safe and cared for in a way she hadn't felt in a long, long time.

JACQUI'S HEART POUNDED. Her palms were sweaty. Her stomach churned.

Her body was in full fight-or-flight mode. She was leaning toward flight when Reid pressed his hand gently on her back and urged her into the oversize lobby at the Hynes Convention Center.

Her fear had little to do with the threat to her life. She could tackle complex equations and come up with solutions to problems that had the rest of the world scratching their heads, but the idea of spending the entire day with strangers trying to talk up her invention had her wanting to hide.

Finley Jackson, the bodyguard—personal security agent, she'd called herself—walked at Jacqui's other side as they navigated the crowd and got the badges that would gain them entrance to the conference. When Dad had insisted on getting Jacqui a bodyguard, she'd pictured a big, buff bruiser of a man, but the agency had sent a slender and attractive woman who stood not much taller than Jacqui's five-five height. Before either Jacqui or Reid could ask, Finley had explained what qualified her for the job. She'd been a sniper in the military and then spent ten years on protective duty in the Secret Service. After retiring, she'd opened her own martial arts studio before becoming a bodyguard.

"My stature makes people think I'm easily defeated." Finley had met Reid's eyes, then Jacqui's. "I'm anything but."

Jacqui didn't doubt it.

Finley had met with Jacqui and Reid at the hotel the evening before, and together they'd come up with a plan for the conference. Jacqui hadn't wanted the world to know she'd hired a bodyguard, so Finley would remain at Jacqui's side all day, playing the part of a mentee.

"Most of my job consists of keeping you out of situations that require me to intervene," Finley explained. "That means you'll never be alone. I'll be watching for people who are overly interested in you, people who look like they might be armed, and people behaving suspiciously. Mostly, I'll just be walking beside you, surveying the scene."

With Finley on one side and Reid on the other, Jacqui felt safe. It wasn't fear for her life that had Jacqui itching to bolt.

It was the people and suits and handshakes and, her least favorite activity on the planet, small talk.

They were heading into the arena when she spotted Braden coming toward her. His eyes were narrowed, his brows lowered, and his trademark smile missing.

Based on the way Reid and Finley tensed, they saw him too.

"It's okay," Jacqui said under her breath. She stepped out of the crowd and stuck her hand out to shake. "Glad to see you, Braden."

But he walked right past her outstretched arm and embraced her. "Thank God you're all right."

She allowed the hug for a moment before she leaned away. "What did you hear?"

He stepped back and held her at arms' length. "Your brownstone burned down?"

"Not all the way, but—"

"But someone died, right? I just heard from Ted, who heard from Dudley Paige at Mass General, that a friend of yours was trapped and couldn't get out."

She had no idea who Ted was. But Dudley Paige was an old

friend of Dad's. The Boston medical R and D community was small, so Jacqui wasn't surprised that word had gotten out about the fire. The rumor mill seemed to be churning at top speed already, and the conference had just gotten started. Like most truths put through the mill, what came out didn't precisely match what had gone in.

"Something like that," Jacqui said. "My house sitter died at the scene."

"I'm so sorry." Braden's cool blue eyes studied her. "Are you all right? Do they know what started it?"

She was reeling from seeing him, from the fears she still harbored about him, and from the fact that he knew—and that by the end of the day, everybody would know—what had happened at her brownstone.

She shouldn't be there. She should be mourning, or managing the house, or doing... anything else but this.

Reid must've sensed her distress because he stepped in. "They're still investigating the fire. It was tragic." He stuck his hand out. "Reid Cote. Business consultant."

Braden shook it. "I'm glad to meet you. Glad you're helping. Business isn't exactly Jacqui's thing." He gave her a wink to soften the words, not that she was even a little insulted.

"We have some literature for you." Reid reached into his laptop bag and pulled out a stack of brochures.

Braden flipped through the one on top. "This is great. Thanks."

"And I'm Finley." The bodyguard stuck out her hand. "Old friend of the family, but new to this industry. Jacqui was kind enough to let me tag along today."

"Hi, Finley." Braden shook her hand, but his attention wasn't diverted for long. To Jacqui, he said, "Is there anything I can do for you? I've been praying, of course. I'm sure you're heartbroken."

Jacqui swallowed the grief his words raised. "I'm still trying to process it. My dad is managing the house, and the police suggested I keep my distance from Annie's family while they deal with it, so"—she shrugged—"I figured I might as well come."

Braden smiled for the first time since he'd approached. "Because I know how much you love these kinds of things."

"Oh, yeah. This is my jam."

He laughed. "Your *jam?*"

She managed a slight chuckle, thinking of the teenager who was managing the ice cream shop while Jacqui was away. Bree used the expression all the time. Chocolate ice cream was her jam, and so were water skiing and art classes. "I got that from one of the kids I work with." At the confusion in Braden's expression, she said, "Long story."

There was a reason she hated these things. She was terrible at them.

"You have a new job?" Braden's voice was low, worried.

"No, no. Just helping out a friend until the lab is rebuilt."

"Which will be when, exactly?"

Reid cleared his throat, shooting a pointed look at the people swarming all around. "This probably isn't the place to talk about it."

"Right. And I still need to get my badge." Braden gripped her upper arm, giving it a gentle *I'm here for you* squeeze. "I'll see you in there."

He stepped into the long line waiting to check in.

Jacqui, Reid, and Finley entered the exhibit hall, where booths were set up in neat rows, promoting everything anybody in the medical R and D industry would want. Everything from lab equipment to software to consulting services. In years past, BNB'd had a booth, but this year, Don had let the deadline slip away, too focused on Lola's illness to even consider it.

The only benefit to a booth would have been having a place to stow their stuff. Reid was carrying the bulk of the literature Martha had designed and printed. Jacqui had a few brochures in her bag. Now it was time to get to work.

She was still trying to figure out how to get started when Doreen Nadler approached. "Miss Beal."

Jacqui's back straightened. "Miss Nadler. Nice to see you here."

Not true, but it seemed the right thing to say.

The woman's smile was so contrary to the look she'd worn during their meeting a few days earlier that Jacqui was tempted to take a step back in surprise.

Doreen nodded at Reid and Finley but didn't greet them further. "I read the article in the paper this morning about your company."

The article had been Martha's doing. She'd sent out a press release the evening before explaining Jacqui's *groundbreaking invention that could ultimately save millions of lives*. She hadn't loved the hyperbole, but Martha had pooh-poohed her objection. "It makes no promises, and it *could* do that, right?"

It was possible. Depending on what was developed with it, it might have even been probable.

Apparently, the article was doing its job.

Doreen said, "I don't know what's going on with the ownership of BNB—"

"There's nothing going on." Jacqui forced a smile but feared it looked more like a grimace. "I own the majority of the company, though I still value Don's insights. I'm looking forward to the day, when he's feeling up to it, that he comes back to work."

It was the line Martha had given Jacqui to say whenever anybody mentioned Don or his ownership in BNB.

"And the lawsuit?" Doreen asked.

"There is no lawsuit, Miss Nadler." Jacqui stepped closer, lowered her voice, and held eye contact. "I have tremendous respect for Don Burgess. I know you do too. I think we just need to give him time to grieve." She stepped away again. "Meanwhile, I'm working hard to keep the company he helped build strong. We're already receiving proposals from companies interested in the exclusive patent rights. I hope Boylston makes the short list."

Reid squeezed her elbow, a slight touch that told her it was time to move along.

Thank heavens he was there.

Jacqui nodded once. "Enjoy the conference." She turned and walked away.

Heart pounding, head swimming, somehow she'd done it.

Reid whispered in her ear, "Perfect."

The next couple of hours were a blur. Jacqui had conversation after conversation, and in each one, she used the lines Martha had given her. The press releases Martha sent had resulted in a couple of newspaper articles and even more blog mentions. By lunchtime, Jacqui had overheard more than one person talking about her company and her invention. Somehow, what had felt impossible two days earlier—finding a reputable company to purchase the exclusive rights to her patent—now seemed not only possible but inevitable.

Braden found her as people were streaming out of the exhibit hall for lunch. The smile on his face indicated that he'd had the same results as she had. "You're the talk of the convention."

She started to respond, but Reid tapped her on the elbow. At the sight of all the folks nearby, she headed for an empty corner where they'd be out of earshot of passersby.

Braden glanced at Finley, then gave Jacqui a pointed look.

"It's okay," Jacqui said. "She's been with me all morning."

His smile returned. "I bet you'll have a handful of proposals by the end of the conference."

"I hope so."

"I overheard some stuff about the lawsuit this morning," he added, "but in the last hour, all the buzz has been about the neuron."

Jacqui had told Braden about the rumors that Don was going to sue her. She didn't add that she thought Don had started those rumors himself or that he was working against BNB. Braden seemed to have taken her at face value. Either Braden had no idea of the seriousness of the rift between them, or he was an excellent actor.

The more time she spent with Braden, the less inclined she was to believe he was working against her.

Reid questioned Braden about everything he'd heard and everyone he'd spoken to that morning while Jacqui stepped back to enjoy a welcome breather. She wasn't used to all the activity, the chaos, the swarm of people, and it had exhausted her.

Reid and Braden had moved on to conversation about where they should get lunch. Jacqui couldn't have cared less and was reaching for her phone to check her messages when she felt Finley tense beside her.

The woman's cool hand wrapped around Jacqui's upper arm, and Jacqui looked up.

Don was approaching the group, press-on smile in place. "Jacqui."

"How are you, Don?"

Braden reached out and shook his hand. "How've you been? I've been praying for you."

The fake smile seemed to tighten at the corners. "That's very kind of you, son." Don's attention turned to Jacqui. "Seems like you've generated some interest in our cell today."

"We created something amazing," Jacqui said. "It's only natural people would want to know more about it."

His expression softened, and for a moment, he looked like the kindly old man she'd known for so long. "I was really sorry to hear about the fire at your place. And the woman—your house sitter, right?"

Jacqui wasn't fooled by the tenderness on his face. "A young woman, an *innocent* woman who had her whole life ahead of her, was murdered."

Anger was wafting off Reid like a strong scent. She grabbed his arm, hoping to be an anchor, to keep him still and quiet beside her.

"I heard." Seemingly unaware of Reid's animosity, Don shook his head and reached out as if to touch her.

She flinched, and he dropped his arm. "I'm glad you weren't

there. I'm glad you're safe. Whatever differences you and I have had, I would never wish you harm."

Could that sincerity in his words be real?

If it was, then who'd set the fire at her house?

No. It had to have been Don. Nobody else had anything to gain from her death.

"Anyway," he added, "I just wanted to say I'm sorry about your friend."

For the first time in months, she recognized the man she'd considered a mentor for so long, the grandfather figure she'd loved. In his eyes were grief. Grief and regret and profound loss. She remembered the funny, vivacious woman Don had shared his life with and felt nothing for him but sympathy.

Don nodded to Reid, Finley, and Braden before meeting her eyes and holding her gaze. "I'm glad you're well."

Her throat tightened. She swallowed but couldn't make herself speak.

He turned and walked away, shoulders hunched, weary and broken.

The four remaining stood silently a moment before Braden said, "Man, he looks older." He faced the rest of them. "Did that feel weird, or was it just...?"

Braden took in Reid's expression, which was filled with fury. Obviously, Reid hadn't fallen for Don's act.

Had it been an act?

Jacqui had no idea.

"I'm obviously missing something," Braden said.

Reid forced a smile and slapped him on the back. "Don't worry about it. Let's get lunch."

CHAPTER TWENTY-ONE

They were just finishing up lunch at the crowded deli when Reid's phone dinged with a text from Denise. She and Ella had arrived safely, and she was eager for him to come by.

"Everything okay?" Jacqui asked.

He'd told her the night before about Denise's plan to be in Boston that day. Eager as he was to see Ella, he hated to leave Jacqui's side. "Denise wants to meet in an hour."

Jacqui's eyes widened, but she schooled her expression quickly. "Okay."

"I can put her off, meet her later. I hate to—"

"Ella comes first, Reid. Go." She glanced at Finley. "I've got all the help I need."

When Reid had first met the bodyguard, he'd been skeptical. But he'd been watching her all morning, and the woman missed nothing—including his close scrutiny. She'd seen Don coming and known the man was a threat long before Reid had noticed his presence.

Braden had gone to the restroom, but he'd be back. Before Reid had met Braden, he'd been inclined to believe the man was working against her, but there was something about him, something both innocent and trustworthy, that had Reid agreeing with Jacqui's assessment. Braden was on her side. Reid guessed Don was working with someone, but it wasn't her assistant.

Jacqui would be safe with them. As much as he wanted to stay at Jacqui's side, he couldn't wait to see his daughter.

"Take the car." Jacqui dug into her bag and came out with the keys. "I'm not going to need it."

"You sure you don't mind?"

"Of course not. Have fun."

Reid said good-bye to Finley, then kissed Jacqui on the cheek. Only when he stood to leave did he see Braden returning from the bathroom. His eyebrows were raised. He hadn't missed the kiss.

Maybe Reid shouldn't have done that. Maybe Jacqui didn't want Braden to know they were together.

Maybe Reid *did* want him to know it. Braden was younger than she was, but not by much. Reid didn't want the guy getting any ideas.

Reid met Braden halfway. "If you don't mind, I'd appreciate it if you'd stay with Jacqui this afternoon. No need for you two to split up again."

"Fine by me. You aren't staying?"

"I'll be back tomorrow."

In the car on the way to Denise's downtown hotel, Reid put Jacqui and her problems behind him and prayed. He'd need God's help to get through this meeting with Denise. "Please, help me keep my little girl with me," he said in the quiet car. "Please don't let me lose her."

Reid pulled into a parking garage that cost roughly the per-hour equivalent of his college tuition and made his way to a suite on the second-to-top floor. Because the famous Denise Masters couldn't possibly stay in a run-of-the-mill hotel room.

That was not the attitude he should start with. And who cared what Denise did with her money? It was hers to spend however she saw fit. She had earned it, after all. He paused outside the door and prayed for patience, for wisdom, for understanding.

Approximately four seconds after he knocked, the door swung open, and Ella crashed into his legs. "Daddy!"

He lifted her, breathing in her little-girl scent and relishing the feel of her in his arms.

For a moment, he said nothing, just held her, and everything felt right with the world.

And then the fantasy dissipated.

"Ella," said a woman whose voice he didn't recognize. "You're not supposed to answer the door without permission."

Reid looked past his daughter to a black woman with a head full of micro braids that reached beyond her shoulders. They'd been pulled into a side ponytail. He recognized the pink ponytail holder as one of Ella's and smiled.

Ella pushed back from him and looked over her shoulder. "Sorry, Celeste." Then to Reid, "This is Celeste. She's my new friend. Isn't she pretty? I was doing her hair. She keeps her hair in braids like that all the time. Aren't they cool? I wanna do my hair like that, but she said it would take a long time, and sometimes it pinches. Mommy said not this summer, but maybe another time. Can I, Daddy?"

He tweaked his little girl on the nose. "We'll see."

Ella wiggled to get down. As soon as her feet hit the floor, she grabbed his hand and pulled.

He stepped into a living area complete with couches, chairs, a small round kitchen table, and a full kitchen. Beyond the floor-to-ceiling windows, he got a glimpse of the city.

"Come on, Daddy. I wanna show you our room."

"I'm not sure that's such a good idea." He figured neither Celeste nor Denise would appreciate that.

Denise stepped out from one of the rooms off the side of the living area. Her hair, which used to be brown, had been dyed blond. He wanted to hate it, but the truth was, it looked good. She looked good. She wore a lightweight floral dress that showed off her trim waist. On the face that always looked so done-up in photographs, she wore a little mascara and lipstick, but nothing to cover the smattering of light freckles she'd had as long as he could remember. For a moment, he saw the girl he'd fallen in love with.

"Reid."

"Hi, Denise."

Her attention shifted to their daughter. "Ella, sweetie, remember what we talked about."

Ella gripped Reid around his waist but spoke to her mother. "I don't wanna leave him."

The words must've inflicted a wound, because Denise flinched. She covered it with a smile. "You and Daddy are going to go do something this afternoon"—she gazed at Reid—"right?"

"Children's museum or aquarium?" he asked.

Ella shouted, "Aquarium!"

"Good choice."

Denise said, "Right now, you and Celeste are going for a walk, okay?"

Ella left her father's side and took Celeste's hand and tugged her toward the door, talking to Reid as she went. "She's gonna buy me some of those polka dot ice cream things. They're so good. I'll save you some."

"Yum. Be sure to stay with Celeste."

Ella rolled her eyes. "I *know*, Daddy." She shook her head at the nanny/bodyguard as if to say, *parents, am I right?*

Celeste offered a conspiratorial smile, and the two left.

The door closed behind them, leaving Denise and Reid alone together for the first time since...

Since Denise had left them.

"You need anything?" Denise was studying him with wary eyes.

"Nope."

She grabbed a bottle of water from the fridge and nodded to the table. "Should we—?"

"Sure." After she took her seat, he settled on the cushy, upholstered chair. "Nice place."

She shrugged. "Ella's having fun. She's jumped on every bed." Denise's smile was slight but seemed genuine, as if she found their daughter amusing. No, delightful. "Where that kid gets her energy, I'll never know."

"You probably shouldn't let her—"

"Please don't." The smile faded. "She's tiny. She's not going to hurt anything."

"It's just not a good habit. We need to teach her to respect other people's belongings."

Denise inhaled a deep breath and blew it out. "Any other parenting tips before we get started?"

"I'm just saying—"

"I know you're better at it than I am. You don't need to keep reminding me."

"I'm not..." He clamped his mouth shut. "Sorry."

She set her bottle of water on the table, and he opened it for her, just like he always had. He set the bottle and cap in front of her.

"Thanks."

He shrugged.

She sipped.

The silence was heavy with all the things they'd never said to each other.

Normal couples, when they divorced, had conversations. They hashed things out.

He and Denise had never had the opportunity. He'd come home to find her bags packed. She'd walked out without a word of explanation apart from, "I can't do this." Their divorce had been handled by lawyers. After it was finalized, she hadn't contacted them for years.

Now, she seemed determined to worm her way back into their lives.

He wasn't about to break the silence. Denise was the one who'd called this... meeting, for lack of a better word. She was the one who wanted to change their arrangement. He'd let her lead.

She set the bottle down. "I want more time with her."

"So you said."

"I don't want to go to court over this."

"Joint custody?" He didn't hide the incredulity. "You don't really want that."

"You don't know what I want, Reid. I'm not the same woman I was six years ago."

"No, now you're rich and famous and—" He managed to cut himself off before adding *even more selfish.*

"And lonely and missing my little girl like you wouldn't believe." Her eyes filled, and she swallowed hard. As if she were trying not to cry. As if she really meant it.

He reminded himself that the woman played pretend for a living. And she was really good at it.

"I know you don't believe me." Denise was unnaturally still, hands pressed flat on the table. Shoulders lowered and back. He couldn't tell if she was posing for a reason, or if something else was going on in that head of hers. "I don't know what to do about that," she said. "I don't know how to convince you—"

"Maybe if you could go back in time and not leave us in the first place." *Her.* He'd meant to say *not leave* her *in the first place.*

"If only I could." The words were soft as if not spoken for him. They hovered over the table like smoke in a bar.

A moment passed, and then she added, "I've regretted it for years, you know? All the fame and money. I love being an actor. I love taking words in a script and bringing them to life. I know you think it's stupid, but it's what I was born to do. But the rest? I'm sick of it. I'm sick of the fame. I'm sick of having cameras in my face all the time, of not being able to leave the house without makeup on for fear someone's going to take my picture and concoct some story about me, as if not wearing makeup must mean I'm in the middle of some big breakup with a man I barely know, a man I never even dated. I'm sick of total strangers shoving scripts at me and asking me to play the lead in their indie films. I'm sick of people wanting to be friends with me not because of me but because they think I can do something for them."

Oh, the perils of being rich, famous, and beautiful. But Reid didn't say that, just nodded for her to continue. He didn't want to interrupt what he was sure was a well-rehearsed monologue.

"When Ella was kidnapped—"

"Don't go there, Denise." His heart pounded. "You couldn't be bothered to—"

"I was in the hospital."

He sat back. Stunned. "You said you were on location."

"I didn't want anybody to know. It's a long story, but—"

"Why?"

"My agent was working on getting me a part, and he didn't want word to get out."

"You could have told me."

"We needed to keep it under wraps."

"That's a ridiculous excuse. You really think I'd run off to the gossips rags to tell them? You should have told me." Reid forced a deep breath to calm his racing heart. "But what I meant was, why were you in the hospital?"

"It's a long story."

He made a show of checking the time on his phone. "I'm not in any hurry."

She sipped her drink, set it down. Shook her head. "No. I'm sorry, but no. I want to work with you on this, but my medical issues are none of your business."

"They're my business if they affect our daughter. Which they obviously did, if you couldn't—"

"I don't have to tell you any details about my life. Now, do you want to discuss Ella, or should we meet in court?"

The fact that she wouldn't tell him why she'd been hospitalized told him the reason might be something he could use against her. Maybe a good private investigator could find out. Maybe, if he dug enough into her life, he'd find the ammunition to fight her. And it was becoming clearer all the time that there would be a fight.

In the past, whenever Denise had pressed him for anything regarding Ella, he'd only had to bring up her history, and she'd back down. Not anymore. Something had changed, something significant.

This wasn't an act, and Denise wasn't going to be intimidated or guilted into giving up.

There was something else too. She was alone. She could have had her agent or her lawyer or any number of people with her there. Whenever he'd seen photos of her in the past couple of years, since the first superhero movie, she'd been traveling with what could only be described as an entourage. Friends, agents, bodyguards, hangers-on. He had no idea. But she'd brought none of them to Boston with her. Just Ella and the nanny.

He needed to stop thinking he was dealing with the guilt-ridden woman who'd abandoned them. Denise was different. She was stronger and more determined than ever.

He was almost afraid of the answer, but he asked, "What do you want?"

"I don't think she'd like online school. She's too social for that, at least right now."

That Denise had figured that out all on her own impressed him. And made him nervous. "I agree."

"Her home is in Coventry. I don't want to take her away. As much as I'd love to have her half the time, that doesn't feel feasible at this point."

He should have been comforted by her words, but her tone only raised his blood pressure higher. She was coming off as entirely too reasonable. How could he defeat her if she persisted in behaving so rationally?

"I think your suggestion about the holidays was a good one," she said. "I figure we can trade off who gets her for Thanksgiving and who gets her for Christmas."

Though he hated the thought of not seeing Ella for every holi-day, he said, "Okay."

"And we can do the same with Easter and the Fourth of July."

"Easter doesn't work. It's a one-day holiday. She wouldn't have time to fly out and be back for school."

Denise nodded. "But I could go there. To Coventry."

"You haven't been to Coventry in years. You haven't seen your parents—"

"I'm well aware of my shortcomings as a mother and a daughter."

He had to stop doing that, to stop reminding Denise of all her failures. When had he become so bitter, so angry? The calmer she was, the more his own faults came to light. It was as if, rather than fighting back, she was simply lifting a mirror, showing him himself. He didn't like what he was seeing. "You're right. I'm being unfair."

She sat back, eyes wide, as if the words shocked her.

That was how much of a jerk he'd been. Not that she didn't deserve it. But maybe it wasn't his job to judge.

"You'd do that?" he asked, trying to keep disbelief out of his voice. "You'd come to Coventry to be with her?"

"I was thinking I might get a place there, maybe on the lake. So she wouldn't always have to fly out to see me."

He felt sick to his stomach. This was not going the way he'd planned. If Denise wanted a place in Coventry, then she was truly serious about spending more time with Ella.

"She has a few school vacations a year, right?" Denise asked. "I figure, the years I have her for Christmas, I'll take her for April vacation, and you can have her for February vacation. The years you have her for Christmas, I'll get her for February vacation."

Reid nodded, numb.

"And, since you get her the whole school year, I want her for six weeks every summer."

"No." The word came from deep inside. He should shut up. He should pray about it. But instead, he said it again. "No. No to the summer. No to the vacations. Just... no."

"I realize this is hard for you," Denise said. "I realize—"

"No." He pushed back his chair and stood, heart pounding so loudly he worried she could hear it. "You left her. You didn't call us for *two years*. And now you want to swoop in and play *mommy*? Forget it. She's mine."

Denise stood as well. "Just think about it."

"You aren't good for her. You don't know how to be a parent. Good parents teach values and morals. Good parents are *there*. You..." He shook his head, tried to clear it. Tried to sound like a rational person, not a crazy father. But what came out was, "You can't teach what you don't have."

"You know nothing about me."

"Oh, I know you. I know who you are. I know the woman who walked away from her family and—"

"I can't take that back. I would if I could."

He stepped around the table, got in her face. "Would you? Would you really give up the fame and the money for Ella? I don't think so. I think you want it all. Well, guess what, lady. You can't have it all. Being a parent takes time, time you've never been willing to offer her."

Denise's eyes filled with tears, but she didn't back down. "Step away. Now."

He did, squeezing his hands into fists, trying to regain his self-control. "I'm sorry. I shouldn't have—"

"I hope you got that out of your system, because I will not let you speak to me that way again. What I did was wrong. More than wrong. Some would say unforgivable. Nevertheless, I hope someday you'll forgive me. Ella has. I've forgiven myself. Even God's forgiven me. Maybe one of these days, you'll practice what your faith preaches and do the same."

The words were stab wounds, piercing his heart. She was right. God help him, Denise was right.

A phone dinged in the other room.

She walked away, returned a moment later, and said, "They're on their way up."

Reid couldn't form words. He swallowed. Tried to get himself under control.

"I'm not asking for the world here, Reid." She crossed her arms and leaned against the kitchen counter. "She's my daughter, and I love her. Please, just think about it. Pray about it."

~

Fortunately, Ella had so many stories about all the fun stuff she'd done with her mother and Celeste since she'd flown to California that she didn't seem to notice Reid's mood that afternoon. They walked from the harbor hotel to the aquarium just a couple of blocks away and marveled together at the fish in the tanks, Ella chattering and Reid doing his best to concentrate and not think about the things Denise had said.

The fact was, Denise was right, at least about one thing. Six years had gone by, and still, Reid hadn't forgiven her for walking out on Ella.

For walking out on him.

She'd been dramatic, no doubt. In high school, she'd created drama, and not in good ways, imagining offense when none had been intended, assuming intrigue when none had existed. But he'd always been able to talk her down from those ledges. By the time they were in college, she'd matured, or so he'd thought. In high school, in college, and in their marriage, he'd found her amusing and delightful. She'd kept him laughing.

She'd made him happy.

He'd loved her. He'd adored her. He'd have done anything for her.

And she'd left him.

He'd never forgiven her for that.

All those years, he'd judged Denise for the scars her abandonment had left on Ella's heart.

Never admitting the scars she'd left on his.

Ella tugged his hand. "Daddy, look at those." She pointed at a tankful of colorful fish. "Can we get fishes?"

"Fish," he said. "The plural is fish."

"Can we get some? Mommy has some in a big tank, and they're so pretty. Can we get one like that? I like the red ones. Aren't they pretty?"

He started to agree to whatever Ella wanted, unwilling for Denise to offer their daughter anything that he couldn't match. Or beat.

But he thought better of it. "I don't think so." He ground the next words out, so little did he want to say them. "Maybe you can just enjoy the fish at your mom's house."

Ella shrugged and moved on to the next topic of conversation.

Totally unaware of the battle raging within him.

When they'd gaped at every exhibit, Ella dragged him to the gift shop, where he bought her a stuffed whale that she promptly named Pansy and gave him a long explanation as to why.

They were outside the aquarium, watching the boats in the harbor, when Ella said, "Can we get something to eat?"

Was she hungry already? "Didn't you just have ice cream?"

He knew how little his daughter could eat. And it was only five o'clock. He didn't have to have her back to the hotel for three hours.

"I didn't like it. It's not as good as Miss Jacqui's."

Funny how quickly Ella had forgotten Fred, the owner of the Coventry ice cream shop, though they'd gone there for years before Jacqui started managing the place.

Not that it surprised him. Jacqui wasn't exactly forgettable.

"Miss Jacqui is in Boston," he said, an idea forming. "That's why I'm here. I came to help her with a project."

Ella's eyes lit up. "Can she go to dinner with us? Please, Daddy?"

There was no need for Ella to beg. Reid was longing to see Jacqui, longing for someone to help him manage all the anger and fear still swirling in his gut. Or at least someone to entertain his daughter so he could deal with the feelings for a minute. "Let me call her and see if she's busy."

Jacqui answered on the second ring. The exhaustion in her voice had his hopes deflating, but he asked anyway. "I told Ella you're in town, and she wanted to know if you could join us for dinner."

"Oh. I'd love that." By the perked-up tone, she wasn't just saying it. "I need to do something to shake off the day. I think Ella is just the ticket."

"Excellent." He gave Ella a thumbs-up, and they started walking along the sidewalk crowded with tourists and business people. "How'd the rest of the day go?"

"Better than we expected. In fact, I've already received a number of proposals and requests for more information." She rattled off the names of the companies, and he recognized most as those they'd researched, all good firms with good reputations. "And of course the IntraHeart proposal."

"Have you had a chance to look at that one?"

"Yes. It's everything we hoped."

It was the best news he'd heard all day. If only she'd hurry up and finalize that, the target would be off her back. "The car's at Denise's hotel. It'll probably take us a half hour to pick you up. Are you back at the hotel?"

"I am. Call me when you're close, and I'll head down."

He ended the call feeling more optimistic than he had in hours. They made it to Jacqui's car and headed toward the hotel. Ella, eyes wide as she took in the city streets, was chattering about how different Boston was from Los Angeles. "And it's always sunny, and there are palm trees *everywhere*. And the traffic is just like this."

This was terrible. Horns blazing, drivers cutting others off, some offering helpful hand gestures. Boston had a lot to offer, but the traffic alone would make him crazy.

It took longer than he'd hoped to get out of the downtown

madness. Stopped at a light and close enough that he could see the top of their hotel, he texted Jacqui that they were nearby.

Traffic picked up speed as they neared the hotel. Reid needed to change lanes and glanced in the rearview, spying an SUV behind him, moving too fast.

Cars on his right and left, another in front. He was boxed in.

The SUV was closing fast.

The traffic braked at a light. Reid had no choice but to do the same, praying the driver of the SUV would slow down.

He barely had time to brace himself.

The SUV smashed into the back of the Audi, shoving it forward and jerking Reid's head back into the seat.

Ella screamed.

A split second later, the Audi smashed into the car in front, jerking his head forward.

Shaken, he turned to the backseat to Ella. "Sweetie, are you—?"

Movement behind the car caught his eyes.

Two people, both wearing ski masks, climbed from the SUV and headed toward Jacqui's car.

Without thinking, Reid undid his seatbelt and launched himself into the backseat. He didn't know if the doors were locked, didn't have time to check. From the seat beside Ella, he leaned over her and covered her with his body, slipping his arms behind her and holding her tight.

She seemed shocked into silence.

The door beside him swung open, and a masked face peered inside.

Reid wanted to punch that face, kick the man standing there. But he dared not let up his grip on Ella.

A woman said, "Hurry up!"

A hand gripped Reid's shirt and yanked, pulling the fabric against his neck. But he didn't move, just hung on tighter. No way, no way would he lose Ella again. They'd have to kill him first.

And maybe they would. *Please, please God. Please let help get here before they take her.*

Then the man said, "It's not her. Come on!"

From outside, the sound of the city filtered in. People shouting, a faraway siren.

Reid looked out the rear window and watched as the two would-be kidnappers climbed back into their SUV. It did a U-turn and tore down the street, turning at the corner.

He still didn't let go of Ella.

He wouldn't lose her again.

CHAPTER TWENTY-TWO

Finley at her side, Jacqui hurried inside police headquarters. She spoke to the man behind the desk and was directed to the floor where she and Reid had been the day before.

An hour earlier, she and the bodyguard had stepped outside beneath the overhang at the hotel, ready to meet Reid when he pulled up, when a loud crash drew her attention. The way the people drove in this town, she was surprised there weren't more wrecks.

And then she'd seen the Audi.

She'd started in that direction.

But Finley had grabbed her wrist. "What are you doing?"

"That's my car." The pitch in Jacqui's voice rose as she peered at the scene. "That's Reid. And his little girl."

The bodyguard's grip only got stronger. "Come on," Finley said. "Back inside."

Jacqui tried to yank her hand away, but Finley didn't release her. "Jacqui, you hired me to protect you. I can't do that if you don't do what I tell you." She'd tugged Jacqui through the hotel entrance, across the lobby, and into the elevator.

Then, Jacqui had waited in her room, alone, for what felt like hours while Finley found out what was going on.

When she finally returned and gave Jacqui an update, the news made Jacqui's blood run cold.

Since they didn't have a car, Finley had arranged for one of the police officers on scene to give them a ride to the station.

Now, Jacqui spied Reid, Ella on his lap, sitting across from Detective Klein. The sight of them both in one piece pulled a sob up from deep inside. She swallowed it down and practically ran across the room, skirting desks and dodging cops.

Reid turned just as she approached. He stood, bringing his daughter with him. She expected him to open his arms, but he didn't, just held his daughter between them like a shield.

Jacqui stopped short. She reached out and patted Ella's back but spoke to Reid. "Thank God you're all right."

"Yeah."

She caught the worry—and something she couldn't name—in his eyes.

Ella didn't let up her grip on her father. "Hi, Miss Jacqui."

"Hey, sweetheart. How are you?"

She shrugged her tiny shoulders and turned her face back into her father's shoulder.

Never had Jacqui seen the girl so quiet, so frightened. The sight of it had tears threatening again. She lifted her gaze to Reid's and mouthed, *I'm so sorry.*

He shook his head. "Will you take Ella so I can talk to the detective for a minute?"

It took some cajoling, but Ella finally shifted from Reid's arms to Jacqui's. The girl wasn't big for her age, but it wouldn't be long before she was too big to be held. Right now, though she was six years old, Ella clung like a toddler.

Klein nodded toward the elevators. "There're vending machines."

Jacqui walked that direction, Finley at her side. As if there might be danger even in police headquarters.

And maybe there was. Finley had said that the accident most likely hadn't been an accident at all. She'd said that the two masked intruders who'd approached Jacqui's car had nearly stolen Ella away.

Jacqui needed to get it through her thick skull that danger was everywhere. And everybody she cared about was in the crosshairs of whoever wanted her dead.

Don. Or someone working with Don. Who else could it be?

She bought Ella a bag of cheese crackers and a bottle of fruit punch, and they found a bench. Jacqui sat, but Ella didn't scramble off her lap as Jacqui had expected her to. She stayed put and picked at her snack and sipped her drink in silence.

Jacqui tried to draw her out, but Ella didn't say much, only that they'd gone to the aquarium. Jacqui told her about the last time she'd been there and her favorite exhibits. She talked about sharks and crabs and starfish. "I don't know why, but I've always been rather fascinated by seahorses," she said.

Ella glanced up at that. "They're pretty."

"Aren't they?"

"Imagine if we could ride them like real horses?" Ella's voice pitched up at the end as if posing a question. "Maybe mermaids do."

Jacqui smiled. "Maybe you're right. Maybe there are mermaid knights and mermaid princesses and mermaid castles with stables full of seahorses."

For a moment, Jacqui thought she'd succeeded in pulling Ella into conversation. But the child just shrugged and nibbled crackers.

Jacqui had never been great at make-believe, but she kept babbling about the pretend mermaid world, hoping to get Ella's mind off what had happened.

The elevator dinged, and Jacqui looked up just as a blond woman stepped off, a black woman with long braids at her side. The blonde's gaze landed on Jacqui, then Ella, and her eyes widened. "Ella, sweetheart."

Ella turned at her name, then scrambled off Jacqui's lap before she could stop her. "Mommy!" She launched herself into her mother's arms.

Ella's mom lifted her and glared at Jacqui. "Who are you?"

Jacqui stood, Finley at her side as if the actress might pose a threat. "I'm a friend. Jacqui Beal."

"Where is Reid?"

She nodded toward the big room. "He's in there. He's talking to..."

But Denise had spotted him and was already marching that direction, the other woman trailing.

Jacqui and Finley stayed on their heels. Jacqui shouldn't have let Reid's daughter go into Denise's arms. Yes, Denise was Ella's mother, but Jacqui had been asked to watch her. Until Reid said differently, Ella was Jacqui's responsibility.

Denise was still a good ten feet away when she shrieked, "How dare you?" Her voice was so loud and shrill that people from all over the room turned to watch.

Jacqui figured such scenes weren't uncommon in the police station and wasn't surprised when most of the cops turned their attention back to their work without so much as raised eyebrows.

Reid stood. "She's okay. She wasn't hurt. She was just—"

"You!" Denise approached and stopped just a foot from him. "You accuse *me* of not keeping her safe. You nearly got her killed!"

"Calm down, Denise. It was a car accident. We were rear-ended."

They were rear-ended, but the *accident* part wasn't technically true. Jacqui wasn't about to say that.

Denise rounded on Jacqui and pointed at her. "Is this the one? Was this the target?"

Uh-oh. Apparently, someone had filled Denise in on all the details. Which was only fair. She was Ella's mother, after all. But by the tone of her voice, she wasn't entirely rational.

Jacqui could see why Reid didn't want this woman to have custody of Ella.

On the other hand, her daughter had almost been kidnapped—again. Maybe her behavior made sense.

Reid's face paled. His Adam's apple bobbed, and he nodded. "I would never let—"

"You put my daughter in danger!" Unlike Reid's skin, Denise's turned bright red. Her eyes bulged. She stepped closer to Reid and jabbed him in the chest. "You were driving the car of a woman whose life is in danger!"

"I didn't—"

"And you!" Denise rounded on Jacqui. "What are you, some kind of mobster or something? Some kind of redheaded Al Capone wannabe?"

Behind Jacqui, one of the police detectives snickered. If she hadn't been the target of Denise's attack, she might've laughed herself. Instead, her stomach clenched into knots. "I'm a scientist."

Denise straightened her shoulders, surprised by the answer but not backing down.

She turned back as if to attack Reid again, but Ella stopped her with a hand on her face.

"Mommy."

Jacqui couldn't see the girl's face, but she could hear the tears in her voice. "Please don't yell at Daddy and Miss Jacqui."

Denise's expression shifted from fury to something else, something closer to concern and grief, as if Ella's sweet words had poured cold water on her ire. She hugged her daughter close, tears leaking from her eyes. "I'm sorry, baby. You're right." To Reid, she said, "We'll talk about this later. You can bet your life a judge will hear about this."

Reid said nothing as Denise marched away, his daughter in her arms. As soon as she was out of sight, he collapsed in the chair and dropped his head into his hands.

Jacqui sat beside him. "She'll cool off." She placed her hand on his back.

He flinched away. When he looked up, he didn't even glance at her. To Klein, he said, "Do you need anything else from me?"

"You were describing—"

"I don't know!" The words came out too loud. When he lowered them, he sounded defeated. "A man and a woman. Their voices were muffled."

"Do you know how tall—?"

"I barely got a look at them. I was focused on Ella."

Klein blew out a long breath. "If you think of anything else..."

Reid was up and walking toward the elevator before Klein finished his statement.

Jacqui kept her seat. "Was this meant to be an attack on me?"

"It looks that way," he said. "Your car's been impounded. We'll have to keep it as evidence for now."

"Do you think it was Don?"

He shrugged. "Reid can't say for sure." He explained what happened when Reid glimpsed the two masked figures coming toward the car. *Oh, Reid.* What a terrifying moment that must have been.

"He was focused on protecting his daughter," Klein said, "not getting an ID."

"I can understand that."

"The SUV was found in a parking garage on Columbus Ave. It'd been stolen. We assume the drivers had another vehicle there, a getaway car. Someone's going to go over and look at their security footage and see if we can find the second one."

"What about fingerprints? There's got to be a way to figure out who they were."

"We're working on it. As soon as we find something, I'll let you know." He focused his attention above Jacqui. "You're keeping her safe?"

Finley said, "Doing my best, sir."

He leveled his gaze on Jacqui again. "I wish we could offer you some protection, but there's not enough manpower. Do me a favor? Make yourself scarce till we can catch these guys. Eventually, they're going to get their hands on you. And it seems they're not worried about how many people they hurt until they do."

The tears she'd been fighting filled her eyes. "You're right." The words came out tight. She should have left the city already. The artificial neuron, for all the good it might someday do, had already caused too much heartache. Reid and Ella could have been killed. Annie had been.

Meanwhile, Jacqui, the target of these monsters, remained unscathed.

She was putting those she loved in danger. The sooner she got out of Boston, the better.

If only she'd come to that conclusion before the attack.

If only she'd come to it before Annie's death.

She should have done so many things differently. If she had it to do over again...

There was no going back, but she would make better decisions going forward. She would do everything in her power to protect those she loved, even if it meant losing BNB, losing her reputation, and losing the neuron she'd invented.

The first thing, though, was to go to Reid and beg his forgiveness.

She thanked the detective and headed for the elevator to catch up with him. But by the time she and Finley got there, Reid was gone.

Jacqui raced down the stairs and spotted Reid as he crossed the glass-fronted foyer. "Reid!"

He must not have heard her, because he kept going.

She hurried across the space and grabbed his arm. "Hey, wait."

He spun, yanking his arm from her grip, clearly poised for a fight.

"It's just me," she said.

"I know."

Oh. He *had* heard her. He'd ignored her.

Now, he stared down at her, mouth pressed closed, hands fisted at his side.

"I'm so sorry this happened."

"Well, that changes everything. As long as you're sorry."

His sarcasm shocked her into silence.

"If you weren't so consumed with making sure your device went to exactly the right company, if you'd just accepted Intra-Heart's proposal, if you'd just learn to trust God with your device instead of feeling like you have to control every little—"

"Are you really accusing me of being faithless?"

"What would you call it?"

She'd call it cautious. She'd call it doing her homework.

But none of that was the point. She started to fire back a response but paused and took a breath. Reid was upset because he was afraid. She didn't want to make this worse than it already was.

But the truth was the truth. "I'm not the only faithless one in this conversation."

He crossed his arms. "What's that supposed to mean?"

"Denise is Ella's mother. She obviously loves her daughter. Maybe you should—"

"You just gave her ammunition to take my daughter away from me."

"What are you talking about?"

"She can claim that I put Ella in danger. That my poor judgment almost got her kidnapped. Again. Because I chose to associate with you."

Ammunition? Surely no judge would blame Reid for the attack. But Jacqui could see what he meant. He'd been in danger because he'd been driving Jacqui's car. Ella'd been a victim because she'd been in Jacqui's car.

"Obviously, I never meant for you or Ella to get hurt."

"People like you never do."

She absorbed the blow, breathed through the pain, and tried again. "Have you asked God about this? Are you following His lead in this custody issue, or are you—?"

"She's not fit to be a parent." The words were blasted like machine gun fire. "I know her better than anybody."

"No, you don't."

He gestured toward the ceiling, the upper floors. "You saw her up there. She's crazy. She's irrational."

Jacqui softened her tone and stepped closer. "And you're thinking clearly right now?"

He glared down at her. "I think I'm seeing this clearly for the first time in weeks." He spun and stalked away.

She watched his retreating back, frozen in place.

When he'd gone outside and disappeared from view, Finley approached and took her elbow. Only then did Jacqui notice the many people milling about in the glass-fronted space. "I can't protect you if you won't let me."

"We're in a police station," she snapped. "How much danger could I be in?"

"Do you really need me to answer that?"

Jacqui registered the kind look on the bodyguard's face. Finley was only trying to keep her safe, and Jacqui wasn't making her job easier. "You're right. I'm sorry."

She was ready to call for a Lyft, but Finley wasn't having it. They returned to Detective Klein and convinced him to get them a ride in a squad car back to the hotel. Jacqui texted Reid. *You want a lift?*

Walking.

On the way back, sitting on the wrong side of the bulletproof glass in the radio car, Jacqui stared at her phone, but it seemed Reid had nothing more to say.

When she was alone in her hotel room, trying not to think about Reid and Ella and Denise and the accident, Jacqui dialed Braden's phone. He sounded perfectly relaxed when he said, "Hey. What's up?"

"I'm not going to be at the conference tomorrow."

"What?" The tone shifted to concern. Maybe even anger. "Why?"

She didn't want to get into it, and though she didn't want to believe Braden was working against her, she couldn't be sure. "There's something I have to take care of."

"Are you leaving the city?"

"No, no." She hated to lie, but she wasn't sure Braden could be trusted. "I'm not going anywhere. I just can't make the conference. I might be around in the afternoon. It just depends how the morning goes." There. If he was working against her, he'd pass that information along, throw the bad guys off her tracks.

How had she gotten herself in this mess? How was she suspecting friends and fearing enemies?

How had she lost Reid?

Tears stung her eyes. She shook her head as if the sadness and despair could be shaken off.

"What about the meeting with IntraHeart?" Braden asked.

In the chaos of the afternoon, she'd forgotten about the meeting Mack had requested. She'd agreed to meet with them the following morning to discuss the lawsuit against them, her expectations, and their proposal.

Braden continued. "Mack gave me the rundown on what they're offering, and it sounds really good. I don't think you should let this opportunity pass."

She still would meet with them, but she'd have to give them a new location. She wouldn't be returning to Boston until she knew she was safe. "I'll take care of that."

Braden blew out a long breath. "Jacqui, isn't this why you're here? I mean, are you ever going to license the rights?"

She put confidence in her voice that she didn't feel. "That's not really your concern."

"Isn't it?" His volume rose. "You haven't even started rebuilding the lab. I want to get back to work. I want to do something besides bang out dents in my dad's shop. I've been patient, but—"

"You can get another job anytime you want." Her words came out harsher than she'd intended. She couldn't seem to soften them when she added, "Nobody forced you to keep working for me." The rest of their techs had moved on. It was just her and Braden now, and it sounded like Braden wouldn't be around much longer.

The thought of it had her slumping on her bed. She didn't want to lose her assistant.

She couldn't rebuild her business by herself. She didn't know if she even wanted to. What would be the point? To develop something that made her a target? At this rate, the neuron was never going to help anybody.

All Jacqui had gone through—which was nothing compared to Ella's trauma and Annie's death—it would be for nothing.

"I've been loyal to you," Braden said. "You promised me you were rebuilding, and I believed you. You think I haven't had better offers?"

"I'm sure you have. I'm trying to—"

"I turned them all down. But now?"

She waited through his long pause, afraid of what he'd say next.

"I liked working for you." His tone was even. "I didn't want to leave."

Jacqui didn't miss the past tense. Her throat closed up. She wasn't sure she could force words out even if she could think of what to say next.

Silence stretched between them. After a minute, Braden broke it with, "That's it? After everything, you have nothing to say?"

"There's more to this." Her voice was high and squeaky. She cleared her throat and tried again. "Someday, I hope I can explain everything."

"Yeah. Whatever."

Three quick beeps told her he'd disconnected.

Jacqui crawled farther up her bed and curled on her side, letting the tears fall.

Was she really crying over Braden? He was a nice man, a smart man. He'd been loyal, or so she believed. And she'd lost him.

She'd lost her business.

And she'd lost Reid.

All for the sake of an artificial neuron that, if Don had his way, would end up in the hands of a company bent on making sure it never did one bit of good.

CHAPTER TWENTY-THREE

Rage poured over Reid hotter than the humid June air. From the moment he'd realized that the accident wasn't an accident at all, the moment he'd known Jacqui was the target, he'd been furious.

He was walking—stomping, more like—down Huntington Avenue. He'd reached the hotel twenty minutes earlier, turned the corner, and headed away from it again. He wasn't ready to face her.

How dare she accuse him of not trusting God with Ella?

Sweat dripped into his eyes and down his back, but he didn't let up. He needed to move. To think.

Why had Jacqui loaned him her car?

Why, why hadn't she signed a contract already? If she'd just accepted IntraHeart's proposal, this would all be over. But Intra-Heart wasn't *good enough* for Jacqui. No, she was looking for the *perfect* company. As if all companies weren't run by human beings, flawed human beings trying to do their best.

Jacqui didn't understand how business worked. There was a reason she'd needed Don. Maybe Don hadn't steered her in the right direction with Tarim, but at least the man understood the world of enterprise.

Not Jacqui. Heck, if not for Reid, she'd still be doling out ice cream and wringing her hands in Coventry, trying to figure out her first step.

Instead, multiple companies were interested, all good companies. Martha and her public relations work had succeeded in turning the rumors against Jacqui around and creating buzz about the neuron. But none of the proposals they'd received were nearly as good as IntraHeart's.

None of the companies interested were as solid as the Cambridge firm.

Still, Jacqui waffled.

Why?

Did she *like* being in danger?

Did she *like* putting those she supposedly cared for in danger?

Or was she just that clueless? Was she so smart she was too stupid to take care of herself? Head-in-the-clouds research scientist and trust-fund kid who couldn't be bothered to worry about the people around her and the damage she was doing to them.

Reid was stepping off a curb to cross a side street when he caught sight of a car barreling toward him. Just in time, he stepped back, losing his balance and nearly falling, feeling the wind from the sedan as it passed, horn blaring.

His heart raced.

Whose head was in the clouds now?

He moved into the shade of a nearby building and leaned against the red brick. What was wrong with him?

His thoughts were out of control. He needed to get himself together. To think straight. But he didn't want to do that. Because when he did, he'd have to face the truth.

None of this was Jacqui's fault.

Jacqui had offered to loan him her car, but he'd taken her up on the offer.

He was the one who'd invited her to dinner, dinner with his precious child. He was the one who'd put Ella and Jacqui in the same orbit even though he knew Jacqui's life was in danger.

Protecting Ella was Reid's job, not Jacqui's.

Yes, if she'd accepted IntraHeart's proposal, then maybe the killers would back off. Maybe not, though. Until the attorney got the new partnership paperwork drawn up, Don would still inherit everything if Jacqui died. Myers was working on it, but he wouldn't have it completed until the next day. A Saturday.

They were all doing their best.

Reid forced a few deep breaths, savoring the slightly cooler air in the shade. He was hot and hungry and wrung out.

And scared. Almost as scared as he'd been when he got the call that Ella had been kidnapped. Because, thanks to his poor decisions, Ella had almost been snatched again.

He'd prevented it, but now Denise had ammunition to use against him.

If she pressed the issue, with her money and her lawyers, it was very likely she could convince a judge that Reid was the unfit parent.

Rather than facing the prospect of losing Ella for a few holidays and weeks in the summer, Reid might lose his baby girl for good. All because he'd failed to protect her. Again.

None of that was Jacqui's fault.

The words she'd spoken to him in that kind, reasonable voice penetrated now. He'd accused her of being faithless, but was he trusting God with Ella?

He wasn't. He couldn't. He'd trusted Him once, and she'd been kidnapped.

And rescued.

The truth was no more than a whisper in his soul.

God *had* protected Ella. Not the way Reid would have liked. If he'd had his druthers, his little girl would never have known that trauma, that terror.

But God could use it. Would use it.

Reid admitted He was already using it.

God promised to work everything for good for those who loved Him, and Ella surely loved her heavenly Father. At just six years old, her faith was strong, stronger than it would have been without the kidnapping.

He hated to admit that. Hated to admit that anything good had come out of that dreadful experience.

God hadn't protected Ella from the kidnapper. He'd let that terrible thing happen to her.

Denise wouldn't be a good custodial parent for their daughter. She was too selfish, too consumed with her career, her needs, her desires. She didn't really love their little girl, not like Reid did.

Right?

He thought back to the woman he'd seen in the police station earlier. She'd been irrational, no doubt. Angry. Furious, even. But in her eyes, he'd seen the truth.

She'd been terrified. Terrified for Ella.

He'd seen something else there, something he didn't want to admit. As fierce as the rage Denise had directed at him, the love she'd directed at their daughter was obvious.

She'd said God had forgiven her. How dare Reid have a higher standard?

At the police station, Denise had acted irrationally.

He thought back to the conversation with Jacqui, the things he'd said. Talk about irrational.

So maybe sometimes love made people irrational.

Maybe love did more than that. Maybe love changed people.

God's love surely did.

Reid's love for Ella had altered him forever.

Had Denise's love for Ella finally changed her?

He didn't know. God help him, he didn't want to know. He didn't want to lose his little girl. He didn't want to spend a single holiday, a single vacation day away from her.

But Denise was her mother. And if Reid was right, if Denise loved Ella, then she had a right to spend time with her.

Ella had a right to know her mother's love.

Still leaning against the cool brick building, Reid slid to the ground. He didn't want to do it. Everything in him raged against what he knew he had to do. But he bowed his head and whispered words that left a wound in his heart. "Ella is Your daughter first. I trust You. Do what's best for my little girl."

Please, please, just don't let me lose her.

CHAPTER TWENTY-FOUR

Jacqui had shifted from crying to praying after Braden hung up on her. For Reid and Ella, for Braden, and for wisdom. The more she prayed, the more confident she was that IntraHeart was the right home for her device.

When the phone rang, she snapped it up, hoping to see Reid's name. It was her mother.

"Guess who's flying to Boston tomorrow!"

Dread filled Jacqui's stomach like poison. Her initial reaction, a strongly worded *No!* was tempered just in time. "That's not a great idea, Mom."

But Mom didn't pick up on Jacqui's fear, just started chatting as if all were well. It seemed Dad had told Mom about the fire but not about Annie's death or that Jacqui's life was in danger. Jacqui wasn't about to worry her with that news either. They'd been discussing it for five minutes—Mom insisting, Jacqui trying to kindly put her off—when Reid's call came in. Much as she longed to hear what he had to say, she let it go to voice mail. "I appreciate the offer, Mom. I do. But I'd rather you not come."

Mom's laugh sounded forced. "Well, I guess I know where I stand."

"I want to see you, of course. But things are so busy. I wouldn't have any time to spend with you."

"I've already bought the ticket."

"My weekend is jam-packed with appointments."

"I need to do some shopping anyway. I can entertain myself." Mom's tone was so casual, so relaxed. Clearly, Jacqui was getting nowhere by being polite.

"What about Dad?" Obviously, Mom hadn't told Dad her plan to fly to Boston. If she had, surely he'd have talked her out of it. "Won't he miss you?"

"Your father's going to stay in New York for the weekend. There's another doctor who wants his opinion. I was thinking of going there to see him, but—"

"You should do that."

Mom sighed, and her voice was lower when she said, "Darling girl, after the fire... It must be upsetting. I feel like I should be there with you."

Jacqui hated to do it, but she had no choice. "I'm sorry, but I don't want you here right now."

The silence on the other end of the phone had Jacqui's eyes filling again. As if she hadn't cried enough that day.

"Well, then. That settles that."

The wounded tone in Mom's voice caused the tears to spill down Jacqui's cheeks despite the relief that coursed through her. She was careful to keep her tone even when she responded. "I'm sorry. It's just not a good time."

"That's fine. I guess you don't need me."

She wanted to argue. She needed her mother more than ever. She wanted to curl up at her mother's side and tell her everything. But she wouldn't put Mom in danger.

"I'll plan a trip to see you soon," Jacqui said. "I should be selling the rights to the neuron this weekend, so we can celebrate."

"All right." Mom seemed to be working to keep her words even. "I'll talk to you later."

Jacqui ended the call and pressed the phone to her chest. Mom would forgive her. When she knew everything, she'd forgive her.

But if the killer got to her, she'd never have the opportunity to make it right.

No, she couldn't think that way.

She sent a quick text to her father. *Mom was planning to come here, but I put her off. Probably hurt her feelings. Please invite her to NY and make her feel better.*

Dad didn't respond right away, not that he ever did. But he'd get the text and do as Jacqui asked. He wouldn't want Mom languishing at home, feelings hurt, all alone.

That taken care of, she listened to her voice mail. Reid was coming back, and he didn't sound angry. The first bit of good news since the car wreck. She knocked on the door between her room and the bodyguard's—Finley had moved into Reid's old room, and Reid had gotten one across the hall—and waited until it swung open.

"Everything all right?" Finley asked.

"Pack your things. Reid's going to be here in a little while. After I send him away, I want to go to my parents' house in Hingham."

Finley's head tilted to the side. Most of the day, she'd maintained the same passive and serious expression, but in that instant, Jacqui saw the women behind the suit and gun. "Reid's not coming?"

"No." Jacqui was going to send him back to Coventry. She'd asked enough of him and done enough damage. She wasn't willing to risk his life. He had a daughter who needed him.

Finley's tender expression faded. "We should go somewhere they can't find you. If you want to leave the hotel, let me look into a safe house."

Jacqui was longing for home. She wanted to crawl between the sheets of her old bed. She wanted to be surrounded by her childhood things. But it was only for one night. For one more night, she could handle anything.

"Fine. But I'd like to leave soon."

Finley was already dialing her phone as she headed back to her own room.

Jacqui closed the door between them and took the suitcase from her closet. She was in the middle of filling it with her clothes when someone knocked on her door.

"Don't get that." Finley was in the room and at the door in seconds, pistol in her right hand. She peeked through the peephole. She turned and whispered, "It's Reid."

"It's okay," Jacqui said.

With the safety bar closed, Finley cracked the door. "Anybody with you?"

"I'm alone."

"Anybody else in the hallway?"

A pause was followed by, "Nope."

The door closed, and Finley flipped back the safety bar and opened the door for Reid. She stepped out of the way.

He slipped inside, crossed the space to Jacqui, and pulled her close. "I'm so sorry." His words, filled with regret, had her tears spilling all over again.

"No, I'm sorry. If I'd just—"

Reid pressed his lips to hers, cutting her off. She felt so confused, so overwhelmed, that at first she didn't know how to respond. But her body took over when her brain stalled.

From somewhere about a million miles away, she heard Finley say, "I'll just be..." And the door closed between their rooms.

Reid's skin was warm, the heat pressing through the thin fabric of her blouse as he ran his hands over her back. She felt the urgency, almost desperation, in his kiss, as if he were drowning and she were his only chance for survival. His need was heady, feeding her own. Everything in her wanted to get lost in it, to get lost in him.

She had to stop. Had to stop this now, before it went too far.

She realized she was gripping his shoulders with the same intensity she'd felt from him. She opened her palms and slid them down his chest, then pressed.

Slowly, slowly he seemed to register what she was doing.

He stepped back. Breathing heavily, he took another step away. "I'm sorry. Again. For…" He shook his head. Looking at the carpet, he rubbed the back of his neck. "Man, I have a lot to apologize for. Maybe I should make a list." But when he looked up, his lips quirked. "Or maybe you're keeping one?"

"There's no list, Reid."

"It wasn't your fault," he said. "What happened with Ella—"

"I was the target."

"Ella's my responsibility, not yours. I shouldn't have taken your car. That was on me. I shouldn't have invited you to dinner. That was on me too. I just… I missed you. I wanted to see you."

He'd missed her? He'd been with the daughter he adored, but he'd *missed* Jacqui?

She'd missed him too. The afternoon had been dismal and difficult without him. Despite his occasional bouts of fear-induced anger, she liked this man. She more than liked this man.

And by the way he was looking at her, it was possible he more than liked her too.

He started toward the bed, then seemed to think better and pulled the chair from beneath the desk near the window. He sat and leaned his head back. "I think I'm melting."

"It's hot out there."

He leveled his gaze at her. "It's hot in here."

She popped her blouse away from her skin a few times, desperate for a breeze or an overhead fan. It *was* hot in there, despite the machine blowing chilled air from the ceiling.

He leaned forward and rested his forearms on his knees. "You forgive me?"

"You were upset."

"I shouldn't have taken it out on you."

True. Rather than make light of it, she said, "Of course. Do you forgive me?"

"Nothing to forgive. You're doing your best."

She lifted her shoulders and let them fall. "You're right,

though. I've spent a lot more time researching companies than I've spent praying for God's guidance." She sat on the end of the bed to face him. "I rectified that in the last hour."

"Oh, yeah? And?"

"We've had a lot of requests for more information and a few proposals, but, after praying about it, I've decided to accept Intra-Heart's proposal. Their offer is more than I had hoped, their plans seem viable, and their reputation is excellent. They have the know-how to use the neuron in multiple different devices. I feel strongly that's where the Lord wants the neuron."

He sat back, eyes wide. "Just like that?"

"Not 'just like that.' We did our research. They're the company I've wanted from the start."

"What about the lawsuit?"

"You were right about that. According to Mack, it's frivolous. The guy was under the influence of painkillers when he fell. The injury wasn't due to any fault in the device. They were going to show me evidence tomorrow, but"—she flipped a hand between them—"I don't need to see it. Mack wouldn't lie to me."

Reid's slow smile spread, alleviating, just a little, the worry that she'd seen etched on his brow. "When will it be finalized?"

"We're supposed to meet tomorrow to discuss it, but their proposal covered everything. I'm hoping they can have the contract ready to send to the IP attorney at the firm. I have a few calls to make to get everything set up, but I don't think it'll be a problem."

"Even though it's Saturday?"

"The attorney will be glad for the overtime hours. I think Intra-Heart will be eager to get it finalized. I just want this whole mess behind me."

"Have you heard from Myers?"

"He's going to have the new partnership paperwork ready by tomorrow too."

"So, it's almost over."

"Almost."

Reid's smile broadened, though the hint of worry lingered in his eyes. Not for her, she guessed, but for Ella and all that still needed to be resolved there. "We should celebrate."

"The thing is—"

"Let's stay here where it's safe. We'll order in."

She shook her head. She was feeling a lot of things right then, some of which she didn't have a name for, but *safe* wasn't on the list. "I've decided to go to a safe house for the night. Finley's setting it up. Since the accident was right outside the hotel, whoever hit you must know where we're staying. I just want to get out of here, away from all of it."

Reid was nodding slowly. "That sounds like a good plan. I'll get my—"

"You're not coming."

He sat back as if she'd struck him. "What? Why not?"

She swallowed the words that wanted out. The words begging him to stay with her. "You've done enough. Finley's taking good care of me. When this is all over—"

"No." He launched to his feet. "I'm staying with you. One more night. I promise I won't"—he pointed from himself to her and back—"it won't happen again. I'll keep my hands—"

"I trust you, Reid."

"Then let me come with you."

As if he hadn't spoken, she said, "Since my car's been impounded, you'll need to rent a car to get back to Coventry. Of course, BNB will pay for it."

He swallowed hard. "Don't do this, Jacqui. I need to stay with you, to make sure you're safe."

She tried to sound confident when she said, "I want to be alone."

His eyes narrowed as he studied her. "You're a terrible liar."

"I have a date."

"Sure you do." He pulled her from her seat on the bed and held her hands. "What's going on, really?"

"My mom wanted to come up. I told her I didn't want her here."

"You're trying to protect her."

Jacqui nodded, not trusting her voice.

"You're trying to protect me."

"You've got a little girl who needs you."

"The safe house should be... *safe,* right?"

"It should, but—"

"Then let me come. Let me be there to look over the paperwork with you. Let me be there when you sign the new partnership contract. I want to be a part of it." He lifted her hands to his chest, and she felt his beating heart beneath them. "Part of all of it—even the hard things. I want to be with you."

Jacqui fought the temptation to give in. The last thing she wanted was to send Reid away, to spend the evening alone in a strange place with only her intense bodyguard for company.

She stared out the window and let herself imagine the worst. Reid, dead, because of her. Ella, fatherless, because of her.

Reid stood behind her. "Please, Jacqui. I need to be sure you're safe."

Before she responded, a knock sounded on her door.

Finley pushed in from the adjoining room and approached it, gun drawn. She peeked through the hole. "It's the detective."

Klein was there? What could possibly have happened? Jacqui's stomach twisted. She stood beside Reid, took his hand, and nodded to Finley, who swung the door open.

The detective stepped in wearing a wide smile. "Good news."

"Come on in." Jacqui nodded to the desk chair, and he flipped it and sat in it backwards.

Finley stood nearby, against the wall, as if the detective might be a threat.

Reid said, "What happened?" Jacqui heard wariness in his voice, the same that she felt. As if they were both afraid to hope.

"I wanted to tell you in person. I just heard from the homicide detective. They were able to get a fingerprint from the window jamb at your house, the one that had been left open."

"And?"

"It was Don Burgess's. They brought him in this afternoon, and he confessed."

"Confessed to what exactly?" Jacqui asked.

"Everything," Klein said.

Jacqui sat heavily on the bed. Reid stood at her side and squeezed her hand.

"The fire," Klein said. "The destruction of your lab. Even today's attempted kidnapping."

Reid shifted beside her, and Jacqui looked up to see his expression. He seemed almost confused.

"What's wrong?" she asked.

"I wasn't convinced it was him."

She was about to respond, but Klein said, "You said you didn't get a good look at him."

"Yeah. But the voice—"

"Maybe he was disguising it in case you recognized it," Klein said. "Anyway, why would he confess if he hadn't done it?"

"Good point." Reid's confused expression melted away.

Klein wasn't finished. "His facts line up. He knew details about the break-in at your lab. He knew about the two separate fires at your brownstone. He knew about today's kidnapping attempt and gave us the name of his accomplice, a woman he'd hired for the job, along with her description. He says she took off after they left the scene. She must've given him a fake name because there's no record of her, but we're shaking all the trees. We'll find her."

"I can't believe he really did all those things." As convinced as Jacqui had been that Don was guilty, she found herself dumbfounded to receive confirmation. "I can't believe he tried to murder me."

Reid squeezed her hand but spoke to Klein. "Do you know why he confessed?"

"He said when he saw the child in the car, he realized what he'd done, all for money. He was racked with guilt."

"Wow."

Reid sat beside her and pulled her against his side. "It's over."

She was almost afraid to believe it.

But the easygoing expression on Klein's face convinced her. If the detective could relax, she could too.

"Only thing is," Klein said, "we're keeping the news under wraps until we have his accomplice in custody. So keep it to yourself."

"Sure, of course," she said. "Hardly anybody knew what was going on anyway. Can I tell my dad?"

"Just warn him not to broadcast it." The detective stood, and they did the same.

Jacqui shook his hand. "Thank you so much for everything you did. I'm sure Annie's family will be glad to know her killer's been caught."

"The homicide detectives were headed to their hotel. It won't bring her back." He shrugged, a little of his joy leaching away. "But at least justice will be done."

At the end of the day, a woman had died, and nothing they did would change that.

Jacqui and Reid walked Klein to the door, promising to be available for whatever he or the prosecution needed from them.

By the time he left, Finley had her suitcase packed and was standing in the door between their adjoining rooms. "I assume you no longer need me."

Jacqui could hardly believe it was over, and so abruptly. "Thank you for keeping me safe. Sorry I made it so difficult."

A smile spread across the woman's face. "I've had difficult clients before. Compared to them, you were a piece of cake." She winked, bid Reid good-bye, and left.

Just like that.

A second after the door closed behind her, Reid whooped, lifting Jacqui and spinning her around.

She laughed. "Put me down, you nutcase."

He did but didn't let go. "Thank God. Thank God."

"I know. I can't believe—"

But he cut off her words with a kiss.

CHAPTER TWENTY-FIVE

While Jacqui got ready to go to dinner, Reid returned to his hotel room, took a quick shower, and called Denise. After her curt greeting, he said, "I'm sorry for what happened today. You're right to blame me. It never occurred to me that the guy would target Jacqui's car, especially when she wasn't even in it." He neglected to mention that he'd been about to pick her up. No need to add to Denise's ammunition against him.

He braced himself for Denise's wrath, but once again, she surprised him.

"I know that." Her voice was calm and steady. "You're the most protective man I know. Do you realize that Ella doesn't even know what happened? She said there was an accident, and then you jumped in the backseat and held her tightly until the police got there. How did you even get your long body over the seat?"

He thought back. One second, he'd been behind the wheel. The next, he'd been in the backseat. "I have no idea. I just jumped, I guess." The memory of it had him choking up, and he swallowed the emotion. "I wasn't going to let her go, not for anything. They'd have had to kill me to get to her. I was just praying the police would get there—or a bystander, or somebody—to stop them before they could take her."

His honest answer was met by a long moment of silence. Finally, Denise said, "You shouldn't have been in that woman's car, knowing her life was in danger."

"I know. You're right. Like I said—"

"Please let me finish. My point is that you're not a perfect parent. You're going to make mistakes sometimes."

"I know th—"

"Reid."

"Sorry." He clamped his lips together.

She sighed. "You're a great father, but you're not perfect. I'm nowhere near as good at parenting as you are. You've had a lot more practice. But I want..." She sniffed. "I love her, Reid. I know I'm late to the party. I know you've known what an amazing person she is since the moment she was born. I didn't get it. I didn't, but I do now. The more time I spend with her, the more I love her."

He squeezed his eyes shut and said nothing. What could he say? One of his worst nightmares was coming true.

But what felt like a nightmare to him would be a blessing for Ella. Jacqui was right about that. Ella deserved to know her mother. She needed a mother's love. Who was Reid to deprive her of that?

Who was he to deprive Denise of the child she'd carried? The child who shared her smile, her joy for life, her love of people.

Denise had made a lot of mistakes, but she was trying to do the right thing now. Who was he to deny her?

"I'm glad," Reid said. "I'm glad you love her." He found, as the words left his mouth, that he meant them. "I want you two to have a relationship, a good relationship."

"That can only happen if we spend time together."

"I know that." He prayed for wisdom and words. "We can figure this out. You and me. We can figure out how to make this work for us and for Ella."

"You're not going to fight me?"

"No." But he chuckled. "I mean, I'll try really, really hard not to be too possessive of her."

Denise laughed. "I guess that's the best I can hope for right now. And I'll try just as hard to be a great mother, to make up for all I've done wrong."

"There's no way." He shook his head and started over. "What's done is done, Denise. Don't try to make up for it. Just be the best mother you can from this point forward. Ella has an amazing, beautiful heart. When you two start spending time together regularly, the relationship will come. You'll both be better for it."

"What about you?"

He closed his eyes and considered his darling girl. And then he thought about the beautiful woman who'd be joining him for dinner. And the all-knowing, all-loving God who'd brought them this far. "Don't worry about me. I'm going to be just fine."

REID HELD Jacqui's hand as they exited the North End restaurant. The Italian food had been the best he'd ever eaten. And maybe that feeling was influenced by the woman he'd shared it with. They walked alongside old buildings, some of which had been there for hundreds of years. Thanks to the many authentic Italian restaurants, the area was a popular spot for tourists and locals alike, and crowds were gathered outside most of the eateries along the road. The largest crowd loomed ahead. When Reid read the sign—*Mike's Pastry*—he wasn't surprised. Even he'd heard of Mike's. "You need a cannoli?"

Jacqui looked up at him, eyes wide. "You're kidding, right? After that meal?"

He shrugged, and she laughed.

"You're a bottomless pit."

He patted his stomach. "I'm a growing boy."

"I don't mind stopping, if you want."

"Nah. I'm good." He could practically taste the famous cream-filled pastries, but there was no sense waiting in line if Jacqui didn't want one.

For the first time since their first date—had it just been ten days prior?—they'd enjoyed a meal without the worry of her business and the threats looming over her.

And even though he knew he would be losing time with Ella, he felt at peace about the conversation he'd had with Denise. He didn't want to share his daughter, but she didn't belong to him. She had a right to know her mother. Maybe, if Reid could learn to treat his ex-wife well, make her feel like he was a friend, she'd buy a place in Coventry. Maybe it wouldn't always be so bad.

He'd have to learn to let go a little. Before he'd met Jacqui, his world had become consumed with Ella. He loved it, truly he did. But it wouldn't hurt him to have a life apart from his daughter. It might even be healthy.

He really hoped some of that life would include Jacqui.

"I suppose we ought to call for a ride," he said.

"I'm in no hurry to get back, unless you are."

Not even a little. "Where shall we go then?"

"It's such a pretty night. Let's walk to the harbor."

Though the faint whiff of the breeze hinted at the ocean, he had no idea which direction to walk. "Can you get us there from here?"

By way of answer, she tugged his hand.

They weaved along narrow streets and within a few minutes, had left the crowds behind. Cars and SUVs lined the narrow one-way street on both sides. Aside from a group of people laughing and joking as they walked about a block ahead, he and Jacqui were alone. At the next corner, the group turned, leaving nothing but peace in their wake.

She bumped his shoulder. "It's so nice, isn't it, just being together?"

"I was thinking the same thing. You and I haven't had much time to enjoy each other without former partners and ex-wives looming over us."

"Maybe it'll be boring." Her voice held a hint of humor.

"Here's hoping."

She laughed. "I just hope you don't find *me* boring."

He stopped and faced her. "You're kidding, right?"

Her shy smile was accompanied by a shrug. "I'm really quite dull. I usually have my face staring at a screen or some component that I'm working on, or running labs, or—"

He silenced her with a kiss. He'd meant it to be a quick one, but sparks ignited, and he didn't want to stop. After a minute, he broke away and pulled her against him. "As long as you always bring those lips, I'll never be bored."

She rested her cheek against his chest. "That sounds like a deal. Of course, there's still the matter of—"

"Let's not." He backed up to see her face, noting the lowered brows, the downturned mouth. "I understand the problems. I don't want to think about that tonight. For tonight, let's just enjoy each other. Let's trust God to work the rest out."

The easygoing expression returned. "Fair enough."

He took her hand, and they resumed their walk.

They were nearly to the corner when a van careened around the corner and stopped right beside them.

Two people jumped out.

Both wearing masks.

Reid pushed Jacqui behind him. But in that split second, one hit him in the stomach with something hard.

He doubled, wanting to scream at her to run but unable to get a breath.

A man wrapped his arms around Jacqui's middle and dragged her toward the van.

Behind Reid, the other person pressed something hard and cold to his temple.

Jacqui screamed. "Don't! Please, don't! I'll give you whatever you—"

"Shut up." The man punched her in the back, and she fell forward onto the floor of the cargo van.

Reid was afraid to move, afraid to flinch.

Looking over Reid's head, the man said, "Shoot him."

A pause, then a woman said, "Someone'll hear. We should—"

"Fine. Bring him." The man shoved Jacqui deeper into the van like a sack of garbage.

The hard thing that had been pressed to Reid's head now jabbed into his back. "Hurry before he changes his mind."

Reid scrambled in behind Jacqui. He was crawling toward her at the very back when pain exploded across his scalp. The pain receded as his vision closed in. Against his will, he collapsed, and everything went black.

CHAPTER TWENTY-SIX

The chill of the concrete floor seeped through her thin sundress and numbed her backside.

Propped against a wall a few feet away, Reid shifted and moaned in his sleep. Their abductor had hit him hard with the butt of his gun. Of course, he'd wanted his partner to shoot Reid, so it wasn't as if he'd been worried about causing a traumatic brain injury. Thank God, Reid had regained consciousness within a few moments of the blow, but he'd been fighting a killer headache ever since.

Jacqui had insisted he close his eyes and try to rest. In any other circumstance, she doubted Reid would be able to, but the injury had made it hard for him to focus.

She longed to join him, to slip into oblivion for just a few moments. But the cold and fear kept her eyes from drifting shut.

They hadn't been in the van for long, maybe twenty minutes after they'd been grabbed, and by the scent of salt water she'd picked up on the walk between the van and the door, they hadn't gone far from the harbor. She'd had a bag thrown over her head before she was manhandled from the van into some sort of cavernous space—based on the echo of their footsteps—and down a steep staircase. She'd been terrified she and Reid were being separated, so when the hood had been pulled off her head and she'd seen him, groggy but alive, she'd nearly wept with relief.

The feeling hadn't lasted.

They were in a windowless room, maybe an old storage area, in a basement. The only light came from the cracked door. The light beyond it wasn't impressive, either. Maybe a lantern or two? She didn't know what kind of building this was, but she guessed maybe it used to be a seafood processing plant. It was empty of people and equipment, so all that remained of whatever had been there was the stench of dead fish.

She sat in the middle of the room, her wrists attached to a wooden post behind her back.

Reid was catty-corner to her just a few feet away, bound to some kind of pipe.

She could see nothing that might help free them. No stray knives lying around. No sharp edges to cut through the thick plastic zip ties. And even if they could get themselves free, their abductors were right outside the door, both armed, one clearly unconcerned about committing murder.

Who were these people? Don had confessed to the fire and the abduction attempt. Was the woman the one he'd hired? If so, who was the man? And why did it seem like the man was in charge?

And why would Don confess and then have others go ahead with his plans? What could he possibly hope to gain? He had to know he wouldn't inherit anything if he were in prison. If Jacqui died, her parents would fight Don for her shares of BNB, and from prison, he would surely lose.

But if Don wasn't behind this attack, who was?

Tarim? Was the company so corrupt that they'd sink to murder in order to protect their profits? The kidnappers weren't Asian—Jacqui could tell that even though they wore ski masks—but there was no reason Tarim couldn't have hired locals to do their dirty work.

If that were the case, had Don been working for them until his guilt compelled him to confess? If so, why wouldn't he have told the police about Tarim's part in what happened?

No matter how many different ways she looked at it, she couldn't make any sense of it.

Whether she understood what was happening or not was irrelevant, really. She and Reid were trapped, and nobody knew it. Jacqui had dismissed Finley. Mom wouldn't be calling anytime soon, not after their awkward conversation earlier. Jacqui had told her dad that Don confessed, so he would assume she was safe. Ella and Denise were probably headed back to California already, not that Denise would be concerned about Reid. By the time anybody realized Jacqui and Reid were missing, it would be too late.

God knew where they were. God knew, and He cared. He would rescue them.

She had to believe that. Shivering in the cold storage room, alone but for Reid's occasional moans, she had never prayed harder.

She didn't know how long they'd been trapped when Reid pushed himself to a sitting position. He reached out with his foot and nudged hers.

"You should rest," she said.

Shaking his head, he glanced out the door. She couldn't see the two abductors out there, but she could hear the murmur of their voices.

"You all right?" Reid whispered. "Did they hurt you?"

"Not really." Her back ached from where the man had punched her, but it was tolerable. It was nothing compared to how Reid must feel. "How's your head?"

"Better." He looked again at the door. "How long's it been?"

"A couple of hours."

"What are they doing?"

She shrugged, but he wouldn't see the movement in the darkness. "Just talking. I can only make out the words when they raise their voices."

"Any idea their endgame?"

"They haven't said anything to me, just told me that nobody would hear me if I screamed. Which is probably true. The place feels deserted."

He stretched his neck. "I don't remember much. I don't know how we got down here."

"I don't know if he carried you or what. They had a hood over my head."

Even in the darkness, she could feel Reid's regard. "You must have been terrified."

"More scared for you, and scared we'd be separated. The man..." She could still see the gun pressed against Reid's temple, hear the man's command that his partner shoot. Thank God she hadn't.

Why he hadn't done the deed himself, Jacqui didn't know. Maybe he'd changed his mind. Maybe he'd feared somebody would hear and see them getting away.

Whatever the man's reasoning, it was clear to Jacqui that God had intervened. He must have a plan to rescue them.

Reid dragged his legs over the floor, obviously trying to find something that could free them, but he had just as much luck as she'd had doing the same thing. He tugged on the pipe he'd been secured to. It held fast, and he muttered something under his breath. Then, he shifted to his feet and stood, sliding up the pipe slowly. It rose all the way to the ceiling, which revealed more exposed pipes, ducts, and wires.

He was half-standing when he stopped. "It's rough here. Maybe I can..." He didn't finish the thought but scraped the zip tie up and down on the pipe. Could he possibly get free?

If he did, what then?

She'd done the same earlier, hoping the wooden post might be rough enough to cut through her tie, but no luck.

Voices rose from the other room. Then, the stomping of footsteps faded.

Quieter footsteps grew closer, and Reid plopped himself back down on the concrete and slumped as if half awake.

The female captor stepped inside. She wore a ski mask, but her brown frizzy hair poked out the bottom. "You two all right in here?"

"Reid is hurt," Jacqui said. "He needs to see a doctor."

The woman's head shook fast. "I could find some aspirin or something."

She obviously wasn't the madman her partner was. Maybe she could be persuaded to help them. "That would be very kind of you. And some water. It's important to stay hydrated after a head injury."

"Yeah, he hit him too hard. Sorry about that."

The woman's accent was more South Shore than inner city, more John F. Kennedy than *Good Will Hunting*. Was she educated, even wealthy?

Realization hit Jacqui, and she lowered her gaze to the floor for fear the woman would see recognition in her gaze.

Jacqui knew exactly who these people were. How should she handle it, though? Say something? Keep it to herself? *Lord?* No sooner had the prayer left her mind than words popped out of her mouth.

"It's Kelly, right?" Jacqui'd heard so much about Kelly and Kirk, Don's kids, but in all the years she'd known Don, in all the time she'd spent with him and Lola, she hadn't met them until the funeral, and even then, she'd hardly done more than offer her condolences.

But now that she'd put it together, there was no doubt in her mind.

And the way Kelly angled back, eyes wide behind the mask, told Jacqui she was right.

"I remember you from your mother's funeral." Jacqui kept her tone comforting. "She was an amazing person. I loved her like my own grandmother."

By the way Kelly shot a look behind her, it was clear she was nervous.

Why?

"You need to keep quiet," she hissed. "If he figures out you know who we are—"

"It's Kirk, right? Your brother?"

Her voice lowered. "He's dangerous."

Jacqui held her eye contact. "I understand, Kelly. From the very beginning, it's been clear you're only doing this because he's making you. I don't know if he's holding something over your head, or if—"

"Shut up." Kelly shot a look at Reid and backed toward the door.

"Please bring the aspirin," Jacqui said, her voice as relaxed as if she were requesting an extra napkin at a restaurant. She didn't know how she could sound so calm when everything inside her was trembling with fear. "If you don't mind."

Kelly nodded once and went out the door. Jacqui hoped the woman would come right back and prayed for the words to say when she did.

From the side, Reid said, "Don's kids?"

Jacqui whispered, "I wonder if they know Don confessed."

Reid moved back to a crouch, found the spot on the pipe, and started sawing away again. Maybe he'd be able to get his hands free.

Maybe Kelly would help them.

Maybe, maybe there was hope.

BEFORE KELLY RETURNED, Kirk's voice carried through the open door. "What are you, sick or something?"

Kelly's voice was quieter, and Jacqui couldn't discern the words.

"I told you to stay out of there."

"He's hurt," Kelly said, voice high and trembling. "I just thought—"

"Don't think. Just do as I say." His voice lowered, and Jacqui couldn't pick up anything else.

So much for Reid's aspirin.

Reid had plopped back on his bottom at the sound of their voices and now met her eyes. "The headache isn't that bad," he whispered.

Perhaps not, but Jacqui had hoped to get Kelly alone again. "Are you having any luck?"

A slight shrug. "No way to know."

He probably wouldn't be able to cut through the thick zip tie in time, but it gave him something to do.

Footsteps announced someone was coming seconds before the door pushed open.

Reid barely had time to plop down on the floor as Kirk stomped in. He crouched in front of Jacqui. "Where's the neuron?"

She'd been surprised the question hadn't come earlier. Now, she answered honestly. "In a safe deposit box at my bank."

He moved closer until his face was just inches from hers, the ski mask not nearly as frightening as his coal-black eyes. "You telling me the truth?"

"I'll give it to you if you let my friend go."

Reid said, "Jacqui, don't."

But she ignored him, focusing on the man in front of her.

Through the tiny hole, she saw Kirk's lips stretch, revealing straight white teeth. "You'll give it to me. One way or another."

He stood up and peered down at her. "The research? Everything a company will need to develop it?"

"It's all with the neuron."

"What bank?"

She told him, and he swiveled and marched out, leaving the door wide open. He shouted the name of the bank. "See if she's got a box there."

Kelly said, "It's not that easy. I've gotta—"

"Shut up and get started. We need to know she's not pulling our chain."

Reid scrambled up to work the zip tie again. "How can Kelly find that out?"

"Remember I told you Don's kids had been in some trouble? In Kelly's case, she's a hacker, a pretty good one. One of her exes got her to hack into an online retailer and steal personal information. She ended up turning him in and only had to serve a little time for it."

"Talented woman," Reid said.

"The brother's the real problem in the family. Don never said much about him, but I had the feeling his legal troubles were related to violence—spousal abuse, assault and battery. That sort of thing."

"I'm shocked. He seems like a big teddy bear."

Even now, Reid could get her to smile.

Jacqui considered the situation from multiple angles. She knew who they were. If Kirk found out, he'd kill them for sure. But Jacqui doubted Kirk had ever intended to let them live.

The masks said differently, though. Why bother with masks if she and Reid weren't going to survive to tell the tale?

Maybe Kirk hadn't shared that part of the plan with Kelly yet. The masks were for her benefit.

Both brother and sister were quiet in the other room.

Aside from the gentle scraping sound as Reid worked the zip tie against the pipe, it was quiet.

Jacqui guessed it was four or five in the morning. The bank wouldn't open for hours. And when it did, what would happen? Jacqui would need to retrieve the items from the safe deposit box in person.

Reid would be the incentive they'd use to make sure she did what she was told. She'd give up the neuron and all her research to keep him alive. Ella needed him. If Jacqui was the reason he lost his life, she'd always blame herself.

But *always* wouldn't be a very long time, because once Kirk and Kelly had what they needed, Jacqui and Reid would both be dead.

CHAPTER TWENTY-SEVEN

In the dim light coming from the other room, Reid could clearly see the determination on Jacqui's face. She wasn't giving up.

Reid wouldn't either. He'd fight to the death. There was no way he was going to roll over and die. He knocked softly on the wall behind him, and Jacqui looked his direction.

"I'm impressed."

She blinked, confused.

"You're so strong, so fearless."

Her shoulders slumped. "I'm trying."

"That's all we can do. That and pray."

Jacqui's was the clearest, brightest mind he'd ever known. Maybe she'd come up with some way of escape.

She bowed her head. A moment later, he heard her muttering, praying. Maybe as she sought the Lord, God would give both of them some idea what to do.

Because this wasn't working.

He quit running the zip tie along the pipe. He couldn't check his work, but it didn't seem as if all that scraping had done anything but exhaust him. Thanks to his half-up, half-down position, his legs ached. And yet after all he'd done, he felt no indentation in the plastic. It slid no differently as it scraped over the rough spot than it had when he'd begun. There had to be another way to get free. There had to be, because Reid wasn't going to die there, and he sure as heck wasn't going to let Jacqui die there.

He sat and then slid his arms further down the pipe. It turned at the floor, and he scooted along with it, following it to the corner.

As he moved to the back of the room, with the door cracked wider and more light flooding the room, he was able to make out an old, rusted machine on the wall behind Jacqui. Maybe the pipe went all the way there. In the shadows, it was impossible to tell.

He kept scooting, praying neither Kelly nor her brother would come in.

He was nearly to the corner when Jacqui whispered, barely audibly, "We need to tell Kelly about Don's confession."

Reid stopped, considered the point. "Why?"

"She's scared. If we can get her alone, we can convince her they're going to get caught, no matter what they do. Then maybe she'll help us."

It was a good idea, but they needed to think it through from all angles. "What makes you think so?"

"I think I know what happened. Don unlocked the window at my house, but I'm betting he didn't climb through it himself and set that fire. I'm betting Kirk did that. You saw Don yesterday. He was genuinely distressed about Annie's death. Even after everything, I can't believe he would have tried to kill me. No, I think Don wanted Kirk to find the neuron and the research, and so he unlocked the window for him. I think the fire was all Kirk's idea. But when Don was arrested, he had to either confess or tell the police his son was guilty of murder. Rather than send his son to prison—"

"He confessed."

"Exactly. And I'm thinking that Kirk believes the police will think Don did this. They won't be able to prove it, but they'll believe it was Don, just like with the fire. Kirk figures Don'll never rat him out, and he'll never even be a suspect."

Reid reached the machine and followed the pipe to where it connected. "But with Don in jail—"

"The police aren't stupid. They're going to figure out Don's confession wasn't authentic, and when they do—"

"Who else would a person go to prison for but a loved one? His own son."

"Exactly."

Reid found where the pipe connected to the machine. There was a bolt there, and it felt grainy, maybe rusty. If he could just…

Footsteps warned him someone was coming. As fast as he could, he scooted back to the corner, turned, and was almost back to his spot when Kirk stepped inside. He stared at Reid a long moment. It was as if he knew something wasn't right, but he couldn't quite make out what.

Reid stared back.

After a minute, Kirk focused on Jacqui. "Looks like you were telling the truth about your safe deposit box."

Jacqui said nothing.

"You have the key?"

"You should, seeing as how you took my things."

Kirk stomped out, yelling, "Check her purse!"

Reid returned to where he'd been at the start.

A minute later, Kirk walked to the room and dangled a set of keys an inch from Jacqui's face. "Which one is it?"

"If you'll back up a little, I'll try to see."

The man grumbled but pulled his hand away.

"Why don't you set them down on the floor and fan them out?" she suggested, her tone calm, almost to the degree that she sounded like a teacher attempting to reason with a foolhardy pupil.

His back to the door, Kirk crouched and laid the keys out on the floor.

"And now, if you'll just get out of my light."

He huffed but, still crouched, scooted to one side so the light from the door fell on the keys.

Jacqui studied them. "Third from the right."

Kirk lifted it, and the other keys and keychain dangled below his grip. "This is it?"

"It is."

"What else will you need to get into your box?"

"My driver's license. And I'll need to sign something at the counter before they let me back."

"Will I be able to go in with you?"

"I have no idea. I've never attempted to take another person with me."

Kirk turned his attention to Reid. "How about you? You ever try to take someone with you to view a safe deposit box?"

"Can't help you."

The man glared at him, then at Jacqui. Finally, he rocked back on his heels and stood. "Bank lobby opens at eight." And he marched to the door.

"Excuse me," Jacqui said. "I need to use a restroom."

He snickered. "Suffer."

"If I don't use a rest room, I'm going to lose control of my bladder. And if I do that, I'm going to get a lot of raised eyebrows at the bank. Even if they can't see a urine stain, they'll surely be able to smell it. The last thing we want is to garner extra scrutiny."

"Yeah. I'm so sure that's your worry."

"I assume my friend's life will be in danger until I give you what you want, correct?" When he didn't argue, she continued. "So yes, it is my worry. I'm trying to do everything I can to protect him."

The man's gaze shifted from Jacqui to Reid. "Must be nice having her put herself on the line for you like that. Nothing a guy likes more than being rescued by a woman."

Kirk wasn't wrong, but Reid didn't rise to the bait, just held his eye contact.

"Fine, I'll take you," Kirk said.

Reid almost argued, but Jacqui beat him to it.

"I'd feel more comfortable if the woman took me. You understand."

"You understand I don't give a rat's backside what makes you comfortable."

Jacqui stared at him, not backing down. After a minute, Kirk shrugged. "Don't matter to me. You try to escape, I'll shoot your friend in the head." He turned toward the door, calling, "Hey, get over here!" on his way out.

Jacqui shot Reid a look. He dared not say a word with Kirk so close to the door, but he tried to project confidence in his expression.

Maybe Jacqui could convince Kelly to help them.

If not, Reid was going to have to figure out how to get free, or they were both going to die.

CHAPTER TWENTY-EIGHT

At least an hour passed before Kirk cut the zip tie connecting Jacqui to the post. He left those that kept her hands together. Before he took her from the room, he dropped the black hood over her head again.

Kelly took her arm. "This way. Don't give me trouble, okay? Your best chance to get out of this is to just do what he tells you."

Jacqui walked beside her up the stairs and onto the first floor. It was warmer up there, the air damp. When she'd come through the night before, this cavernous space had been dark, but now light filtered through the hood. She couldn't make out anything and wasn't sure if that was because the room was empty or because the fabric was too thick. But natural light meant windows. The scent of fresh air encouraged her further. Somewhere, something was open to the outside. If they got away and couldn't get to the door, they could always go out a window.

She believed God was going to save them, one way or another. Maybe Kelly would be a part of His plan.

Jacqui couldn't say anything about Don, though, until she was sure they were alone. For all she knew, Kirk was creeping along behind them.

She heard the creak of a door and was gently pushed into a darker room.

"Can you please take off this hood so I can see?" Jacqui asked.

"He doesn't want me to."

"I won't tell if you don't."

There was a long pause, and then the hood was snapped off her head. The only light in the bathroom came from the open door, but the little Jacqui could make out was rather disgusting. It had a toilet and sink and stunk as if it hadn't been cleaned in months. Maybe years.

"The plumbing doesn't work," Kelly said, "but you can use the toilet. Better than going in your dress, right?"

She lifted her hands behind her back. "Any chance you can cut that?"

Before Jacqui could react, her dress was lifted and her panties pulled down. The woman said, "Sorry. Sorta intimate, but—"

"Better than going in my dress," Jacqui supplied. She bunched the skirt in her hands and hovered over the toilet and managed to make it work. Asking to go to the bathroom had been a ploy to get Kelly alone.

But also, a ploy to empty her bladder.

When Jacqui was finished and dressed again, Kelly lifted the hood to drop over her head.

"Are you aware that your father is in jail?"

Kelly's arm fell to her side, the hood with it. "What?"

"He confessed yesterday. To the break-in at our lab, to the fire, to my house sitter's death, and to the car wreck yesterday. His arraignment won't be until Monday, so he's spending the weekend in jail."

The woman stared beyond Jacqui.

"I thought that might be news to you. If you were thinking of pinning this on him—"

"Not like that. We just thought... We figured they'd suspect him, and like the other night, he'd have an alibi. How did he get past that? He was on the Cape."

"I don't know, but he convinced the cops he did it, so—"

"This is bad."

"The cops are going to figure out that he lied, and then they're going to look at the only people he'd be willing to spend the rest of his life in prison for. Who else but you and Kirk?"

Kelly's fear and worry felt palpable.

"You don't have to do this," Jacqui whispered. "Just make a call. Help us out of this. Turn your brother in."

"He'll kill me."

"Not if he's in jail."

"I need the money. I'm gonna lose my kids."

"I have money, Kelly. I have millions in a trust fund. Whatever you need, you'll get. I promise. Just help us out."

A long moment of silence had Jacqui wondering if she'd made any impact on Kelly at all. Then, the woman dropped the hood over Jacqui's head and gripped her arm. "Hurry. We gotta get back before he comes looking."

"Are you going to help us?"

Kelly didn't answer, and Jacqui, tempted as she was to press the question, kept her mouth shut and prayed.

All the way across the room, down the dark staircase, and into the basement, Kelly said nothing.

She escorted Jacqui back into the storage room, took off her hood, and had her sit again.

Reid was leaning against the wall as if he hadn't moved since she'd left.

Kirk followed them in with a fresh zip tie. He looped it through one of the ties around Jacqui's wrist and attached it to the post.

"You were right. She wanted to get me alone." Kelly was staring down at her when she added, "They know who we are. And Dad's in jail. He confessed."

Kirk swore loudly, ripping his ski mask off. He was bearded and balding and wouldn't have looked at all scary if not for the menacing expression on his face as he glared down at her.

"You're lying."

Jacqui said nothing, just glared right back at the man. But inside, her heart sank.

CHAPTER TWENTY-NINE

Reid's heart was pounding. It'd taken every ounce of self-control not to show how out of breath he was when Jacqui was returned to the room. He'd had to scramble back to his spot on the wall fast lest Kirk discover he'd moved.

When Kelly told Kirk about their father, Jacqui's shoulders slumped. Reid understood how she felt. They could use the woman's help. But he thought maybe, maybe they'd be able to get free without it.

The abductors were arguing in the other room, voices raised as if they didn't care a whit if Jacqui and Reid overhead. Jacqui was listening hard, barely paying Reid any attention. Apparently, Kirk thought the information about Don's confession irrelevant to what they were doing. So what if their father was in jail? They were going to sell the neuron and make millions. They could disappear and never be seen again.

By the sound of tears in Kelly's voice, she didn't like that idea. Apparently, she was doing this so she could see her kids more, not leave them forever.

Cry me a river, sister.

If she really cared about her kids, she wouldn't have gotten into this mess in the first place.

Reid prayed they'd keep arguing long enough for him to get this taken care of as he scooted to the back wall and around the corner.

Jacqui turned to watch as he made his way to the old machine. "Tell me what you learned."

"There's a staircase to the left. The sun's up, and the upstairs room is bright. I couldn't see much from the bathroom, but there must be lots of windows."

"Good, good."

"I know she told him, but I still think she might help us out in the end."

Outside the room, the arguing continued.

Reid felt safe talking if they kept their voices low. "It's not going to matter. I'm going to get us free. When I do, I'll create a distraction, and you run."

"What?" Her voice was a vehement hiss. "We have to stay together."

"No. You have to run. It's my only chance."

That silenced her for a moment, and he hoped she would agree.

Technically, he should be the one to run. They wouldn't kill Jacqui until they had what they wanted, but Reid was expendable. He didn't say that.

He wasn't leaving without Jacqui.

"I'm not leaving you here," Jacqui said.

He'd figured as much. "Then we'll both have to try to get free."

He found the bolt connector on the machine. He'd already loosened it while Jacqui was gone, no small task without a wrench and with his hands tied behind his back. But with God's help—and he was pretty sure God must've been involved—Reid had managed to turn it. Now, he rotated the bolt more. Each turn was a challenge, but he worked at it, scraping rust against rust, tempted to yank the thing free. That would make noise, though. Without the element of surprise, they would fail for sure.

Finally, the bolt came loose, and Reid shimmied the two pipes apart just enough to get the plastic tie through the opening. He stood and stepped away, earning Jacqui's wide-eyed approval.

He walked back to the place where he'd started, thankful to be able to do so standing up. His head was still pounding, and nausea churned in his stomach, another symptom of the concussion. He'd worry about that later.

He sat as he'd been sitting before. If Kirk came in now, he'd never know Reid had freed himself from the pipe. Unfortunately, with his hands still behind his back, he was useless.

He needed to get them in front, and with his long legs, that was going to be tricky. Fortunately, to go with his long legs, he had long arms as well. Now, practically yanking them out of their sockets, he managed to move his joined hands across the floor below him, past his hips, under his butt, and finally below his knees.

If Kirk came in now, Reid would be not only caught but utterly defenseless.

He scraped his shoes off, pulled his feet up and through the loop of his arms, squishing his body like a contortionist. His shoulders ached. His arms screamed with the stretch.

And then, just like that, his hands were in front.

Out of breath and sweating, he paused to rest.

Jacqui mouthed, *Wow.*

Yeah. He wondered if, back when God had designed him, He'd been thinking of this moment. When Reid was in grade school, other kids had teased him about his *monkey arms.* He'd grown into them—to a degree. And they'd sure helped him in sports. Being able to reach over opponents' heads to make shots, being able to stretch from first base to make catches. Playing ball, he'd been thankful for his long arms. He'd thought they were a gift so he could be a sports star.

But now he knew the truth—God had given him the freakish arms for just this moment.

The conversation outside the room entered his consciousness again. Kelly said, "If you cared about your children—"

"I'm doing this for them." Kirk's voice was low and angry. "I want to be able to give them whatever they need."

"What if they need you, huh?"

He scoffed. "All I have to offer is money. And that's all yours want from you. They're better off with their dads anyway."

Reid blocked their voices out. Barely above a whisper, he said, "Warn me if they come."

"You need to run," she said. "If I get caught, you need to go."

He returned to the machine. "That's not going to happen."

"Reid, Ella needs you."

Ella.

He couldn't think about her.

He prayed he'd find something sharp enough to cut the zip ties binding his hands.

He had no idea what the machine was. It had levers and pipes. Maybe some kind of washing mechanism. But no sharp edges.

Ella did need him.

But he couldn't see any way to save both himself and Jacqui. And if it was going to be one or the other, she would be the one to walk away from this.

And Ella... Ella had her mother.

Denise loved her. Denise wouldn't raise her like Reid would, but she'd raise her with love, as she'd been raised with love. Denise could do it.

He couldn't let his thoughts go there. Wouldn't.

He studied the length of pipe that had been connected to the one he'd been tied to. It was about a foot long and had another connecter bolt on the opposite end. It could be used as a weapon. He unscrewed it and jimmied the pipe free.

"Reid, we have to stay together. I'm not going to leave you."

He heard the tears in her voice and understood how she felt. No way would he leave her there, but that was different. It was his job to protect her, not the other way around.

Women and children first. That was how it worked in rescues. That was how it would work here.

"If we can't both get free," he said, "then run and get help."

"We have to stay to—"

"If we can't, then run. It's the only way."

She kept arguing. He ignored her. He had to think.

Now he had a weapon.

All well and good, but if he couldn't cut the tie holding Jacqui in place, they weren't going anywhere.

Holding the pipe between his knees, he resumed his search. There had to be something...

Kirk's voice rose outside the room. "You will do what I say!"

"I'm sick of being told—"

The loud *smack* had Reid cringing.

Focus, Cote.

Running his hands all over the machine, he found a bit of sharp metal. He had no idea what it was and couldn't see it, but he gripped it and tried to pull it free. It wouldn't budge.

Come. On.

He pulled harder and felt it give, but not enough. With his over-large hands, he couldn't get the right angle. The thing was bigger than he'd originally thought. At least a couple of inches long, it might be too long to get out of the mechanism without making noise.

He pulled again, then had a thought.

Rather than try to pull it, he scraped one of his zip ties across it. Winced when it sliced his skin. Adjusted, tried again.

And then, just like that, his hands yanked apart.

One smacked into the machine, the sound resounding like a clang.

Kirk said, "What was that?"

Hands free, Reid was able to get a grip on the metal. He yanked.

Footsteps.

"Reid, hurry!" Jacqui's whisper-shout wasn't necessary. He was working as fast as he could.

The metal piece came loose.

Reid held it tightly and swiveled.

The pipe fell from between his knees and clattered to the floor just as Kirk stepped in the room. "Hey, what the—!"

Grabbing the pipe as it rolled away, Reid dove toward Jacqui. He pressed the jagged metal into her palm and lunged toward Kirk as the man was reaching for his gun.

Reid swung the pipe like a bat, aiming for his head. But Kirk shifted, and the pipe hit his shoulder. He fell against the wall.

Jacqui yelled, "Reid, watch out!"

He turned as Kelly stepped in the room, gun raised.

From the corner of his eye, he saw Jacqui stand and dive at the woman, arms still bound behind her back. They both rolled out of sight.

Kirk was reaching for his gun.

Reid kicked him in the head and was reaching for the weapon when he heard a scream from the other room.

He bolted out the door to find Jacqui on the floor, the woman standing over her with the gun lifted. Blood oozed from her arm.

He took all that in as he tackled her. "Run!"

Jacqui struggled to her feet and bolted across the empty space toward a wall. He wanted to get the woman's weapon, but Kirk would come out any second. They were literally out-gunned. Their best option was to escape.

He was nearly to the wall where Jacqui had disappeared when a shot rang out, the bullet whizzing past his head as he reached the corner.

He ducked around it and followed Jacqui up the narrow staircase. He caught up with her, snatched the metal from her still-tied hands, and sliced the plastic in one swift movement. "Go, go, go!" They were easy targets in the small space.

Jacqui reached the top.

Reid heard footsteps behind him and dove onto the upper floor as another gunshot rang out.

He scrambled to his feet.

Jacqui had reached the door. She was yanking, pushing, pulling. "It's locked!"

The room was ringed in windows, some broken, some open. All were up against the high ceiling.

Kirk was stomping up the stairs.

Reid leaned against the wall beside the staircase, pipe raised. Looked around.

An old metal cabinet stood against the back wall. If Jacqui climbed it, she could reach the broken window above.

He pointed. "There. Go."

"We have to stay together!"

"It's our only chance."

She hesitated a split second, then bolted for the cabinet.

Kirk stepped from the staircase.

He was swinging his gun toward Reid when Reid swung the pipe.

Kirk must've seen the blow coming. He ducked, dodged it. With no space to aim his weapon, he countered with a punch and hit Reid's forearm with the butt of his gun.

Reid lost his grip on the pipe. It whirled away. If he dove for it, he might have a chance.

But Kirk's gaze had moved beyond Reid. He spotted Jacqui climbing the cabinet and aimed his pistol.

Reid let the pipe roll out of reach and tackled Kirk just as he squeezed the trigger.

The shot went wild.

They wrestled, fighting for the weapon. But Kirk, using the butt-end of the gun, pummeled Reid in the head.

The head that had already suffered one blow that night.

Everything went fuzzy.

Obviously sensing Reid's weakness, Kirk pushed off him. One look at the window told him what Reid already knew to be true.

Jacqui had escaped.

Thank You, Father. Reid wasn't going to survive, but if he died to save her, it would be worth it.

Get her to safety, Lord. And protect my sweet little girl. Help Denise be the best mother she can possibly be.

The thought had his heart breaking. He'd so looked forward to seeing his daughter grow up. To walking her down the aisle. To holding her sweet babies in his arms someday.

He was going to miss that. He was going to miss all of that. But God would hold onto Ella every day of her life.

All those thoughts flitted through his mind as Kirk railed and cursed and stood and aimed his gun, screaming. Reid didn't want to hear the man's words, but they interrupted his prayers, the bittersweet thoughts of Ella growing up without him, the tender memories of her life. He wanted to focus on that, not on the madman in front of him.

The madman was screaming. "Get back here! Get back here or I'll kill him. I swear I will."

Reid stared up the barrel of the gun, trying to pull back memories of Ella.

Kirk quit shouting. He just stared down at Reid, his face filled with rage. And fear. And then, both of those emotions melted away, replaced with resignation.

Reid closed his eyes, ready to face God.

But a *thunk* had them popping open.

Kirk winced.

The gun flopped from his hand.

All Reid could see from his vantage point was a two-by-four poised to hit again.

It swung and connected with Kirk's head a second time.

Kirk fell over.

Behind him, Jacqui lifted the board once more.

Reid stood, dizzy, head pounding. But amazingly, incredibly, surprisingly not dead.

Kirk moaned and reached for the gun.

Reid grabbed it and stepped on the man's hand. "Don't move, or she'll hit you again."

Jacqui's eyes were wide. Tears streamed down her cheeks. The board was still lifted over her head.

Reid aimed the pistol at the man on the ground. "I got this. You can put that down now."

She lowered it, dropped it. It fell with a clang. "I told you, we had to stay together."

An utterly inappropriate laugh blew from his mouth as he turned toward the staircase, half expecting Kelly to emerge. She didn't, though. It seemed she was content to let Kirk do the heavy lifting. Reid kept his gaze there, just in case, and nudged Jacqui's shoulder. "I should have listened to you. You're obviously the smart one."

CHAPTER THIRTY

It all happened so fast.

Jacqui was smiling, thinking about how Reid could always make her smile.

Though he was watching the stairs, his laugh floated in the air.

The man on the ground rolled, kicked Reid's hand.

The gun clattered to the floor.

Kirk dove for it.

A flash of horror filled Reid's eyes. He tackled Jacqui, and they both hit the cold concrete floor. Reid covered her with his body.

A shot rang out.

Then another.

Reid didn't move, not a muscle.

Kirk had killed him.

As footsteps closed in, she knew he was going to kill her too. It was over. There was no way he would get his hands on the neuron now. And the only way he and his sister would escape prison would be to eliminate all the witnesses.

She was trapped beneath Reid's body. She couldn't move, couldn't escape. All she could do was pray. Pray someone would come. Pray God would protect her.

And then, the most amazing thing happened.

Reid whispered, "Are you all right?" He sounded as shocked as she felt.

He still didn't move. But he was alive. How was he alive?

"Are you?" she asked.

He pushed up, looked behind him, and then rolled off her and stood.

Jacqui sat up and surveyed the scene.

Kirk was down, blood oozing across the cement floor beneath his body.

Kelly was standing at the top of the stairs, gun aimed at her brother.

Slowly, she swung the gun toward them.

Reid shifted so he stood between Kelly and Jacqui. "It's okay," he said. "You saved our lives. You can put the gun down."

Jacqui sidestepped so that she was beside Reid.

But he wasn't having that. He moved in front of Jacqui once more but didn't look her way. "Just put it down, Kelly. We'll tell them you saved our lives. We'll tell them you helped us escape. That he was making you do it."

"You'll tell them?" The gun trembled in her hands, but she didn't lower it. "I won't go to jail?"

Jacqui didn't know the answer to that, but Reid spoke as if he were certain. "Of course not. You'll be set free. You'll be able to see your kids."

Slowly, slowly, the gun lowered. As soon as it was pointed at the ground, Reid closed the few yards between them and took it from her.

He turned to Jacqui just as the whine of sirens reached her ears. Maybe someone had heard the gunshots and reported them. Maybe that sound had been there before, but Jacqui hadn't heard it over the roaring of fear and worry in her ears.

Reid pulled Kelly around the corner and settled her against the wall that made up one side of the staircase. "Sit down and stay there, okay?"

She just nodded.

He rushed across the room and checked on Kirk. He met Jacqui's eyes and shook his head.

She turned away, almost unable to take in what it meant.

Reid crossed the room and pulled Jacqui into a hug, turning her so that he could keep his eyes on Kelly.

"We're safe," he said. "It's over now."

CHAPTER THIRTY-ONE

"I want that man charged and imprisoned!"

"Dad." Jacqui tugged on her father's hand, trying to get him to resume his seat in the small room at the police station.

On his other side, Mom said, "Nathaniel, sweetheart. Calm down."

But her father ignored them both, focusing only on Detective Klein. "He almost got my daughter killed!"

Klein said, "We're well aware—"

"For all we know, his confession was part of their plot," Dad said.

"Please, Daddy. Sit down and let him talk."

Maybe it was the *daddy* that had him finally hearing her. He glanced her way and then plopped in his seat.

On the other side of the table, Reid shot her a sympathetic look. Her father'd been railing at the detective for five minutes.

"If you're through?" Klein said, one eyebrow raised.

Dad huffed but leaned back in his chair.

"Donald Burgess recanted much of his confession. He admits that he vandalized the lab last spring, that he assaulted you"—he nodded to Jacqui, earning raised-eyebrows from her father—"and that he unlocked and cracked the window at your place. He admits to having known about the kidnapping attempt yesterday after the fact"—at this, he nodded to Reid—"but not having taken part."

Dad said, "He lied. That can't be legal—"

"He's an accessory to murder, Dr. Beal," Klein said. "The DA will decide exactly what other crimes to charge him with, but you can rest assured that he's not walking away from this."

Dad leaned back. "Okay, then. Okay." But he squeezed his eyes closed, and his lips mashed shut and twisted. It seemed his anger was only a front for what he was really feeling.

Across the table, Reid was watching the scene, watching her, with such tenderness in his expression. He'd done everything in his power to protect her.

He'd told her to run.

He'd dived on top of her when Kirk got the gun.

He'd stepped between her and Kelly.

He had so much to live for, but over and over he'd proved he was willing to die to save her.

She would never be able to express what he meant to her.

Two seats down from Jacqui, Mom was comforting Dad.

Jacqui had explained to her mother why she hadn't wanted her to come to Boston, adding a teary apology, but Mom had brushed off the words. "I knew something was wrong. I didn't know what, but..." She'd wrapped Jacqui in a tight hug. "All is forgiven, sweetie."

Now, Mom comforted Dad. "She's safe now. It's over."

Dad dropped his gaze to his lap, but his shoulders shook.

Tears pricked her eyes as she slipped her hand around her father's arm and leaned against him. "I love you, Daddy."

He settled his head against the top of hers. "I love you more than I can say." For a moment, they just stayed like that. She loved having her father at her side, but she couldn't stop looking at the man across the table.

Jacqui had called her parents just minutes after the police arrived on the scene and told them what was going on. She should have done that way back when Don had first vandalized their lab.

Maybe nothing would have changed, but at least she'd have had their support.

After giving their initial statements, she and Reid had been taken back to the hotel to shower and change clothes while her folks had flown in from New York. She and Reid had met them at the police station, where Klein had ushered the whole group into this private room.

Klein cleared his throat. "It seems Burgess enlisted Kirk's help this week. He was hoping to talk you into accepting the deal with Tarim, but failing that, plan B was to break in and steal your invention. He swears the fire was all Kirk's doing."

"Easy to pin it on his kid now that he's dead," Dad said.

Across the table, Reid said, "I actually think it's true."

Dad glared. "And how would you know?"

Reid ignored Dad's aggressive tone. "When we saw him the other day, he seemed genuinely distressed about the fire."

"I agree," Jacqui said.

"Even so," Klein said, "he helped his son commit the act and didn't turn him in after the fact. According to the sister, Kelly, after the house sitter died, Burgess told Kirk to back off, that it wasn't worth killing over. That's when Kirk got Kelly involved. Kelly hasn't been able to get a decent job since she was arrested for hacking, and she needed the money."

Reid said, "What's going to happen to her?"

Klein turned his direction. "The DA will take the fact that she saved you into account, but she's still guilty of kidnapping. She'll serve time."

"I figured." He met Jacqui's eyes. "When I told her I didn't think she'd go to jail, I lied."

"Thank God you did. You saved our lives."

"Anyway"—Klein focused on Jacqui—"unless you have more enemies you want to tell us about?"

"Not as far as I know," she said.

"We have your statements. If you think of anything else we

need to know, give us a call. Otherwise, I'll turn this over to the DA. He'll be in contact."

Five minutes later, Jacqui, Reid, and her parents stood in front of the police station. The morning sun had given way to clouds and cooler temperatures, and Jacqui was glad for it. It had been a long day, and it was only midmorning.

She was exhausted.

Just as she had the thought, Reid said, "How about breakfast? I'm starving."

She couldn't help the laugh. "Of course you are."

They went to one of Dad's old haunts near the hospital, ordered giant breakfast platters, and ate and talked as if it were just another day.

And it was, except now all the fears and worries she'd been burdened with for months were gone. That afternoon, she'd sign the contract with IntraHeart. She could have rescheduled for Monday now that the pressure was off, but she wanted it done. The sooner the better.

She wanted out of Boston. She wanted to go back to Coventry, to her little lakeside cottage. She wanted to sleep for about a week. And then...

And then. That was the question.

And suddenly, she knew the answer.

Leave it to her blunt father to bring it up before she was ready to share.

"I guess you'll start rebuilding your lab right away," Dad said. "You don't have to wait for the insurance money when you can use your trust fund."

"Why don't you give her some time to think?" Mom said. "She's been through a terrible ordeal."

"She's got a plan." Dad lifted his coffee mug in Jacqui's direction. Their plates had been cleared. It was eleven in the morning on a Saturday, and the place was bustling with customers, but thanks to their table in the corner, she had no trouble hearing the confidence in Dad's voice. "I figure you've got it all worked out."

Jacqui shifted from her father to Reid. The intensity in his gaze bore into her soul.

She'd almost brought this up the night before—all the obstacles to their relationship. Truth was, there was really only one. She lived in Boston, and he lived in Coventry. Coventry was Ella's home, and Reid wouldn't take her away from everything she knew. Maybe, if not for the kidnapping, he'd have considered it, but now?

Ella needed to be where she felt safe. She would always be Reid's first priority after God.

Except that wasn't true. Reid had nearly died—had nearly left his daughter fatherless—to protect Jacqui.

Maybe they could both be his first priority.

Even so, she would never ask him to uproot his daughter to be with her.

In the very back of her mind, an idea had been forming. She'd lived in Boston for years, and she liked it. She did. But being in Coventry the past few months had taught her some things about herself. She needed sunshine, she needed to hear birdsong, to see beauty. She needed companionship, and not just from the people she worked with.

She needed Reid.

They held eye contact for a long moment, so long that Dad cleared his throat. His voice was lower, less confident when he said, "What's the plan, Jacqui?"

She turned to him and smiled. "I'm going to rebuild right away."

"I knew it." He leaned toward her, smiling widely. "I thought maybe you'd go to work for someone else, but you'll find someone to manage your business for you. You're not wired to have someone telling you what to do. Your mind needs space to create, to come up with more brilliant inventions."

Dad was right. He was exactly right. She'd been honest with Reid the day before when she'd said her gaze was almost always on a screen or a machine. She'd invented the neuron that way, but by the time she was done with that, she'd felt burnt out. The destruction of her lab had, in a strange way, been a gift because going to Coventry had pulled her out of that funk. "That's exactly what I need. Space to create. Space to think. That's why I'm building the lab in Plymouth."

Dad smirked. "Plymouth? What's there? That's an hour south at least, almost to the Cape. The traffic alone..."

He kept talking, but she was focused on Reid and the slow smile spreading across his face. The look of pure affection in his eyes. Because he knew where she meant.

"...you'll be going against the flow at least," Dad said, still talking about the traffic to Plymouth, Massachusetts. "So that's something. But still, why so far out of the city? If you want to go south, Maybe Quincy or—"

"Not that Plymouth, Dad. The one in New Hampshire."

Dad sat back against the booth. "What? What are you—?"

"It's a university town. I'll be able to find techs."

He scoffed. "Plymouth isn't exactly Harvard."

Dad wasn't wrong. It would be a challenge to find the people she needed. And the space. She'd have to purchase all new equipment. And the business end of things—she'd either be hiring someone or having to learn it herself. She didn't want to learn it herself, so...

Maybe it was a bad idea.

But one look at Reid's exultant expression, and she chastised herself. "I'll bring people with me." Would Braden come? He was a Boston local, but maybe she could talk him into relocating to New Hampshire. She prayed God would work that out.

And as she lifted the silent prayer, all her other worries faded like the steam rising from her coffee mug. Relocating to New Hampshire hadn't been her plan. But it was His. And His plans could always be trusted.

"Jacqui, you need to think about this," Dad said.

Mom's gaze flicked from Jacqui to Reid, and a small smile graced her lips. She understood. Dad would, too, in time.

"I'll live in Coventry," Jacqui said. "It's beautiful. There's a lake and hiking trails and skiing nearby."

"You don't need those things," Dad said. "You need an educated labor force. You need—"

"Dad?"

He pressed his lips closed.

"This is where the Lord is leading me."

Dad stared at her, blinking, seemingly unsure of what to say.

But Mom reached over and took Jacqui's hand. "Then it's where you must go." She turned to Dad. "Isn't it, Nathaniel?"

His glance skipped from Jacqui to Reid and back. "If you're sure."

She held out her free hand, and Reid slipped his in it. He lifted her knuckles to his lips, watching her over the top.

It was with considerable effort that she forced her gaze back to her father. "I'm sure, Dad. I've never been more sure of anything in my life."

CHAPTER THIRTY-TWO

"You did it."

Space had been rented, equipment delivered. Jacqui had even managed to lure a few techs to Plymouth. They'd start work on Monday.

The person she was most excited about had been there a week already. He nudged her shoulder. "You should be proud of yourself."

She turned to Braden. "I couldn't have done it without your help."

"I'm just glad you took me back."

"I'm just glad you forgave me for not telling you what was going on."

"If I'd known, I'd have been more supportive."

"You forgive me for keeping you in the dark?"

"Of course," Braden said. "You forgive me for pressuring you to make a decision before you were ready?"

She smiled at her assistant. He was so much more than that now. He was her friend. "Obviously."

He laughed, but Reid interrupted with a shout from the other side of the room. "If you're finished with your mutual admiration-appreciation-apology thing over there, I could use some help."

Braden chuckled as he crossed the space, passing machines and computers and all the items she'd purchased to outfit her new lab. He crouched where Reid was finishing up a bookcase. She could have had it professionally assembled, but he'd insisted he could do it.

She figured he was regretting that decision now.

"Miss Jacqui, look!" Ella had found Jacqui's new leather chair and was sitting in it, spinning it round and round.

"Careful. You're going to make yourself sick."

But Ella's only answer was, "Wheeeee!"

"Ella Cote," Reid's voice was stern.

"Leave her be," Jacqui said. "She's not going to hurt it."

Reid smirked at Jacqui, then shook his head.

She really needed to keep her mouth shut. Reid was Ella's father, and Jacqui would have to work hard not to go against him like that. But really, it was just a chair.

Ella had gotten back from her mother's house the day before, having spent Thanksgiving in California. Next year, Denise would get Ella for Christmas, and Reid was already dreading it.

But he was at peace with the agreement they'd made. And Ella seemed as happy and confident as ever.

Reid and Braden moved the case into place against the wall, and then Reid stepped back and surveyed his work.

Braden punched his shoulder. "Very impressive." The sarcasm was evident in his voice. "And you did it almost all by yourself."

"Shut up." But Reid's voice held only laughter. He crossed the room to Jacqui. She expected a kiss, maybe a squeeze to her hand.

But he lifted her and spun her around. When he set her back down, he said, "Congratulations."

"I haven't done anything yet."

He turned her to face the room and settled behind her, hands on her shoulders.

Shiny new equipment, shiny new computers, shiny new furniture. She couldn't wait to dig into her latest idea. It'd been germinating for months. She had notebooks filled with plans and formulas. All she'd needed was the place to make it happen.

And the people to help her.

Reid said, "You've already done so much."

Jacqui thought of the artificial neuron and the teams working to develop products. She'd heard from Mack, who'd related some of their ideas. Great ideas, ideas that would change lives.

The one she was most excited about was the device they were developing for Alzheimer's patients, which could enable them to access their memories again. It could help people recognize loved ones they hadn't recognized in years.

That was all she'd wanted, to change lives.

She hadn't known to ask for the rest of this. Assistants who'd become friends. A little girl who was not her daughter, but whom she loved as if she were.

And the man at her side.

They'd been dating. Good old-fashioned dating. Movies and dinners, walks near the lake and hikes in the mountains. They'd taken Ella swimming and boating, to parks and museums. For nearly six months, they'd been feeling out this relationship. It'd been born of Reid's loneliness and Jacqui's need for help. It had grown under pressure, been fertilized by Reid's sacrificial protectiveness and then Jacqui's sacrifice of her home in Boston.

It had started in June as a seed, then a tiny sprout. But time and adversity had matured it quickly. Now, she couldn't imagine her life without this man beside her.

And she wouldn't have to.

The engagement ring Reid had given her was safely tucked away in a little velvet box. The day after Thanksgiving, while Ella was in California, Reid had taken Jacqui to the official start of Christmas season in Coventry's town square. She'd watched as the tiny lights on the twenty-five-foot tree had twinkled to life, mesmerized by the beauty of it against the dark lake and starry backdrop.

When she'd turned to see Reid's reaction, she'd found him on one knee.

He'd looked as if he had a world of things to say to her, but he couldn't seem to spit them out.

She couldn't form words herself. She'd gazed at the beautiful diamond he held out to her, tears spilling from her eyes, and simply nodded.

After Reid had slipped the ring on her finger, he'd kissed her, and the crowd had erupted in applause.

It had been a magical moment. Tonight, they'd tell Ella, who Jacqui had no doubt would be thrilled. And then the planning would begin.

Now, as she surveyed her new lab, she was eager to get to work. But more than that, she couldn't wait to become Ella's stepmom.

She couldn't wait to become Reid's wife.

She trusted that God would guide them every step of the way, and she couldn't wait.

THE END.

Thank you for spending your valuable time getting to know Jacqui and Reid. I hope you enjoyed reading it as much as I enjoyed writing it. If you did, then you won't want to miss Braden and Carly's story. Turn the page for more about TRACES OF VIRTUE.

When doing what's right goes terribly wrong...

From her deathbed, Carly Garcia's mother asked Carly to look after her stepfather and her sisters. Carly is doing everything in her power to keep that promise, but now she has a new life to protect, this one innocent and vulnerable. She visits her ex to tell him a truth he doesn't deserve to know... and witnesses his murder. Now, Carly's on the run from killers whose faces she never saw.

Braden Reilly is building a career in Coventry, New Hampshire, happy to put the drama of his crime-ridden Boston neighborhood behind him. When a woman he's spent years trying to forget shows up on his doorstep, his first instinct is to turn her away. But the bruises on her arms and the fear in her eyes have him offering her sanctuary. The story she tells him makes his blood curdle.

Together, they must discover who's behind a murder nobody believes occurred before the killers catch up to Carly and her unborn child.

Don't miss this plot-twisting thriller, the latest in the addictive Coventry Saga from a USA Today bestselling author.

Standalone Novellas

A Package Deal

One Christmas Eve

Faith House

ABOUT THE AUTHOR

Robin Patchen is a *USA Today* bestselling and award-winning author of Christian romantic suspense. She grew up in a small town in New Hampshire, the setting of her Nutfield Saga books, and then headed to Boston to earn a journalism degree. After college, working in marketing and public relations, she discovered how much she loathed the nine-to-five ball and chain. After relocating to the Southwest, she started writing her first novel while she homeschooled her three children. The novel was dreadful, but her passion for storytelling didn't wane. Thankfully, as her children grew, so did her writing ability. Now that her kids are adults, she has more time to play with the lives of fictional heroes and heroines, wreaking havoc and working magic to give her characters happy endings. When she's not writing, she's editing or reading, proving that most of her life revolves around the twenty-six letters of the alphabet. Visit robinpatchen.com/subscribe to receive a free book and stay informed about Robin's latest projects.